THE SUMMONING

There was a silence. Gerbert had ti[me to]
comprehend the strangeness of it: that he stood
at his ease, conversing with a bodiless head.

"Take me," said the Jinniyah.

He was speechless, staring.

"Take me with you," she said. "I am an ora[cle. I]
am meant for the high places. This is prison, [it is]
waste. They use me almost never. They speak [to me]
only when they must. Take me where I can be [what]
I was meant to be."

"Steal you?"

"Free me."

"I don't have the spell for that."

Emotion could not twist that graven face, but
the voice rang like iron smitten on iron. "Take me
with you!"

"You are not mine to take."

"I choose you. I name you master. I will serve
you, amuse you, prophesy for you. I have waited
here, until you should come. I am your servant and
your destiny. Through me you shall fulfill your dream."

He gasped like a runner in a race. "You are a
devil. You tempt me. You lure me to my destruction."

"I am a Jinniyah and you slave. I tell you what
will be. If," said the Jinniyah, "you take me with
you. You go to Rome; the prince of your faith will
honor you; kings will owe their thrones to you. Your
Church itself will bow before you."

Gerbert's hand stretched of their own accord. . . .

Bantam Spectra Books by Judith Tarr
Ask your bookseller for the ones you have missed

A WIND IN CAIRO
ARS MAGICA

ARS MAGICA

Judith Tarr

BANTAM BOOKS
NEW YORK • TORONTO • LONDON • SYDNEY • AUCKLAND

ARS MAGICA

A Bantam Spectra Book / September 1989

ISBN 0-553-28145-3

Published simultaneously in the United States and Canada

Bantam Books are published by Bantam Books, a division of
Bantam Doubleday Dell Publishing Group, Inc. Its trademark,
consisting of the words "Bantam Books" and the portrayal of
a rooster, is Registered in U.S. Patent and Trademark Office
and in other countries. Marca Registrada. Bantam Books,
666 Fifth Avenue, New York, New York 10103.

PRINTED IN THE UNITED STATES OF AMERICA

O   0 9 8 7 6 5 4 3 2 1

To Varda and Chris
as a gift:
A little something that I made myself

Acknowledgments

To Professor Jaroslav R. Pelikan, who, in the course of a seminar on the medieval papacy, suggested that Pope Sylvester II and I might find one another congenial;

to Brother Richer of St.-Rémi, for the history;

to William of Malmesbury, for the legend,

and to Gerbert himself, for the letters which so clearly reveal the man—

with a bow to all the friends and associates who put up with me during the writing of this novel.

The night is far spent, the day is at hand; let us therefore cast off the works of darkness, and let us put on the armor of light.

—ROMANS 13:12

PROLOGUE

Aurillac, A.D. 965

The monks' chanting had long since faded into silence. There was only wind keening about the stones of the tower, and the mighty stillness of the stars. But in that stillness, if one had ears to hear, was a thin high singing.

Gerbert shivered without noticing that he did it. That was only his body. His mind was afire. "But don't you see? It rises in the east. It travels up the sky. Then it turns and retraces its steps. Then it turns again and goes on as before."

"Wherefore," intoned his companion, "*planetes*, as the Greeks would say: 'wanderer.' "

"Of course it wanders!" Gerbert stopped short. Brother Raymond was laughing at him, and not trying to hide it. "You are hardly dignified," he said severely, "*magister*."

His teacher grinned and stretched. "Dignity is for overaweing farmers' sons when they fidget over their grammar. Not for perching on towers at high midnight, when God and the abbot know we should be sensibly asleep."

"What's more sensible than astronomy?" Gerbert dropped back on the tiles and filled his eyes with stars. "If I could just *show* people how it works . . . if they could feel with their own hands, see how it all moves, how it sings . . ."

3

Judith Tarr

"That's heretical," said Raymond.

This time Gerbert did not fall into the trap. Not quite. "Theory is excellent in its place. But it's practice that one remembers. You taught me that."

"It was born in you. I merely let it grow."

There was a silence, with music in it. No one else admitted to hearing it; and yet it was there. Gerbert knew that, as he knew that he was Gerbert. Brother Gerbert of the abbey of St.-Géraud in Aurillac, in the county of the Auvergne, in the duchy of Aquitaine, in the kingdom of the Franks, in the faded and crumbling Empire of the West, in this world that God had made.

He lay on his back atop Saint Gerald's tower and opened his arms to the sky. "I want," he said. "I want to *know*. There is so much—so much—"

"I've taught you all I know," said Raymond.

Gerbert sat up so quickly that his head spun. "Brother! I didn't mean—"

"You didn't," Raymond agreed, serene. "You'll fly higher than I. I'm but a master of grammar. You'll be . . . who knows what? Anything you want to be."

"I want to matter." Gerbert paused. Suddenly he laughed. "Listen to me! Abbot Gerald's charity, Richard the farmer's youngest cub, the one who was born asking questions. There's wool in my head and earth between my toes, and never a drop of noble blood to excuse my arrogance."

"There's this," said Raymond, rapping Gerbert's tonsured crown. "This sets you level with kings: this, and what is under it. Never forget that. Nor ever forget that it also sets you level with slaves. There is only one nobility where we are, and that is twofold: of God and of the mind."

"Therefore you are my master, because you stand before me on all my paths."

4

"Except astronomy."

Gerbert drew breath to argue. He could see Brother Raymond's face in the bright starlight, round and comfortable, much less apt for dignity than for sudden laughter. The laughter was winning now.

"Look!" said Raymond suddenly, his mirth melting into wonder. "A shooting star. And out of the eye of the Eagle. That's an omen."

This time Gerbert knew that he shivered. *For me*, he thought, but did not say. Another star fell as he stared, and another, and another: a shower of stars. The great music quivered with the power of it.

In that quivering came a new note, a thrill as of laughter, a thrumming that was not quite discord. It was alien, inhuman, yet perfectly a part of night and sky and stars.

They came out of the north, riding up the arch of the sky, singing in high sweet voices, laughing, gathering and scattering and gathering again in a whirling, skyborne dance. Some rode mounts of air and darkness. Some flew on wings of light. Their beauty smote Gerbert's heart.

Raymond murmured beside him, words of shock and of sanctity. The shock came late to Gerbert, and then unwillingly. That wild beauty, that music that was all of earth and nothing of Christian man, was the child of old night: the witches in their Sabbat, worshiping their black Master in starlight and in wickedness.

They were all naked. They had no shame. The women—not all of them were young, not all were good to look at, and yet they were splendid in their magic. They swooped laughing over the huddled darkness that was Saint Gerald's abbey; they circled the tower—Gerbert shuddered deep, and told himself that it was horror— thrice, widdershins, chanting in no tongue he knew. Their power hummed in his bones.

Brother Raymond lay flat on the tiles, cowl pulled over his head, gasping out fragments of psalms.

Gerbert could have. He could have done anything he willed to do. He crossed himself, to prove it. The witches swept in closer. Their eyes were burning bright. They called to him. "Come, brother. Come! Cast off your chains and fly with us!"

He was on his feet, with no memory of movement. His habit was like iron, binding him to the earth. His body in it was air and fire.

One of the witches came down close enough to touch. She was young; her body was full and sweet; her hair was bronze, her wings were gold. She did not speak. She beckoned; she smiled.

Gerbert's hands were on his habit. The magic was wild in him. His shoulders itched wondrously where wings strained to swell and bloom.

"I want," his tongue said, clumsy now, with his mind all fixed on that lovely, laughing face. "I want to know.

"To *know*." His hands dropped to his sides. The itch in his shoulders turned to pain. "Not simply to be, and to be wild. To know." He met the witch's eyes. They burned. He did not flinch. He spoke quite calmly, though his heart thudded under the coarse black habit. "Your way is never mine."

Her hand stretched. Almost, almost, she touched him. Almost he swayed into that touch.

"No," he said. It was the hardest thing he had ever done.

Be with us, the witches sang. *Be.*

"No," he said again. Again he signed himself with the cross. Not for any power it might wield against them. For its power over himself. He could all but see the chains it wrought, that bound him more tightly than ever to robe and vows and cloister. They were too strong for any witch to break. Even for the one who lingered though the rest had abandoned him to his idiocy; who yearned still, who dared to hope that he would yield.

He turned his back on her. He knelt; he clasped his cold and shaking hands. He began, painfully, to pray.

He would not, dared not look back. And yet he knew when she surrendered, when she turned from him and fled to the company of her kind. Once he had seen an arrow torn out of a man's side. It was like that: a rending from the heart of him.

He should have been glad of his victory. But all that was in him was pain.

Part One

THE NOVICE

Barcelona, A.D. 967

1

Bishop Hatto surveyed his newest acquisition with a critical eye. The acquisition stood straight and resisted the urge to fidget. He was not, after all, a raw boy fresh from the fields. His hands were clean, his tonsure tended, and his habit almost new. His face, he could not help. "Plain as a post," his sisters had judged it when he was younger and more inclined to fret over it. "But honest," they had added, meaning to be charitable.

Sisters could be a very great trial.

He swallowed. Probably he would never see them again. Brother Raymond had seen his star rising, the night before he left Aurillac, but that star had risen far from the Pleiades, in the realms between Mars and Jupiter. Not for him the small sunlit spaces, the rounds of the cloister and the fields, the moments parceled out one by one of trying to understand and be understood by the flock of his kin. He had wanted to matter in the world. Now it had begun, and he was here in this far country, before this lord of the Church, being measured and, no doubt, found wanting.

The bishop had been speaking for a while before the words took on meaning. "—of Spain?"

Gerbert blinked stupidly. "What—" His brain floundered, steadied, gave him what he had not been heeding.

11

"What do I think of Spain? My lord, I hardly know; it's so soon." He stopped, began again. "The light is different."

Bishop Hatto had a prelate's face: clean-carved, princely, and readable only when he chose to permit it. Gerbert's learning had been in other languages. This could have been anything from disdain to amusement.

Well then, he thought. Let it be the latter. "In Aurillac," he explained, "the light falls softly, slantwise, but bright for all of that. It has green in it, and gold, and something like honey and amber. Here in Barcelona, the sea changes it. And Spain. It's wider; it's whiter. It has edges. I think . . . my lord, I think it could cut, if one let it."

The bishop said nothing. Gerbert's fists ached with clenching. There, now. It was out. Aurillac's shining prodigy was mad, and quite openly and guilelessly so. And back he would go with the next riding of pilgrims, with a message for his abbot, coldly and regally polite, but most uncompromising. The primate of the Spanish March had neither time nor charity to spare for a witling who saw knives in sunlight.

The primate of the Spanish March nodded calmly and said, "Indeed, it cuts. This is the edge of Christendom. Beyond us is the sword of Islam. We live between blade and blade; our light is the light on forged steel."

Gerbert looked hard at that still and priestly face. Were the deep eyes glinting?

"And yet," said the bishop, "you are here. That is bravery."

"I'm not a fighting monk, my lord."

The bishop glanced from the nondescript body to the square clever hands, and almost smiled. "There is more than one kind of battle. What is it that you look for here?"

That, Gerbert could answer. "Knowledge, my lord. To know, and then to teach . . . but you know that."

"Suppose that I did not. What would you say?"

"Why, my lord, I would say—I would tell you that the West is sadly fallen. What men knew once, they know no longer, nor want to know. It is all iron and edged blades, and lord smiting lord for a fistful of power. They dream of empires, and they kill for a furlong of wasteland.

"But I, my lord, I want to know what the world is. In Aurillac they gave me all they had. Grammar. A little rhetoric. A great vacancy where all the rest should be. Dialectic, the high logic—that's known, a little, in Gaul. But the greater arts, the arts I yearn for, those are lost. Arithmetic, geometry, astronomy, music. The *quadrivium:* the fourfold path. No one knows it; no one can teach it. Do you know what I've heard folk say—folk who should know better, monks and priests with a claim to learning? They say that the lesser way, the threefold way, is endurable—just—in that it teaches one to read Scripture. The greater arts serve no purpose other than to lead men astray; they should be banned, as magic is banned, for magic is what they are."

"No," said the bishop. "No. Magic is another thing altogether."

Gerbert realized that he was gaping. He shut his mouth, searching for words. Words without magic in them. Safe words. "I want—I want the greater arts. I want to master them; I want to take them home and teach them, and kindle a light where the darkness is deepest. It's pride, I know, my lord. But my abbot seemed to think that what I wanted was worth reaching for."

"And that you were capable of reaching for it."

"Well," said Gerbert. "It's the wanting. It stretches the fingers. Sometimes it stretches them enough."

Suddenly, astonishingly, the bishop laughed. "Indeed, Brother! Sometimes it does. We begin in the morning. Simple arts first. Do you know anything of numbers?"

"I did the abbey's accounts for five years, my lord." It struck Gerbert late, and the harder for that. "We? *You*, my lord?"

"I." The bishop was stern again, his mirth gone. "I have some slight store of learning."

"But," said Gerbert. "I thought—I a farmer's son, and you so great a lord, and all your servants, and some so learned—"

"Even the Lord of Heaven deigned to dwell for a space as a carpenter's son. Should I be more haughty than He?"

Gerbert stared at his feet, shamed for once into silence.

"Tomorrow," said the bishop. "Here in my study, after the first mass. We shall see where you need to begin."

"Well?" said Bishop Hatto when the young monk was gone.

"Perhaps," said a shadow by the wall. It did not move, but what had seemed only darkened air had become substance. Human substance: a man in black, black-bearded, with eyes that glittered as he rose. Shadow slipped back like a veil, drawing into itself; neither the stranger nor the bishop took notice.

Bishop Hatto's brows were raised. "As uncertain as that, my friend?"

"Nothing is certain but the will of Allah." But the man in black was smiling, settling himself opposite the bishop, studying the chessboard laid out on the table. Lightly, almost absently, he shifted an ebony imam to face an ivory bishop.

"Ah," said Hatto, half in dismay, half in admiration. "There I think you have me."

"In four moves," the Moor agreed.

"Five," said Hatto. "The young Gaulishman, now. If he should be even half of what I think he can be . . ."

"Between *can* and *should* is a width of worlds. There is a boy—"

"A man, if a young one. He's past twenty."

"A boy," the Moor repeated, gentle but immovable. "Bursting with eager ignorance, and quite as perfectly Christian as ever a monk should be. If I had let him see me, and know what I was, he would have been appalled."

"My dear friend, you hardly look—"

The Moor smiled whitely in a face that had rather more in it of Ethiopia than of Arabia, and swept a long hand from turbaned head to slippered foot. "A heathen, your most Christian excellency. A black and literal Saracen. Need that babe see more than that, to know that I am all he must abhor?"

"You wrong him, I think," Hatto said. "In all my years I doubt I've met a mind to equal his. That passion of his, to *know*—"

"But to know what? In his country even simple numbers are a branch of the forbidden arts. As for what I would wish to teach him . . ."

"He did not cross himself when I spoke of that Art."

The Moor paused. Then he shook his head. "That is no proof."

"Well, then," said Hatto with the air of one who saves the greatest persuasion for the greatest necessity. "I say that he has the power in him. I say that as one who sees it. You know what eyes I have, Master Ibrahim. You know how I came by them."

The dark eyes lowered, but never in humility. "My fault, my Christian friend. I healed your eyes' affliction. I fear I healed it all too well."

"I was hardly glad of it when first I woke to it. But now, I see God's will in it. It showed me a great light in a darkened chapel. It led me to an abbot's hope and pride."

"Such hope as this?" asked Ibrahim.

Hatto sighed. "The Art is all forgotten there, if it was ever known. The power resides in the black tribe, the old pagans with their demons and their Sabbat. Good Christians shun it with all their hearts and souls. But," he said, "this boy has it. I think he has the strength to accept it."

"But should he?"

The bishop threw up his hands. Suddenly he laughed. "Listen to us! I should be protesting; you should be doing battle for so promising an apprentice. He could be quite perfectly content in what he thinks that he has come here to learn: numbers, music, the study of the stars. All those, I can teach him. And yet he has so much more in him; and there is the debt I owe you and your Art. I would offer him, if you would take him."

"Would he permit it?"

Hatto quelled the spark of triumph. It was not yet—not quite—won. "Would you ask?"

Ibrahim stroked his long silken beard. "You tempt me, clever infidel. Oh, you tempt me. True power is as rare as rubies. If he can bear to face its presence . . . if he can master all our bitter disciplines . . . what a mage he would be!"

At last the bishop allowed himself to smile. "Will you ask?"

The Moor's brows met, but his eyes bore no anger. "I will ask," he said. "I will never compel."

Hatto nodded. "That is enough," he said.

2

"Moors?" Brother Rodolfo stopped even pretending to copy the bishop's letter. "Of course I've seen the Moors. We have them in our city."

Gerbert swallowed impatience. "I know that. I've seen them, too. They're everywhere. But why? How can your lords allow it? They're the enemy."

"They live here." Brother Rodolfo was patently enjoying himself. No doubt it was a favored sport, to shock young newcomers from darkest Frankland. "Our lord bishop is their faithful patron."

"That's not so!" said Gerbert, outraged. "His Christian excellency would never sink so low."

"Don't let him hear you say that, Brother. He has dear friends among them. Haven't you heard the story yet?"

Gerbert scowled and said nothing. Rodolfo took that as permission. He settled to it with great contentment, and with a tale-teller's flourish. "When my lord was still a young priest, before he had his bishopric, he took sick. He was a perfect Christian then; he detested the infidel as any good believer should. His illness was dire, and the doctors agreed that it was mortal. They had all despaired of him.

"The worst of it for him was not that he would die. It

17

was that he would die blind. He could face death, but death in the dark was more than he could bear.

"At first he had refused the ministrations of Moorish physicians, though there were and are none better in the world. As his case grew more desperate, his friends prevailed upon him to suffer the touch of unbaptized hands; but none could give him more than a few moments' surcease. He was dying still, and he was still blind.

"Then at last, as he began to sink into the utmost dark, one came with hope. If he would take it. For that hope resided in one man in Barcelona, a Moor and, worse by far, a magus. When my lord heard that, he closed his ears and his mind. Not for his very life's sake would he submit to sorcery—not if it would cost him his soul. He turned his head away from all pleading and composed himself for death.

"As he stood at the gates with the oil of anointing on him, a voice spoke out of the night. It was a man's voice and no angel's, but none had seen him come. He was simply there, a turbaned Moor clad all in black. It came as no little shock that he was young. Little older than you, Brother, but strong for all of that, and possessed of a remarkable presence. No one moved or spoke as he approached the bed and stood looking down.

"He said again what he had said as he came, quietly as before, neither gentle nor harsh, as one who states a simple truth. 'You are a fool, sir priest. Ignorance may excuse you. It will certainly kill you.'

"My lord was dying, but he was not yet dead. He turned toward the sound of that voice; he raised himself. With all the breath that was left him, he said, 'My body may die, but my soul will live.'

" 'Ah,' said the stranger. 'Does your faith permit suicide, then?'

"That brought my lord almost to his feet, and all but

18

slew him, casting him into the stranger's arms. The man was slender, but he was strong; he bore easily that weight of anger and of death. He laid my lord down again, for all that he could do, and said, 'I have been sent to heal you. And so I will, resist me though you may.'

" 'No,' my lord said, the merest thread of sound. 'Before God, you will not.'

" 'Before God, I must.' And the stranger laid hands on our lord, and not one of his friends could stir to his aid. The man prayed over him—infidel prayers, but prayers they were, and no curses or invocations of devils. He prayed long and long. Years, it seemed to those who watched, held helpless by his power.

"Slowly, so slowly that at first they were scarcely aware of it, they realized that something had changed—was changing. My lord was healing. The pallor of death had left his face. And as he grew stronger, the mage grew weaker, until the balance held level between them. Then the mage fell silent. Their hands had locked. And their eyes. My lord could see. The fire that had burned in the mage now burned in him.

"With a crack like the breaking of a world, they fell apart. My lord's people would have fallen on the sorcerer, but my lord himself rose to stop them. He shielded the infidel with his own body. He said, 'Who touches this man, dies.' "

Brother Rodolfo stopped. He was silent for so long that Gerbert presumed that he was done. "And they were friends forever after."

The Spaniard shook himself. "What? Friends? Not precisely then. My lord was grateful—he knew his duty. But he was hardly delighted to owe his life to a Moor and a sorcerer, however white the sorcery had been. It was still sorcery."

"Then how—"

"Time," Rodolfo answered, "and teaching. And the mage himself. Quite simply, they took to one another."

"But," said Gerbert. "An infidel. A magician."

"A white magician," Rodolfo pointed out, "and, by his lights, a pious man. Moors have no bishops, and no priests to speak of, or Master Ibrahim would be one."

Gerbert shook his head. He could not absorb it. Bishop Hatto and a black infidel. Bishop Hatto and a sorcerer. Bishop Hatto who was both an excellent bishop and, by all accounts, an excellent Christian; and, in Gerbert's own experience, a great scholar and a great teacher. It was too much to take in.

Homesickness stabbed him deep. No one at home had ever torn him with so many contradictions. One was a Christian or a pagan, a good man or a bad. And one did not imperil one's soul with the sleights of magic.

Against his will he saw again the stars from Saint Gerald's tower, heard the laughter of witches, drowned in soft wild eyes. The power stirred in him and began, softly, to sing.

Fiercely he beat it down. He was a man of God. If Abbot Gerald had known what in truth he was sending his brightest star to face, he would never have allowed it. But it was done. Gerbert was here. He was studying what he had come to study. With God's help he would emerge unscathed, in body and in soul.

But ah, mourned a hidden part of him, how sweet it would have been, to see, to know, what the power was.

The day after Rodolfo told his tale, Gerbert faced his lessons with thudding heart. For a long while he was certain that he could not go at all. How could he face this man, now that he knew what he knew?

It took all the courage he had, but he did it. Part of it

was cowardice: fear of his master's reprimand. But some of it was the old craving for what the bishop had to teach. He found that he could bury himself in the cool serenity of numbers, and forget who it was who taught them. And such numbers—new ones, wonderful ones, one symbol for each that was less than ten, utterly unlike the awkward, heaping letter-numbers of the Romans: 3 for III, graceful curving 8 for VIII. One could work wonders with them. That they were Arabic—that did not matter. Some magics, even a good Christian could accept with a joyous heart.

Bishop Hatto straightened from the worktable and granted Gerbert one of his rare, brilliant smiles. "Yes," he said as coolly as ever, but the smile lingered in his eyes. "Yes, that is how you do it."

Gerbert basked in the warmth of unwonted praise. He laid down the pen and flexed his cramped fingers, too happy even to grimace at the wandering bird-trails that were his calculations. At his best he wrote a passable hand, clear if hardly elegant. This was frankly a scribble; but it was a victory.

He took up the pen again and reached for a fresh bit of parchment, and waited.

The bishop laughed, startling him utterly. "So eager still! Do you never tire?"

"Oh, yes, my lord," said Gerbert. "But when I've struggled long and hard, and then at last I understand, I forget everything but that."

"Indeed," Hatto said. "Our hour was up long ago, and I have duties waiting. And a task for you, once you've eaten and rested a little."

That was nothing unusual. Hatto always had a use for a quick hand or a quick wit. Lately he had set Gerbert to work doing his accounts, and once or twice writing letters. Gerbert wondered which it would be today.

The bishop was slow to enlighten him. "You've gone pale since you came here," he observed. "How long has it been since you last saw the sun?"

Gerbert blinked, surprised. "My lord?"

"Too long," said Hatto. "Obviously. We have to remedy that. Come, now: have you found your way yet round Barcelona?"

"Yes, my lord. You made me learn, when I first came. I studied the map you made."

"Did you walk the ways on your own feet?"

Gerbert nodded.

"Do you remember them?"

He nodded again.

"Good," said Hatto. "I have an errand for you."

He did indeed. Gerbert was on it before he had time to think, with two servants following, carrying between them an ironbound chest. Gerbert had seen what went into it. A bolt of silk and two of fine linen. A box of medicaments from Toledo. A vial of attar of roses. Sundry oddments, all rare, all precious. A king would not have refused such gifts.

They were not for a king. They would all go to an infidel, a Saracen: the sorcerer of Rodolfo's story. Damn the Spaniard—had he known what the bishop intended? Had Hatto even put him up to it?

"Today," Hatto had said in Gerbert's dumbfounded silence, "is the remembrance-day of my escape from death. I never forget the one who brought me back. Go to him, Brother, if you will. Bring him my gifts and my unfading gratitude. He will try to refuse them; you must persevere. When he offers recompense, let him give you the copy of

Pythagoras which I had asked him to render into Latin. It's time you had a new book."

Gerbert could not say a word. He could only go where he was bidden.

A Saracen. A sorcerer. Perhaps he could simply leave the box with the porter, and come back untainted. Hatto's punishment could not harm his soul. A magus' presence most surely could.

Harm? Or tempt?

The world was a blur about him. The sun was a featureless dazzle. People passed like flotsam in a flood: a babble without sense, a jostle of bodies. Some of them must have been infidels. Gerbert neither saw nor cared.

Sense flooded in, all unwelcome, and all too soon. Here was the street. The fountain that marked it trickled heedlessly into its basin. A woman drew water from it: dark, veiled, Saracen.

Gerbert's throat was dry, but he could not drink where an infidel had drunk.

This, said the cool voice of logic, *is ridiculous.* Here was he, armored in his habit and his faith, with his bishop's trust for shield. There was the house, a colonnaded wall that spoke of old Rome, a gate wrought in iron with Arab intricacy. No dragons crouched within.

Oh, indeed, no. Worse than dragons.

Folly, said logic.

He gathered his scattered wits and clenched his trembling fists. "God guard me," he muttered in peasant dialect.

And laughed, sharp and short, because both the words and the tongue were so perfectly fitted to his cowardice.

The servants were carefully oblivious to it all. He led them toward the gate and raised his hand to beat on it.

Soundlessly it swung back, leaving him standing like a fool, hand raised to strike the air. In the shadow behind was a darker shadow, a sudden shimmer: the movement of a hand, beckoning. With the valor of the lost, Gerbert passed within.

Sudden coolness, echoing night; sudden blinding light. His mind, independent of his will, made sense of it: a brief vaulted passage, a turn, a courtyard smitten with sunlight. There was nothing sorcerous in it, unless there were magic in the trees that bloomed in basins all about, filling the air with sweetness.

His guide came clear before him. It was, he saw with a shock, a woman, and veiled. Her eyes were large and very dark; her brow and her hand amid the veils were the color of a marten's pelt. A demon? A Nubian?

He crossed himself. The great eyes glinted with mockery. The woman turned with flowing grace and led him through the court.

It was all most ordinary, for Spain. The woman walked like a woman, if a young and remarkably graceful one; her scent was fleeting but earthly, and it was one he knew: attar of roses. The servants walked as they had through the streets, stolid, unafraid. No wonders unfolded about them, save what one expected in the house of a wealthy man in Barcelona: a man who seemed less inclined to opulence than to a studied simplicity. One of Hatto's secretaries fancied himself a judge of elegance; he had seen fit to teach Gerbert a few of its many degrees. Therefore Gerbert recognized quality in the plainness of the woman's robe, and in the carving of a lintel, and in the hanging of a rug on a whitewashed wall. The only magic in it was the alchemy of taste.

Gerbert's stride broke. He should have been glad. He was not. He was disappointed.

So much dread, and all for naught. He would have laughed if he had been alone.

He was almost calm when he came to the end of it: a

chamber like any of the others, plain, with a rug and a table and a low divan. The woman's gestures bade him sit. She brought him cakes, fruit, a cup of something cold and sour-sweet. Shame of his fears had made him bold. He nibbled a cake, sipped from the cup. No bolt of lightning struck him; no poison knotted his vitals. The cakes were pleasant. The sherbet was excessively odd. He tasted nothing in either that could have been sorcery.

When he had thus accepted the hospitality of the house, the woman bowed with glinting eyes and went away. She left the cakes and the cup. Gerbert took up another of the former, wondering what it was made of. He knew almonds, but the rest was strange. One could learn to like it. He tried the sherbet again, and grimaced. Too sour, and yet too sweet. Its undertaste was bitter.

"Yes," someone said in excellent Latin, but with an odd accent, "that is rather an acquired taste."

The man had come while Gerbert was preoccupied, soft on slippered feet. He was a little surprising, even when one knew that he was younger than the bishop. One always expected a mage to be immensely old. This one was barely into middle years; his beard was black without trace of grey, his face unlined. The woman could have been his sister: they had the same eyes, and the same dusky skin. What her features were, Gerbert had not had time or wits to see. This man looked not at all like a Nubian. His lips were full in the rich beard, but his nose was thin, arched, the nostrils fine and flaring.

He bowed with exquisite courtesy and sat on the carpet, his grace like the woman's, but fiercer, a man's grace. His long hand indicated the cup which Gerbert had forsaken. "The sweetness is not native to the fruit; alone, it often seems excessively bitter. It grows as lemons do, but its color is paler; it grows large, clustered like grapes on its tree. I find it fascinating."

"Do you like the taste?" Gerbert could not help it; he had to ask. It was that madness of his, to know. Even here, before a heathen sorcerer.

The sorcerer smiled. "It grows on one. Would you prefer orange or citron? We have both."

"Thank you," said Gerbert, "no. Sir." Belatedly he rose and bowed. "Brother Gerbert of Aurillac," he named himself, "in Bishop Hatto's service."

"Ibrahim ibn Suleiman," responded the sorcerer, "in the service of God."

Gerbert was taken aback. Somehow he scrambled himself together. "I bear gifts, sir, from my master. He says that you must accept them, in token of his gratitude that never fades."

"I need no token but his friendship."

"But, sir," said Gerbert, "it makes him happy."

Perhaps he had surprised this master of mages. The dark eyes had widened a fraction; the lips seemed almost ready to smile. "Does it indeed? Surely then he will please me by accepting a gift in return."

"He said you'd say that, sir. He said to ask for the Pythagoras you've been translating for him." Gerbert paused. "From the Greek, sir?"

"From the Greek," said Ibrahim.

"You read Greek? Is it difficult? It's like Latin, I've heard, but the letters are different."

"Arabic is harder," said Ibrahim. "And yes, it is remarkably like Latin."

Gerbert drew a breath of wonder. "Greek! Then you know Aristotle, you must. And Plato. And Hippocrates: do you know Hippocrates?"

"Certainly. He is one of the masters of my art."

"Magic?"

As soon as he had blurted it out, Gerbert bit his tongue. But the mage was calm, unruffled. "Magic, indeed, a very little. And medicine. My first training was in healing."

Gerbert's cheeks burned. "Then you—you aren't—"

"I am a student of the high magic, of the Art as we call it. God has ordained that my incapacity should be least evident in the healing of the body and the spirit."

"As you did with my lord bishop," said Gerbert.

"Just so." The deep eyes were level. "Are you afraid of me?"

"Yes." Gerbert was. He was also calm: calm as a rabbit under the hawk's shadow. The servants were no help. They had set down their burden when he was not looking, and gone away, abandoning him. He was all alone. "They say your arts are of the realms below."

"Yet you came to me?"

"I obeyed my lord's command."

The mage leaned back on his elbow, all at ease. "Perfect obedience! Would it comfort you to know a truth? I am no servant of Iblis, whom your people call Satan. My art is the white art; my allegiance is to the light."

"That can't be," Gerbert said. "Sorcery is evil. God forbids it."

"Sorcery," said Ibrahim, "yes. I am not a sorcerer."

"But isn't it all the same?"

"Hardly." Ibrahim straightened and tucked up his feet. He had a look which Gerbert knew well: eager, intent. A teacher's look. "Magic has its orders and its divisions, as does any other branch of learning. Most simply, there are three: the white and the black, and the broad realm between. In the learned magic, the distinction lies somewhat in method, but chiefly in purpose. To heal is of the light; to destroy is of the dark."

"Like prayers and curses."

Ibrahim nodded, pleased. "Very like. But a prayer beseeches the aid of a saint or of God Himself; it cannot compel. The will of the one who prays is subject to the will of divinity. A white spell differs. It does not presume to command God, Who is above all compulsion. Yet it seeks to work the mage's will on the powers of heaven and earth. The magus masters them; he shapes them to his ends."

"How can that be anything but evil? It goes against the law of God."

"God's law ordains that a spell worked in His name be fulfilled by His will."

Gerbert frowned. "I don't see . . . It's arrogant. To assume that one knows what He intends."

"Any of His priests assumes exactly that, in everything he does."

Gerbert's frown deepened. The man was right, damn him. And Gerbert should have seen it. And yet . . . "Why then do they bid us shun all works of magic?"

"Fear," answered Ibrahim. "Ignorance. Confusion of the high learned Art with its black shadow. The power in itself is neither good nor evil; it simply is. The mind of the magus shapes its purpose." He paused, a breath only. "I have heard that in your country the same fear and ignorance have banned the arts of the Quadrivium."

"Not banned them," Gerbert said. "Let them slide into neglect. But numbers can't call up devils."

"Can they not? The art magic grounds itself in the seven liberal arts. The three arts of language and its use; the four sciences. It is all one in the face of God."

Gerbert's head shook of itself. "No. No, it can't be that simple. Or—or that beautiful."

"Why should it not be? It is part of God's creation. He has not given it to every man, that is true; it is too strong for that, and too perilous. So likewise is any knowledge. In the wrong hands, even the words we speak can destroy a reputation or a life."

"Surely something must be safe," Gerbert said.

"Silence. Perhaps. The mute existence of the beast."

Gerbert shuddered. "God save me from that. And from the snares of the devil."

"May He favor your prayer."

Gerbert looked at Ibrahim. His eyes, he knew, were wild. "You *believe* in Him."

The magus bowed his head. "I am the lowest of His servants."

"But," said Gerbert. "But it's—not—" He had risen without knowing it. "How can they all have lied to me?"

"They did not know."

"God in heaven!" Gerbert spun about. The words were in his mind: *Get thee behind me, Satan!* But he had a little sense left. He did not say them. He managed a travesty of a bow, a babble that passed for farewell. The sun was fierce on his throbbing head, the city a blessed, numbing clamor. Blessed because it was simple, human earth. Because there was no magic in it.

3

Any sensible Christian would have taken refuge in the cathedral, or in any shrine or chapel in a city full of them. Gerbert came to himself down by the quays, in the shadow of the Mount of the Jews. His back was to the city; his face was to the blue splendor of the sea. A ship disgorged treasures out of the east, its master bellowing to his crew in the bastard Latin of Catalonia, while the merchants chattered in a tongue that might have been Arabic. They were Muslims, certainly: bearded, turbaned, robed and foreign. None was as dark as Master Ibrahim.

Gerbert sat on a coil of rope and drew up his knees. He wanted, foolishly, to cry. If he had been only a little younger, he would have hit something.

The merchants' chatter had risen in pitch. The ship's master, as if to counter them, had lowered his voice to a roar. A horse burst out of the hold and plunged down the gangplank. It was a handsome beast, one of those the Arabs bred. It looked more like a stag than a horse, with its great eyes and its delicate muzzle and its slender legs; but Gerbert had heard that its kind were wonderfully strong.

It was a black bay, and spirited. Something in it made

Gerbert think of the magus. Maybe it was only the way its nostrils flared, drinking the wind.

Gerbert glared at the defenseless air. There was no getting away from it. The world had infidels in it. That was no harm to his soul. But magic . . .

It terrified him. Because it tempted him. He should not even think of it; he wanted it.

He straightened, stiff. There. It was out. "I want it," he said. "I want to know what it is."

He knew what it was. Forbidden.

Why?

Because it was evil.

Master Ibrahim had said that it was not. Priests in Gaul condemned the study of the stars as sternly as they condemned the study of the art magic. Gerbert had sworn in boyhood to do battle against that first kind of ignorance.

And the other?

"How can I know?" he cried aloud. "Who can help me?"

No one. Brother Raymond atop the tower, babbling psalms as the witches rode on their Sabbat—that was how the world would bid him be. But he had not wanted to, not then. He had seen beauty in it. He had yearned for it. And, yearning, fled.

It had been a different kind of flight. That had been wild magic, with darkness in it. He had wanted more. Light; learning. Reason and knowledge, where the witches could offer only instinct.

Suppose that all of this was the devil's trick, a clever snare for his vaunted cleverness.

Suppose that it was not. For all that he could do, he found in Bishop Hatto no taint of evil. Nor—he made himself admit it—could he find any in Master Ibrahim. Power, yes. Passion. But of evil, nothing.

Gerbert turned his stiff and aching face to the sky.

The sun had passed its zenith, but its strength had barely waned. It had no answer for him.

He had choices. Leave; go back to Aurillac; refuse all hopes of glory. Stay, but turn his back on magic. Stay, and face it, and accept the truth: that he wanted it. Had wanted it since first he heard its name.

He could burn for that.

He breathed deep, shuddering. He could burn; or he could teach. Mathematician or magician or both, he would be a prodigy in Gaul. Why not embrace it all?

His heart hammered. He had wanted to know. Now he could know more than he had ever dreamed of. It was here, in Barcelona. In the bishop who knew the four high arts. In the infidel who knew the one great Art.

"God," he whispered. "God in heaven, guide my feet."

He rose. He had to go back. He had forgotten Bishop Hatto's Pythagoras.

Terror rocked him. Tomorrow. He would go for it tomorrow.

No. It must be today. Tomorrow he would have no courage left.

The gate was shut. For all his hammering and shouting, he gained only silence. No one came. When fist and throat were both a single ache, he turned away. God's mockery or the devil's, what matter? He had been offered the choice. In his folly he had fled it. Now it was lost.

Slowly he began to walk. His feet dragged. He was ready truly, now, to weep.

"Brother. Brother Gerbert."

It was a woman's voice. He looked up dully.

It was she: the woman who had let him in. She had a basket on her hip; savory scents wound out of it. "I saw you knocking," she said. Her voice was young, her Latin startling. Did she smile under the veil? "I was fetching our dinner; I cry your pardon."

"Have you no servants?" Gerbert asked her.

Her eyes glinted. "Sometimes. Sometimes not. They have caprices."

She had begun to walk again, toward the house. Without thinking, he followed her. A woman speaking Latin, and she not a nun. Astonishing.

She seemed to have no fear of him. Maybe, to a Moor, a monk did not count as a man. It piqued him a little. He was still new enough to manhood to want it to matter.

The gate was unlocked, rather to Gerbert's chagrin. The woman led him past it, and waited while he closed it behind him. "The master is waiting for you," she said. "He has your book."

She meant him to find his own way onward. Clearly she had duties; he was keeping her from them. But he said, "I thought women of your people had no learning."

"Did you?" She sounded amused. "You will find him where you left him." She bowed, all grace. "*Salaam.*"

One could learn, Gerbert decided, to hate the custom of the veil. It let a woman read his every thought, while she hid behind it, secure in her secrecy. He could not even know what she looked like.

Probably she was hideous. He glanced about to get his bearings, and set off across the courtyard. It was not the direction she had taken. He thought he was glad of that.

Master Ibrahim seemed not to have moved. The bishop's chest was gone, likewise the cakes and the cup. The magus had a book in his hands and a smile of greeting for Gerbert, calm as if the monk had never left him.

"Sir," said Gerbert, "I forgot—"

"Here," said the magus. "I kept it for you."

Gerbert took the book, remembering to bow, to murmur thanks. He should have dismissed himself then. He did not. He stood mute, blank. What he had meant to ask was all scoured away.

From somewhere, words came. "Sir. Sir, do you teach?"

He had startled the magus. Or—delighted him? Dismayed him? All of them. "I teach," said Ibrahim. "What would you learn?"

"Whatever I can. If," Gerbert said, "there is no evil in it."

Ibrahim's lips twitched. "You are a difficult pupil, I see. You set conditions on my instruction."

"Only if they're needed, sir."

The magus nodded. "Wise enough, for a beginning." He drew himself up. Suddenly he was stern. "Only a little while ago you fled in horror of all that I was. Now you come back and ask to learn what I can teach. Why? Do you think to trap me?"

Gerbert's wits were coming back, if slowly. "I don't set traps, sir. It's only . . . I was afraid."

"And now you are not?"

Cold, that, and hard. Gerbert faced it as steadily as he could. "Oh, I am. But now I know why. Ignorance. And wanting it, and not wanting to want." He paused. "Is it like that for you? It always is for me. I was a farmer's son. I should never have been able to want more, but I did. I wanted what the priest had, when I saw him in church on holy days: his Latin; his wisdom. I was afraid, but I asked. He gave me what he had. Then he told me that there was more, but that I could only have it if I went into the abbey. That was terror. How could I leave all that I had ever known—my mother, my sisters, everything? I was only nine years old. I couldn't do it. But I had to. It was God calling me, Father Abbot said. He still calls me. He called me to Spain. Now He calls me here.

"I'm always afraid," Gerbert said. "There's always something higher to aim for, and every time there's farther to fall. What can I do but reach and pray?"

"Nothing," said Ibrahim.

"Exactly!" said Gerbert. "But I can't. I've always been one for doing. I've never been able just to be."

"If you would be a mage, you will have to learn."

"Mages act. Mages make."

"And they know when to do neither." Ibrahim fixed him with a black and burning stare. "If it is power you desire, and power alone, then I am no fit teacher for you. Go rather to kings, or to a master of the black art. I do not traffic in ambition."

"I'm not—" Gerbert stopped. He watched his fingers clench and unclench in his lap, rapt as if he had never seen them before. "No. That's not so. I am. But that's not what I want magic for. Power in the world will come or not, as God pleases. I won't use your Art to win it."

"So you say now."

"What oath will you accept?"

"None," said Ibrahim. "Yet. There will be time later, and vows which you must take, if you would master the Art."

"Then," said Gerbert, breathless. "Then you'll teach me?"

Ibrahim bowed his head, raised it.

The child in Gerbert, which was altogether too much of him, wanted to leap up and sing. The man kept him still, held his smile a fraction short of a grin. Nothing could keep him from shaking. He did not trust his voice at all.

"Your bishop must give you leave," said Ibrahim, "and time. You are, after all, his pupil and his servant."

Gerbert went cold. He had forgotten. His memory for duties was never worth much when he had better things to think of.

"Ask him," said the magus. "If he assents, I will teach you."

Gerbert did not bolt back to the bishop's palace. He plodded, head down, numb with all that he had felt since he heard Rodolfo's story. Now he would face reality again. The bishop would forbid him to imperil his soul with the study of magic, and he would acquiesce, because he must.

Or he would run away and become a magus, because that was what he was born to be.

He could be calm, contemplating it. He was far enough gone for that. He would take what Ibrahim offered; or if Ibrahim would not do it against the bishop's will, then another magus would. There were others in the world. There must be.

So far, he had come, in a night and a day. If this would damn him, then he was lost already.

Impetuous, his elders had always judged him. And headstrong. And once his mind was made up, not heaven itself could shake him.

Why, he thought as he passed the guards at the bishop's gate, he was growing into wisdom. He knew himself. He laughed, startling a gaggle of nuns from the cloister on the garden's edge. Their disapproval quelled him, a little. He dipped his head and murmured a blessing; they had perforce to do the same. As he left them, one clear cold voice followed him. "Levity," it said, "has no place in the house of God."

Nor did magic. But he would have both. He straightened his shoulders and went to face his master.

Hatto did not keep him waiting long. It was almost time for vespers; the bishop was ending the day's round of audiences. He received Gerbert in the quiet of his study, taking Ibrahim's book only to hand it back to its bearer. "This is yours," he said.

Gerbert looked at it and at the bishop, and swallowed. A book was the most precious thing in the world, and now he had two: the psalter which Abbot Gerald had given him when he left Aurillac, and this. "My lord," he said. "I'm not—I'm— There aren't words enough. How can I thank you properly?"

"You can look after your book," said Hatto, "and study it. Master Ibrahim will have added a reflection or two of his own on the work of Pythagoras; you may find it useful."

Gerbert clutched the book and bowed. He was all at a loss. After such a gift, how could he tell the giver what he had decided to do?

The bishop regarded him in concern. "Come, Brother, are you well? Have you eaten at all today?"

Gerbert nodded. "Master Ibrahim was hospitable."

Hatto's eyes sharpened. "Indeed. You were gone for a very long time. Did you find one another congenial, then?"

"No!" It came out as a yelp. Gerbert drew a deep breath. "No, my lord. Not—not exactly." Hatto said nothing. Gerbert could not meet his eyes. He scowled at his sandaled feet. "My lord, he horrified me. What he is, what he does . . . it was too much for me."

"Therefore you fled him."

"Yes, my lord," said Gerbert, though it hurt to say it. He stiffened his spine, dragged up his eyes, put on courage that felt rather too much like defiance. "But I went back. I fetched Pythagoras. I—talked to Master Ibrahim."

"To good purpose, I trust."

Hatto's face was as cryptic as a page of Arabic. "We talked about magic, my lord," said Gerbert. He paused, and let it all go at once. "He wants to teach me. I want to learn. It frightens me, how much I want it."

"Yet still you want it."

"I can't help it, my lord."

"No," said Hatto. "I suppose you cannot." He considered his laced fingers, turning them until the amethyst of his ring caught the light and flamed. "What would you do if I forbade you?"

Gerbert was braced for that. He answered steadily, "I would tell you what I tell you now: that I must learn, and that I will learn. No one has ever been able to stop me."

"That is arrogant."

Gerbert bowed his head. "Yes, my lord."

"Honest," said Hatto, "as always. Has it occurred to you that you could deceive me and do as you will, with none the wiser?"

"I'm a terrible liar, my lord," Gerbert said.

Hatto laughed, startling him. "You may never be a saint, Brother, but neither will you please the Lord of Lies. What would you do if I gave you leave to study magic under Ibrahim the Moor?"

It was a jest, it must be; or a test. Gerbert found that he was frowning. It was not his place to rebuke his master, but his brow would not smooth for prudence. "My lord, if indeed you gave me leave, I would thank you with all my heart, and wonder what Mother Church would say to both of us."

"Mother Church," said Hatto, crossing himself with honest devotion, "has no firm law against the high white Art. I know what it is, and I say that it is dangerous, but I believe that you are one whom God has given the capacity to master it."

"You know? You've known all along?" Gerbert said it

almost before he thought it. "You said to Abbot Gerald, 'I would teach him whatever wisdom Spain may have to offer.' You didn't mean only numbers. You meant *this.*"

"Yes," Hatto said.

"It was all a test and a trap. You tried me in your arts, to see if I had the wits to master another Art altogether. You sent me to the magus—knowing—" Gerbert choked into silence.

Hatto's voice was quiet, almost gentle. "I did. But I never bound you with compulsion. I left you free to choose, if you could perceive that there was a choice. I leave you free now. You may go back to Aurillac without constraint, and with my goodwill."

Gerbert shook his head. "I'm not free. I can't choose that, not now. And you know it."

"No," Hatto said, "I do not know it. You thought that you came here to learn numbers. You have learned enough of them to find your way through the rest. Magic was no part of it, nor need it be. Unless you choose."

"I have chosen. As you knew I would."

"As I hoped."

"Why?" Gerbert demanded. "You're no magus. Even I can see that. Why do you offer me up like a sacrifice?"

"I have no art, but I have eyes. A magus gave them to me. They see what is there to see."

Gerbert stared at his hands. Square hands, clever-fingered, as able with hoe or adze as with the pen, but no good at all with a sword: a peasant's hands, or an artisan's. The body beyond them was nothing to notice, neither tall nor short, neither broad nor narrow, neither weak nor exceptionally strong, simply there. He looked like what he was. A poor freeman's son in the black habit of Saint Benedict's Rule. Mages— "Mages look like Master Ibrahim."

"Mages look like anything at all. Do you judge a child's intelligence by the prettiness of his face?"

"But I don't *look* like anything," said Gerbert.

"You look like yourself. To these eyes, as I see you now, a very presentable young monk, somewhat pinched with petulance. And a white light that is your spirit, that names you seeker and scholar and, if you have the strength, magus."

Gerbert looked at him and thought that, perhaps, he understood. It had been the same with Brother Raymond. The master could see what the pupil was; could guide him, even if he went where the master could not follow.

Brother Raymond would never have expected it to end in this. "Then you give me leave? I'm to study the Art? And the Quadrivium, too—you won't take that away from me?"

"Certainly not," said Hatto. "The Art and the arts belong together. You will have both."

"From both of you."

"If your excellency will permit."

Gerbert looked down, abashed. He had been getting well above himself. Now, much too late, he remembered who he was, and who Hatto was. Hot shame burned at all he had said to his lord and teacher.

"Humility can be overdone," said Hatto, "but a modicum thereof has been known to be useful. Remember that, Brother." His words were stern, but then he smiled. "Or at least, remember what tact is. You'll need it if you're to deal with mages."

"I'll try, my lord," Gerbert said.

"Do that. Now, sir: shall we see to the singing of vespers?"

4

Gerbert had cause to remember humility. Or perhaps the bishop had meant humiliation.

The Quadrivium had its difficulties, but those were never too great for Gerbert's wits. They were quick, quicker than anyone's, and he never tried to deny it. But they were of little use in mastering magic.

Spells, yes. Even spells in languages dead since before the Flood. Letters, words, rituals—his mind drank them all and found them sweet. Yet they were only trappings.

"Magic is deeper than words," Ibrahim told him. "Magic goes down to the heart of things. Reason and logic help to define it, but beneath reason and logic, magic is. Your mind must learn it all, names, spells, powers, workings of will in heaven and earth. Then it must forget them. Only by forgetting may it master them."

"That is nonsense!"

Ibrahim had set Gerbert to work recording and remembering the names of the Jinn under the earth and the Afarit of the air, and gone away on business of his own. He often did that. It was a method of his: giving the pupil free rein, he called it. He simply pointed Gerbert to his library, set him a task, and left him to it.

He had a library. Oh, indeed. In Gaul the word could encompass half a dozen books in a locked chest in an abbey's closet. This was wealth unimaginable: a whole room full of books. Gerbert had been set to count them once, and to mark the resting place of each. There were a hundred and forty-four. Not all or even most were books of magic—those were locked in the chest in the corner, under the seal of Solomon woven in a rug worth nigh as much as the books themselves. The rest lay on shelves built to their measure, and there were wonders among them. When Gerbert had fulfilled his task to his master's satisfaction, his reward was to read whatever he liked. He was limited, in that he knew no Greek and little Arabic, and barely enough Hebrew to pick his way through the names of the archangels. But there was Latin enough to last a while, and some of the others were beautiful with gold and jewel-colors.

Gerbert's outburst found him in the midst of this, hunched over a table laden with books and scrolls, cramping hand and eye and mind with a name of the utmost unpronounceability.

"What *use* is it?" he cried to the air. "Why bother to learn it at all, if my only purpose is to forget it?"

He received an answer, soft and much amused. "Not to forget, except with the consciousness. Your bones will remember."

Now there was another thorn in his side. The lady of the gate was not Ibrahim's sister, she was his daughter. She was younger than Gerbert, and not only could she read all the languages which he had barely begun, she was well advanced in study of the Art itself.

It was not that he had any illusions about feminine fragility, of body or of mind. He did not even mind that

44

she was infidel as well as learned. What he could not bear was that she was better at it than he.

She never tried to deny it. "I began younger," she said once, "and I grew up with it. And I have a talent for it."

More than he. And much more patience. She could sit for hours, reckoning every characteristic of every herb ever deemed useful for either magic or medicine, and never do more than frown with the tedium.

"Discipline," she said. And if she wanted to drive him wild: "Women are better at that. Especially young ones. Their humours aren't always in a roil, pricking at them to run about and kill one another."

Discipline, he had responded icily, did not preclude impertinence. Maryam only laughed.

She had decided that he was family: she no longer wore her veil in front of him. She was not hideous, but neither was she pretty. She was too foreign; too much like her father. Of her mother she never spoke. There was a sadness there, and perhaps a smolder of anger.

Now he saw none of that, only her wickedly solemn expression as she sat across the table and opened a book. He could not see which it was. "I know what you want," she said. "You want to cast off all your drudgery and work an honest spell."

That was true, but it was none of her affair. He scowled at her. "Even I know that it never does to be hasty in a high art. When I'm ready to work magic, I'll be allowed to work it."

"But you would give your heart's blood to see a little of it before that."

"So I'd like to see a working or two. Is that a sin?"

She shrugged. "I wouldn't know. I'm not a Christian."

"Have *you* worked magic?" he demanded.

"Of course," she said.

She was baiting him. He breathed deep, twice, and resolved not to succumb. Grimly he turned back to his crabbed and illegible scroll, seeking out the next name in the sequence. It kept blurring in front of his eyes. He kept hearing Ibrahim's voice. "To name a spirit is to master it. Yet have a care that your strength suffice for the mastery, or the spirit will suborn you, and win back its name, and exact due punishment for your temerity."

To name a spirit is to master it.

There was more to it than that. Rites, rituals. Invocations of power. Gerbert was ready for none of them.

He looked up under his brows. Maryam was deep in her book. "What kind of magics have you done?"

She did not start, which meant that she had been waiting for him to ask. He was learning to read her; he was mildly proud of that. "Magics," she said, nonchalant. "The servants are mine." The soundless, bodiless hands that labored in the house, on occasion, when it suited them. "And the garden, how it flourishes. We have roses in winter."

"That's simple," Gerbert said. "One grows them under glass."

He had pricked her, though she barely showed it. "I made the glass. I persuade the roses to grow."

"The sun can do that," said Gerbert.

"You are mocking me," she said, but her coolness had heat under it. "Is that why you're here and not in Frankland? Did you drive them to distraction, until they drove you out?"

"Not unless they did the same to me."

"Ah," she said. "Blame them for your own shortcomings. You'll hardly make a mage while you persist in that."

He set his teeth on the hot words. This was Master Ibrahim's doing, he had begun to suspect: setting this needle-tongued minx on him, to see if he would crack.

To name a thing is to master it.

He actually smiled as he went back to his drudgery.

"Would you like to see magic?"

His smile shriveled and died. He had all he could do not to throw his book at her head. "Yes, I'd like to see magic. No, I'm not going to steal a glimpse before I'm ready! Will you go away, or do I have to chase you?"

"What if I say you're ready?"

"I'd say you were mocking me."

"So I would be," she said. "But Father says you are. He says to come when you finish here."

Gerbert gaped. Then he growled. Then he threw the book, but not at her head.

He had his own kind of temper. He finished as he was commanded, and he did not count the hours. Then and only then would he go to find his master.

Maryam was long gone. Even she could not stand against the perfection of peasant obstinacy.

It was an odd house, this one. From any one place it seemed solid enough, but the longer Gerbert studied in it, the larger and stranger it seemed to be. He would pass rooms that reminded him of others he had seen before, but that were subtly different. Corridors multiplied; doors appeared where he remembered walls, and walls where he could have sworn were doors. And always there were things that he could not quite see. Maryam's servants, which were invisible, but which his bones kept telling him that he could see if he tried. Other things less tangible yet: twinges in his bones, flickers on the edge of vision, nigglings like memories that would not, quite, come clear.

But strangest of all was that he knew no fear. He had never had night terrors as other people did: even as a little child he loved the dark, and took delight in what it showed him. Yet here, in this place half out of the world, he should have been stark with terror, and he knew it; and he was only fascinated.

Fear was something that he saved for the great matters. Learning. Loving. Wanting.

He found Master Ibrahim by the prickling of his nape, by the shifting of a shadow, by a whisper in the air. The magus sat in a room gone dim with evening, lamplit and quiet. He wore his wonted black, but he had laid aside his turban. A cap covered his shaven skull; a jewel glowed in his ear, a moonstone waxing with its mistress the moon.

Gerbert bowed as had become his custom, and sat at the mage's feet. He had learned not to speak until Ibrahim gave him leave. He was allowed to fidget, judiciously.

Tonight he was not moved to. His head was full to bursting with names; he was tired. He did not know if, after all, he wanted to see magic. Had he not seen it already, just in coming here?

Effects only, Hatto would have said. Of causes he had seen nothing.

What use, if he could not do it himself?

He swallowed a yawn. Ibrahim seemed lost in contemplation. The lamp flickered. It globed them both in light; it made all the world without, a featureless darkness.

Gerbert did not know why he moved. He wanted to, that was all. He reached, and the light was in his hands. It was cool, like fishes' breath. It rested pulsing in his palms. There was something that one could do with it, could will, could wish . . .

It quivered and went out.

Ibrahim's voice came soft in the darkness. "Bring it back."

"But I don't—" Gerbert broke off, began again. "I don't know how."

I can name every one of the Jinn, he wanted to say. *I can recite the rolls of all the orders of angels. You never taught me to make a light that sleeps in my hands.*

He did not say it. "You know how," said Ibrahim.

How? With names? None of them seemed to fit, except for Lucifer, and Gerbert was not minded to invoke that one. Not quite yet.

With will? He strained until the sweat broke out on his brow. He willed until his ears buzzed and his eyes went dark. Nothing.

With words? Which ones? They ran through his head, all tangled, all useless.

He slumped, exhausted, growing angry. This was all nonsense, all of it. *"Fiat,"* he said, "damn it. *Fiat lux."*

Inside him, something shifted. Something swelled; something bloomed. He stared dumbfounded at his fingertips. To every one clung a spark of light.

The moment he thought about them, they flickered. He pulled his mind away from them, and they flared up. They coalesced; they settled, round and cool and blinding-bright, in his trembling palm.

Master Ibrahim's smile gleamed out of the night. Gerbert blinked at him, half dazzled, half bewildered. "Was that an incantation?"

Ibrahim laughed. "Hardly! And yet it served its purpose. Now do you see?"

"I see . . ." Gerbert found that he could close his fingers about the light, and it would shrink; then it would swell again, if he not quite willed it to. It was delicately improbable, like walking a tightrope with an egg balanced on one's nose. "But if this is what it is, what are all the rites and rituals?"

"Guides," the magus answered. "Protections. Defenses against the ignorant."

Gerbert's head had begun to ache. The light pulsed.

It wanted to float free. He did not want to know what it would do if it escaped. He willed it to go out.

It only swelled larger.

His brows knit. "Words and will are simple. This is *hard*."

"It is," said Ibrahim.

Gerbert glared at the magic he had made. It had grown again. The ache in his head was fiercer. He had lost the way of it; he could not do it.

Half out of temper, half out of despair, he willed it to grow larger still. It quivered and sighed and dwindled to nothing.

Somehow Gerbert had lain down on the carpet. Perhaps he had fallen over. He was not interested, much. "I know children like that," he said. "Contrary."

"It is a child," said Ibrahim, "but it will grow." He seemed pleased; God knew why. He cradled Gerbert's head with serene and physicianly competence, and poured into him something cool and bitter-sweet.

Gerbert was too far gone to be wary. He merely blinked at the magus and tried to decide whether he liked the taste. He thought that perhaps he did.

"Here is the secret," Ibrahim said, "and the price. Magic is not wrought without consequence. The greater the working, the greater the cost."

"This was great?"

"For you, yes. Were letters easy, when first you learned them?"

"Arabic isn't," Gerbert muttered.

"Surely," said Ibrahim. "Now, sleep, and be content. You have power; you have it in you to master it. I shall take joy in teaching you."

You haven't till now? Gerbert would have asked. But his body was far away, and sleep was near, and sweet. He fell into its arms.

5

There was more to it than that, of course. If Gerbert had not been aware of it, Maryam would have been sure to remind him. Having proven her fitness as a trial to his soul, she advanced to an eminence even more alarming: that of his teacher.

She was skilled, he had to grant her that. She could madden him as no one else could, and goad him into succeeding in spite of both of them. Sometimes he would happily have killed her. Others . . .

He could talk to her. She knew less of the Quadrivium than he had thought she did; oddly enough, he was not too strongly tempted to gloat over it. Somehow and another, he found himself exchanging lessons with her. Arts for the Art. There was a certain symmetry in that.

Sometimes he wondered at the magus' willingness to leave him alone with her. Even in Gaul, young women were not entrusted to the mercies of very young men, even monks who wanted to be priests. In Spain, in a Muslim house, it was unheard of.

There were the unseen servants, to be sure. And he was not tempted. Much. Even after he had decided that while she was not pretty at all, she was beautiful. Much too beautiful for the likes of him, like the Shulamite of that

51

great Song which might have been written for her: *I am black, but comely, O ye daughters of Jerusalem.* . . .

When he was a little foolish with lateness and hunger and too-long working, he had sung it to her. Not all of it. Even the little had made him blush. She had saved him with laughter and a bowl of lamb in spices, and with not saying what they both knew very well. She was not for him.

Friendship was enough. They had that, slow though he was to comprehend it. When he was not fretting over being young and male and sworn to vows which he had never meant to break, he knew how precious rare it was.

It was there in the center of his thought, as they sat in the garden in the still and dreaming heat of noon. She had conjured a breeze to cool them; he had been sensible and laid aside his habit for a light Moorish robe. The back of his mind, and his magic with it, labored to coax a rose to bloom on a bare branch. The rose was recalcitrant, but he had raised an impressive crop of thorns.

Frustration crouched at bay as he watched Maryam. She measured the sun's angle with a stick and a string, recording it at intervals of the water clock which Gerbert had made as a gift to her father. In between, for an hour and more, she had been reckoning with numbers. She was good at that, as with everything; she liked the way they yielded to her will, much swifter and smoother than magic, with no price to pay after.

The blooming of magic in his mind's core was familiar now, if never taken for granted. Gerbert, always a little startled by what he had made, regarded the rose in rather more surprise than usual. It was indubitably a rose, a bud just unfolded, velvet-petaled, sweet-scented, perfect. But he had never seen a rose so dark. Its color made him think of darkest wine. Its center was deep and wondrous gold.

"It's beautiful," said Maryam.

"It's you." He blushed. "I meant—I— It's not *controlled.*"

"True," she said. "You can't let the magic wield you. If you should invoke a spirit of fire, and end with a succubus . . ."

"I suppose *you* have never made a mistake in your life," he snapped.

"I may have made a few," she said. "On occasion. Here and there." She went somber suddenly, so suddenly that she startled him. "Once, badly. Very . . . very badly. So badly that I almost killed my magic, and myself, and anything else that touched me."

He would never have spoken if he had been thinking. But he was off guard, and she hurt—hurt more than he could bear to see. "Tell me," he said.

She did not move, and he knew that she would not speak. His will, rousing too late, was glad. Then she said, almost too soft to hear, "I was doing what I should never have done. I witched the lock of the chest in the library. I took out the books my father had never let me see, except once, when he told me what each was: which of them I could read, and which must wait."

Gerbert knew. Ibrahim had done the same with him.

"I only wanted to look at them," she said. "Not to use them, or even to read them beyond a glimpse or two. I was curious, that was all. I knew I wasn't ready for them; I thought that that would protect me. I thought then, you see, that magic was mostly words—even though I had seen that it was more. I couldn't read Latin, either, beyond a word or two; what I could read, I couldn't understand, and therefore I thought it couldn't harm me.

"But magic is more than words, and the magic was awake in me, wanting to grow. It made me do what I did. And I let it. I let it wield me. I didn't know the words that

53

passed my eyes, but the magic didn't need me to know. It only needed the words.

"Magic is like a horse. It has a mind of its own, and a will to act, and strength beyond anything human. But, like a horse, it needs the restraint of a human will. A trained human will. I was like a child on its father's warhorse. It carried me, but only where it chose. And when I touched it with the spur, it ran wild.

"I don't know exactly what it was that I did, or worked, or summoned. My memory seared itself away, and my father will never tell me. But when I came to myself, I was barely alive, and my—my mother was gone."

She was dry-eyed, telling it, but that tearlessness bared grief more terrible than any weeping. "She had come in in the midst of it. She was a master of the Art, older than my father, and stronger, but weakened then with carrying what would have been my brother. It had been a hard bearing, and all my father's arts, together with her own, had hardly been enough to keep her from losing the baby. But they were winning the fight; she was a month from her time, and he was thriving, and she was even able to walk about a little, with help, if she was careful.

"She was in the garden when she knew what I had done. She ran—she *ran* to the library. She raised her power to defend me. But there was my brother, who needed defending even more than I; and she was weak, and there was the law of magic which knows no breaking. The working killed her. My brother . . . lived a little while. Not long; and that was merciful. The magic had done something to him. He wasn't human. He wasn't anything that should live in this world."

Gerbert found that he was holding her, rocking her as if she were a child still. He wished that she would weep. It was not good for her, this tearless stillness.

She pulled away from him with sudden, painful force. "I know what you're thinking. You think I'm horrible. Because I went on. Because I killed two people, and one an unborn baby, and after I had done it, I didn't cast off the magic that had done it."

"How could you?"

She stared. He had surprised her.

"I suppose," he said, "that if the magic is there, but one doesn't know it, or hasn't awakened it, one can cast it off. Or never acknowledge it at all. I tried. I succeeded, for a remarkable while. But once it's awake, there's no denying it. You can only learn to master it. Worse by far if you had tried to kill it, and failed, and it had devoured you."

"It can be killed. There is a way. Like cautery: burning it out."

"And what would have been left of you after?"

"Enough. I would have been a maimed thing, but no more than any woman is: a servant and a bearer of children. I would have atoned for what I did."

"That would have been a great sin."

Her lip curled. "How Christian."

"Call it what you like," he said. "What would you say? It was written that you be what you are. For you to kill your magic would be as black a crime as if you killed yourself. This way you honor your mother's memory and vindicate her death, by becoming the mage she would have wanted you to be."

"That's not why I do it. I do it because I can't bear not to. I'm selfish, Brother. Selfish and a coward."

"Oh, come," said Gerbert. "You're human. You're a better mage than I'll ever be. Maybe not a better teacher, but you'll do for the purpose."

She hit him without force, with less of anger than of unwilling laughter. Her eyes had brimmed and overflowed.

She shook the tears away; they kept coming in spite of her. "Damn you, I needed that. I never told anyone before. Whom was there to tell? Father doesn't need the pain. We've no family at this edge of the world."

"Friends?"

"Friends." This laughter was more bitter than the last. "Who'd befriend me? Good girls don't read, let alone think. Slaves are slaves. Men are out of the question."

"What am I?"

His bitterness shocked her out of her own. She hugged him, quickly, before he could pull away. "My friend. My brother—I think of you as that. Does it offend you?"

His throat had closed. He shook his head.

A little of the old wicked light had come back to her eyes. "And you're not ugly," she said.

He opened his mouth. She stopped it with her hand. "You're not. Stop thinking you are. You've the sort of face that ages better than any pretty boy's. It will suit you when you need it, when you've risen as high as you want to rise."

"Who says I want to?" he might have said, but did not. He knew how sulky it would sound. Instead he said, "I know what I want to do."

She drew up her knees and clasped them. "Do you? What is that?"

He had not been thinking when he said it. He had only wanted her to stop talking about himself. There were many things he wanted. What he wanted to *do* . . .

His breath stopped in his throat. By God and all the saints, he knew. He had to stand up to get it out; he had to move, pace and turn, pace and turn, throwing off words like shots from a sling. "All this. All this magic. It's all scattered: bits here, bits there. The heart of it, that's one, and solid, but the ways to it are as many as there are teachers of it. Your father takes a little from Hermes, a little from the Moorish mages, a touch from Africa, a bow to Greece, Persia, the Jews, the Chaldees; he mingles them, he makes them his own. He has a system, but there is no overriding *system*. A way of studying them all, in order, as we study the lesser arts.

"Suppose," said Gerbert, "that I found a place, a haven, a school, not of the arts, but of the great Art. It could be part of a larger school, if need be—I know I want to bring the Quadrivium back to Gaul, that dream I haven't forsaken. But with it, for those who have the will and the power, another and higher study."

"You want to found a school of magic in Gaul?"

He stopped, spun. "Does it sound as ridiculous as that?"

"It sounds dangerous. We're tolerated here, but we're here because the world has few welcomes for our kind. In Gaul, from all I've heard, they won't simply drive you out. They'll burn you."

"They won't. Not if I do it as I intend to. Think, Maryam. Why are you tolerated here?"

"Count Borel is a freehanded man. Bishop Hatto is our friend."

"Exactly. The count, and the bishop. That's where to begin. Convince the lords of the world and of the Church that what we do is a high learning—and useful to them. Show them what is possible. Teach them, or their children; make them part of it."

"Implicate them in it," she said. "Can they even conceive of it?"

"Why not? Where I come from, numbers are as close to magic as makes no matter. If I can give them both, in ordered sequence, who's to fault me?"

"Everyone."

"Or no one." He dropped down in front of her. "I want to give magic the order and the honor of the lesser

57

arts: set it beside theology, consort to her queen, crown and scepter of the world that is and was and is to be. I'll teach it to kings. I'll lay it at the feet of the very pope in Rome."

"Why not be pope, if you're aiming as high as that?"

He sat on his heels and laughed a little, at himself, at absurdity. "Now that is nonsense. A schoolmaster is what I'll be. Master of the arts. That's high enough for a farmer's brat from Aurillac."

"That's a dream worth having," said Maryam.

She had surprised him again. Her eyes were bright, resting on him, but they did not mock him.

"When you have your school," she asked him, "will you let me teach in it?"

"Let you? I'd beg you!" He paused. "You really would?"

She nodded gravely. "We'll be old then. And august. People might not mind so much, that I'm not a man."

"I don't mind," he said; and for honesty's sake, "any longer."

"Well. I'm younger than you. When we're old it won't matter. I'm going to be a terrible old woman, Gerbert. That's fair warning."

"Very fair. I suppose you'll want to teach women as well as men."

"Of course. The magic doesn't care what shape its body is. Should I?"

"Never." Gerbert drew a breath. "Imagine," he said. "Imagine it. No more ignorance; no more fear. No more burnings. Magic will be like any great art, honored, respected, welcomed for the good it can do. We'll make a whole new world."

"God willing," said Maryam.

6

Gerbert had thought that he knew what he was born for. Now he knew it surely. This was better by far than the old, selfish dream: the wanting to know all there was to know, for his own glory, for his own contentment. Now he wanted to know it in order to teach it. To enlighten not his single narrow self, but the whole broad world.

It was like the rose which he had made when his mind was on Maryam. It was not what he had intended, a simple, common, scarlet rose; it was infinitely more beautiful. It bloomed unwearying, and where it had begun, on the bare dead bush, sprang green leaves, and buds that swelled into wine-dark splendor.

"See," he said to Maryam. "The magic knows. It gives me a sign."

His mind had never been as clear as it was now, as swift to learn, to master, to remember. Almost of itself it began to set in order what Master Ibrahim taught, and what Maryam added, and even what Bishop Hatto had never ceased to teach him. He pleased them all; he was proud, he could not help it, but it was a clean pride. He was—yes, he could admit it: he was happy.

Even in simple things, things with which a man of nobler birth would never sully his hands. This one was even excusable: he could call it part of his study of music. The bishop had had a new organ made for the cathedral; it was of a design he had never seen before, that one could play with the hands, and no need to leap about like a mad bellringer, hauling with all one's strength on levers and stops. The master artisan had been glad enough of hands that knew what they were about, and a mind that could take in a command the first time, and without mangling it besides.

Gerbert came up out of the bowels of the organ, dusty, oil-stained, and whistling, with an unidentifiable bit in his hand. "Joachim, what in the world is this?"

The master artisan glanced at it. "Harness buckle," he said.

"In an organ?"

Joachim shrugged. "That's the foundry. They like to have their little jokes." He caught the buckle as Gerbert tossed it to him, shook his head, thought visibly about spitting. He did not always remember that he was in the cathedral. Work, as he said, was work, wherever one did it.

The sanctity of the holy place was safe for the nonce. Joachim swallowed abruptly and bowed. Gerbert grinned wide and white in his blackened face. "My lord! Look, we've almost got it together."

Hatto returned the smile, though his glance about was slightly skeptical. "You have?"

"The worst of it's done. The rest is only niggling. And tuning, of course."

"Of course," said Hatto, drawing back as Gerbert clambered through the heaped flotsam, but offering a hand when the young monk slipped. Gerbert found his balance unaided, somewhat to the bishop's relief. He would wash, one could hope, but the smock he wore was beyond

60

redemption. He wiped his hands on it, to little enough effect, looked apology at his bishop, shrugged.

"I think," said Hatto, "that a bath should engage you before I begin. Go; find me after."

Scrubbed clean, in his clean habit, and still somewhat damp about the edges, Gerbert presented himself in the bishop's workroom. The secretaries were hard at it. Hatto himself had taken up pen and parchment, something he was not above doing, if need demanded it.

Gerbert waited in patience, though he burned to know what was important enough to bring the bishop himself with the message. He looked about for something that needed doing, did it. He had copied half a charter before Hatto called to him.

The bishop set down his pen and stretched. He looked tired, Gerbert thought. Gerbert was not sure that he ever slept. He always seemed to be awake when Gerbert was, and Gerbert hardly slept at all. There was too much to be awake for.

Hatto spoke abruptly, without preliminary. "What do you think now of Spain?"

Gerbert was less surprised by the question than he had been once, with three years' custom behind him. "It's splendid," he said.

"Does the light still cut?"

Gerbert answered smile with smile. "Like a fine Toledo blade."

Hatto nodded. "You have the eyes to see: more now than ever. Have you been pleased with your learning here?"

"Well pleased," Gerbert answered, "with all of it."

"Your masters are pleased with you. All of them. I've

61

written to your abbot in Gaul, and told him so. He need have no shame of the hawk he cast into the sky."

Gerbert's heart had stilled. "It's time," he said. "It's time to go back." He did not know what he felt. Gladness, it should be. He was going home. "But I'm not ready!" he cried.

"You are well grounded in all that I can teach."

"The other," said Gerbert. "The other—isn't—"

Hatto frowned. "Master Ibrahim tells me that such studies last lifelong. But an apprentice, you are no longer. He judges you ready to be reckoned a journeyman."

And journeymen . . . journeyed.

"He never tested me."

"Did he not?" In Gerbert's quenched silence, Hatto folded his hands, eyes upon them, brows knit still. "You know that I, with my lord count, have been seeking to raise the Spanish March in the estimation of the world; to prove that our realm is, indeed, worthy to stand level with any in the heart of Christendom. To that end we have agreed that the Church in the March should enjoy a greater eminence. I am, by courtesy and by the fact of my position, primate of the realm. My lord has convinced me that we should seek the blessing of Rome: that we petition for the raising of my see to an archbishopric, with all the authority that that entails. Therefore, when the month is out, we go to Rome, to lay our petition at the feet of His Holiness himself."

Gerbert swallowed through an aching throat. They would go, and he would have escort at least as far as Gaul. He should be honored.

It was not over. It could not be over. Green-girdled Aurillac, drowsing in the sun—no edges in that light, no gleam of strangeness.

Hatto looked up. "You will accompany us. My lord pope, they tell me, has some store of learning, and a great love of its practitioners. I should like him to see what Gaul and Spain together have wrought."

Gerbert had not heard aright. He was being sent back to Aurillac. He had not heard this, that he would go to Rome. To the lord pope. To Christendom's very heart and center. That was for his august age, when he was worthy of it.

"Unless," said Hatto in the stretching pause, "you do not wish it. You may choose to honor your vows to the abbey of Aurillac. They were not intended to stretch past these years in Spain."

Gerbert's head was shaking before his mind had taken it in. "I don't—I don't want— If my lord offers me Rome, I would be a fool to refuse him."

Hatto's face was grave, but his eyes glinted. "The hawk flies high," he said.

"Abbot Gerald will understand."

That was desperation, and guilt, but Hatto nodded. "He will, I think. When he entrusted you to me, he left you entirely to my discretion. I may, if you wish it, free you from your vows to the abbey."

"I don't want to leave the Church."

"That, never. Have you considered the priesthood?"

Often. Gerbert could not say it. He dipped his head: a nod.

"Swear no oaths now," Hatto said. "Take time. Think. Pray. Ponder what is possible, and what is wise. Rome, first. Then we shall see. I should like you to return here, to continue what you have begun. You may choose Aurillac. Or the Holy Father may offer you other choices altogether."

———————

These were enough and more than enough. Gerbert wandered in a daze. Rome. Freedom. To be a priest, and not a simple monk; to stand up before the face of God, and know himself chosen. He, born in a peasant's hut among the sheep, bred to till the earth.

He was not proud. He was terrified.

And in terror, grief. He must leave Spain. That was not a matter for choice. He must leave Master Ibrahim, and the library, and the house that was wider inside than out. He must leave Maryam.

He had known it would happen. But not so soon. Not so completely.

The mage's house was silent. It was not yet Gerbert's time to come there; it seemed empty even of its unseen presences. The gate opened to Gerbert's touch; the cool stillness settled about him.

He meant to find refuge in the library, among books which asked nothing of him but his pleasure. No magic. Something simple, in Latin, to take him out of himself. Something to soothe the wildly fluttering thing that was his mind.

Because his mind could not settle, he wandered, taking a way that before had led him, if indirectly, where he wanted to go. He had not forgotten what kind of house this was; he was not dismayed to find the rooms and stairs and passages only vaguely familiar. The key here, as with magic itself, was will, and that which was both more and less than will. He would go where he wanted to go, because he wanted to go there. Because he also wanted to delay, the house offered him new faces of itself.

He had not known before, how much of the Roman villa still stood beneath and within the Moorish dwelling. It had baths that he had never seen, worn and ancient but still, from the signs, made use of. A door behind them led to a stair, unlit, to be sure, but magic had a remedy. The soft cool light followed Gerbert down into a scent of earth and age and stone. It was clean, if musty. Someone, or some magic, held dust and damp at bay.

The stair ended in a passage. It seemed like any other in the house, straight, stone-floored, its walls plastered and painted white. Here as elsewhere, and as often in the more hidden ways, the whitewash was thin. Shadows gleamed beneath, a memory of line, color: Roman work, unwelcome to good Muslim eyes.

Gerbert paused to peer. He could almost puzzle it out. A vine. A cup, scarlet and gold. A shadow figure, god or mortal. Its hand seemed to beckon him onward.

He had found his refuge, if not the one he had expected. He went almost happily where his feet led him, to a low barred door and a sudden, frozen halt.

There was power here. He had been feeling it for a long while without realizing what he felt. His lip curled at that. Journeyman, was he? Then pray God his master never knew how blind he had been, or for how long.

He laid a careful hand on the door. The power pulsed, responding. It was not inimical, nor did he sense any evil in it. Yet it was nothing he had met before. In summonings . . . perhaps . . .

He shook his head sharply, to clear it. The power called. It *wanted*.

"What?" he asked aloud.

He knew what danger was; what magic could do, if one were unwise, or unprepared, or unguarded. Prudence warned him. He had never been given leave to come here.

He had never been forbidden.

He drew a breath. If this was a test, so be it. He spoke a word of opening.

He did not know what he had expected. A dungeon. A hall of treasure. An enchanted princess.

It was a simple chamber, vaulted and pillared like a crypt. No one had painted over the walls here, or torn up the mosaic of the floor. The colors dazzled him. Gold, scarlet, blue and green and violet, colors of earth and sea and sky, and images of them all. Dolphins leaped in the blue wave; men hunted the stag through the green wood; the eagle flew from cloud to cloud with the lightning in his claw. An emperor sat on a high throne. A shepherd played the flute among his sheep. A nymph bathed in a river, and a faun hid in the rushes, his eagerness all too clear to see.

Gerbert, blushing, cast his eyes about. They caught; he started. In the fascination of walls and floor, he had never seen what occupied the center. A plinth of marble, and on it a shape of bronze. The head of a god, it might be. Or a goddess? The molded ringlets told him nothing, nor the headdress that might have been either helmet or diadem. The face was of a youth or an antique maiden, beauty too pure for gender, strength and fineness both, cast in cool serenity.

No mortal face had ever been so beautiful. Yet, in the white magelight, it seemed almost real; almost alive. The eyes fixed on him as if they could see. The mouth seemed, almost, to smile.

The power had gathered to a center. That center. The image— "God or goddess?" he asked it, wondering aloud in his solitude.

"Jinn," said the image. "Jinniyah."

It was not a human voice. It was the voice one might have ascribed to bronze, if bronze could speak. Clear, melodious, higher than a man's, lower than a woman's. No breath animated it. It might have been a bell smitten, or a horn winded, faint and sweet.

Gerbert had not, of course, heard it. That it was a female of the race of spirits of the earth: the children of Iblis, the Muslims called them, of the infidels' Satan, though those were hardly demons as a Christian would understand it. They could be saved; they could be Muslims. Angels of the lesser ranks, perhaps; spirits wrought of earth and fire. Of earth they had gender, and will. Of fire, magic beyond the reach of mortal men.

The image had not moved or altered. The glint of its eye was only the light, shifting as Gerbert approached.

"Jinniyah," the image said again. Its lips moved as a man's would. A woman's. "What, has he never shown you one of us?"

Gerbert's teeth clicked together. "Not—one like you. "Lady," he added after a pause.

The image could laugh. It sounded like a chorus of bells. "Frankish courtesy! I am *slave*. Or *servant*. Or *Jinniyah*. Titles are not for the geas-bound."

"Geas?" Gerbert asked.

"Spell. Enchantment. Binding. Command. All and none; choose. I am but an oracle. You are a mage."

Barely. He stared at the image. A spirit bound in bronze. For its—her—sins? "You hardly sound oracular."

"My tongue is mine, unless I must prophesy. My binding is light, as such bindings go."

"Why?"

Without shoulders, improbably, she could shrug. "Am I a mage, to tell a mage?"

"I take it back. You are an oracle. You talk in circles."

"Arabesques," the image said. "My nature is my nature."

"Now I understand," said Gerbert. "You talked the wrong man into a rage."

"Not only talked." That, surely, was a hint of smugness. "And not a man. A man would have given me a body."

"*Maryam* enchanted you?"

"You doubt her power?"

"I doubt her pettiness."

"It was hardly petty," said the Jinniyah. "Nor was it she. I am older than that."

"Her mother—?"

"Her mother's mother's mother. They are a strong dynasty. And passionate. Jealous, that first of them was, and with excellent cause. She knew a fine face in a man. Alas for her, she did not know a fine mind to match it. He was a beautiful idiot. Good faith was beyond his capacity; good sense was as far out of his reach as the moon. He was," said the Jinniyah, "a most single-minded creature. But what his mind was fixed on—of that, ah, before God, he was a master."

"What became of him?" asked Gerbert, fascinated, though he had begun to blush again.

"He lived out his life with her. As," the Jinniyah said, "a singing bird. It was, as she pointed out to us both, the just measure of his intelligence."

"He died, surely. And she. Why did she never set you free?"

The Jinniyah smiled. It was not a comfortable smile: it had too little in it of humanity. "I was useful. Waste is anathema to a good housewife, or to a good mage; and wasted I would have been, had I been freed to fly where I would. She kept me while she lived, and perhaps she meant to free me at her death. That, unfortunately, was abrupt; and she had omitted to set down the spell with which she bound me. Her children were hardly minded to devote years and effort to seeking out the spell's undoing, when by it they would lose their oracle. They have been kind, in their fashion. Have they not put me here, with these walls to occupy me, and on occasion their company?"

"How unspeakably dull."

"Better dull on earth than chained in hell."

"There is that," said Gerbert.

There was a silence. Gerbert had time to comprehend the strangeness of it: that he stood here, at his ease, conversing with a bodiless head.

"Take me," said the Jinniyah.

He was speechless, staring.

"Take me with you," she said. "I am an oracle. I am meant for the high places. This is prison, and a waste. They use me almost never. They speak to me only when they must. Take me where I can be what I was meant to be."

"Steal you?"

"Free me."

"I don't have the spell for that."

Emotion could not twist that graven face, but the voice rang like iron smitten on iron. "Take me with you!"

"You are not mine to take."

"I choose you. I name you master. I will serve you, amuse you, prophesy for you. I prophesy. I have waited here, until you should come. I am your servant and your destiny. Through me you shall fulfill your dream."

He gasped like a runner in a race. "You are a devil. You tempt me. You lure me to my destruction."

"I am a Jinniyah and your slave. You go to Rome; the prince of your faith will honor you; he will give you as gift to a king. Princes will learn wisdom at your feet; kings will owe their thrones to you. Your Church itself will bow before you."

"No," said Gerbert, half-strangled. "You lie to win your freedom."

"I never lie. I tell you what will be. If," said the Jinniyah, "you take me with you."

"I am not a thief!"

"You are not. You take what chooses to be yours." The sweet inhuman voice softened, throbbing in his bones. "Take me with you."

His hands had stretched of their own accord. The bronze was smooth, cool, neither alive nor unalive. Magic sang in it.

"Take me," it whispered. "Take me."

It was theft; it was betrayal.

Could one betray an infidel?

He bit his tongue until it bled. That thought was worse than dishonorable; it was vile.

His fingers tensed to pull away. The head came with them. It weighed astonishingly little, as if it were hollow: full of air and fire.

His magic swelled and trembled, magic meeting magic, willing what must be. All that he had labored for, all the paths he had followed, from his father's fields to the tower of St.-Géraud to the mage's house in Barcelona, all had come to one single end: an end that was purest beginning.

This. He breathed a prayer. The image did not burst; the Jinniyah did not take flight in a stench of brimstone. "God is great," she said.

He clutched her to his chest and fought the urge to bolt. Walk, yes. Walk swiftly, but walk steadily. He was no thief. He had gained a servant.

At what price?

His stride lengthened. Out, he must get out. The corridors stretched endlessly. Stairs rose and fell without logic or sense. He could not drop what he held. His arms had convulsed about it. He was bound to it, irrevocably.

Never let the magic wield you.

It was not even his own magic.

At last, a place he knew, a door that opened on light, air, the streets of Barcelona. He fell toward it.

A shadow barred it. Obstacle—obstacle with power, reaching to hinder, halt, take what he carried. Must carry. Could not cast away. The magic uncoiled, lashing. Some last desperate remnant of sanity clutched at it, to beat it aside. Useless. It was its own power now, master of him who was barely a journeyman. What stood in its way, what was power also, raised up against it, rival and enemy, would fall, must fall.

He was strong. That was the horror of it, that he could exult in it: a black and swelling joy, shot with lightnings. No magic in this world was stronger than his.

No little power, this that stood against him, yet it was no match for him. What madness was in it, that it dared to try?

As easily, as contemptuously, as a child slaps at a fly, he smote it down.

The shadow fell. The voice that cried protest was mortal, human, a woman's.

The black exultation of power sank and died. He was empty; emptied. The magic, having wielded him, had abandoned him to cold and stillness and swelling horror. As he saw what he had done. As he saw what he had felled.

Maryam.

The veil had slipped, baring her face. It was waxen grey. Its eyes were wide, astonished. She had had no time to be afraid.

Dead. It rang like a gong. *Dead.*

The magic killed her. Magic—his magic—*he*—

He howled like a beast.

"Take me," said the demon in his arms. "Take. Take. Take."

He wept. He cursed her lying soul to deepest hell. He obeyed her. What else was left to him, save to go mad?

7

Gerbert lay before the altar of the bishop's chapel. The thing that had betrayed him lay on the altar itself, silent now, but not for any awe of sanctity. It would not speak where any but Gerbert could hear. Perhaps it could not.

The bishop's servants reckoned him mad. Rightly. They had not tried to drag him away, nor to do more than watch him, and keep their distance when he tore at himself, and eye the graven image with deep distrust.

He clawed at unyielding stone, welcoming the pain of flesh worn to bleeding rags. "I killed her," he said, his voice raw with weeping. "I killed her."

Robes whispered. He felt in his bones the one who knelt beside him, not touching him. "What have you done?" Hatto asked him, soft yet stern.

He rolled onto his back. Tears dried cold on his cheeks, stinging where his nails had rent them. "I killed Maryam," he said, simply, like a child.

Hatto's breath hissed as he caught it, but his face did not change. He glanced at the altar and its burden. "For that?"

"For my soul's damnation."

"Yet you came here. You do penance. Have you hope of atonement?"

"I want to die."

"Had that been true, you would have stayed to face her father."

Gerbert drew in upon himself, trembling in spasms. "He will hunt me down. He will not let me die. Oh, no. He will want me to atone, and atone, and atone, and—"

Hatto slapped him, hard. "Enough! You are not the first man ever to do murder. Even murder of magic. Get up."

There was power in that voice, if no magic. It drove Gerbert to his feet. It brought men in armor, whom he welcomed with open arms. "Seize me, bind me, chain me. Make me pay."

They did none of his bidding. They only guided him. Back through the bishop's palace. Back to his own small cell, with his books in it, and his pens, and his spare habit. They bade him stay there; they mounted guard.

It was enough. It would have to be. The damned could not pray. The mad could not read. The murderer could only lie on the hard cold floor and let his soul gnaw itself into nothingness.

Or try to. Great passions were alien to peasants' sons, even peasants' sons whose lust for learning had destroyed them. Reason kept wanting to intrude. Grief, yes, that was fitting. And guilt. But hysteria shamed her memory.

"I'm sorry," he said to it. "I'm—so—sorry."

It was not even pitiful. It was too feeble.

His weeping was saner now. He could think around it. They were no thoughts he would ever have wanted to think, but they were necessary. To face what he had done. To set it deep, where he could never forget it, or excuse it, or argue it away. Deep enough even, God willing, to touch his magic.

He shuddered on the stone. Magic. Oh, God, he hated it. *If thy right eye offend thee, pluck it out.*

Pluck. Out.

His body knotted. Simple, yes. Easy. Simpler and easier than facing it. Naming its name. Mastering it.

Master it?

She had. She had killed no one so distant as a sister of the heart. Her magic had destroyed her mother.

Was this how, in the end, she paid? How then would he pay? Who would love him, and fell him unthinking, because he was in the way?

He had an oracle now, to tell him. For all the good it had done Maryam, who had had it before him.

"Maryam," he said, grieving. "Maryam."

They brought him food and drink. He touched neither. He welcomed the pain of hunger and thirst, the ache of a body left too still, too long, on unyielding stone. Pain was a punishment.

How long he lay there, he neither knew nor cared. When they came for him, he went without either will or resistance. He felt light, hollow, emptied of aught but bare being.

Bishop Hatto waited for him. Hatto in his private chamber, with the image of bronze on the table before him, and across the table, still as the image, Ibrahim.

Gerbert's knees gave way. No one moved to help him. He knelt and stared at the magus' face. In this little while, it had grown old.

There was nothing Gerbert could say. They were cold, both of them, and stern. They had tried him, judged him, sentenced him. He knew better than to hope for mercy.

After an endless while, Ibrahim spoke. "Have you anything to say?"

Gerbert shook his head.

The magus' face twisted. A moment only: grief, rage, unbearable pain. Then it had stilled again. "Now," he said, low and rough. "Now you know the truth. What the magic is. What price it exacts."

"Blood," said Gerbert.

"No." Ibrahim bit it off. "Nothing so simple as blood. Did you love her?"

The hot blood rose to Gerbert's cheeks. "Not that way."

"Of course not," said Ibrahim. His contempt cut more cruelly than any lash of anger. "What was she to you, that your power must have her?"

"She was—" Gerbert's voice broke. "She was my dark rose. She was the light of my eyes. She was my friend."

Ibrahim had not moved, but a force like a strong hand closed Gerbert's throat. "She is dead. You slew her. What penance will you do for that, O slave of the Crucified?"

Gerbert shook to his foundations. But he had a voice, after a fashion. It served him. "Anything," he answered. "Anything you name."

"Even servitude in hell?"

"Anything."

Ibrahim looked long at him. He was brave enough, but he was no saint or paladin. He sank down under that black gaze, until he lay as he had lain before the altar.

The magus spoke above him, immensely weary. "I cannot even hate you." Gerbert looked up. He could see only a black robe, a slippered foot. "You did what all young mages do, if they are strong, if their strength exceeds their wisdom. She . . . even she . . ." Almost, he broke. He mastered himself. "You will do anything, you say. Can you do nothing?"

Gerbert could not understand.

"Nothing," Ibrahim said again. "Go, as you had intended. Live. Fly where your ambition takes you."

"But," said Gerbert, "that's not—"

The black eyes glittered. "No? Maryam is dead. I refuse you the comfort of expiation. I demand that you live in your guilt, and hone your power, and become what your destiny wills. I bid you live as she would have lived, had your magic not destroyed her."

Now, at last, Gerbert comprehended. So wise, he had been, in consoling Maryam for the death of her mother. Now he must live by his own, baseless wisdom. It was subtle, that punishment. And just. And in it, no mercy at all.

His head bowed. "As my master wills."

Ibrahim took no joy in that submission. He seemed to forget that Gerbert was there at all: turned, and as if he resumed a speech interrupted, said, "Will you go?"

"You know I must," Hatto said.

"You will not come back."

"That is with God."

"*Inshallah.*" Ibrahim said it bitterly, but not as if he would deny it. "Then it is farewell, my friend. I grieve that it must be thus."

"I grieve with you," said Hatto. "Your daughter—if—"

"She is tended." Ibrahim softened the merest degree. "I am grateful. But she needs nothing now. Nor I. Rest in God," said Ibrahim.

He had almost gone before Gerbert found voice to speak. "Master! You forgot—that—"

Ibrahim did not glance at the image on the table. "It is yours."

Gerbert started, trembled. "It's not—I can't—"

"It is yours," Ibrahim repeated. "It has chosen you. It will serve no other while you serve its purposes."

Gerbert had staggered to his feet. "I can't take it."

"It is not a matter of *can* or *will*. It is only *must*."

"I *can't!*"

Ibrahim turned back a little into the room. "Nevertheless, you will."

"Do you lay it on me?"

"It is laid on you." Ibrahim paused; he seemed to take thought. Or perhaps he had intended all of this, and only played it out because he chose. "What I command, beyond your life and your leaving . . . Kneel."

Gerbert had obeyed before he thought. His knees ached with bruises.

The long dark hands rose over him. He bowed his head beneath their power. "This I lay upon you," the magus said. His voice was soft, but that softness was terrible. "Mage you are, mage you shall be, master of the high and deadly Art. You have seen what price that Art exacts. For the honor of your soul, I command you: Never again betray any who has loved you, or aided you, or given you comfort; nor ever work harm with that power which God has granted you. Wield it wisely and wield it well, and never wield it to gain aught that is of this world. While that binding holds, may you prosper. If you break it, may you know such grief that death itself shall seem a mercy."

"I know it," whispered Gerbert.

"You know only guilt and shame and fear." Ibrahim drew back. His presence had lightened, but his power burdened Gerbert still, bowing him to the floor. "I cannot wish you well. That much of sainthood, I do not have. I wish you long life; I wish you wisdom, and strength. I wish you far from Spain."

"Soon," Gerbert said.

Ibrahim did not reply. He had turned his back. It was very straight, and pitilessly proud.

Far away in the city, the muezzin cried the hour of the Muslims' prayer. Maryam had taught Gerbert the meaning of it.

God is great! God is great! . . . Come to prayer,
O ye Muslims, come to prayer! Come to prosper-
ity, come to prosperity. . . .

Prosperity, thought Gerbert. Ambition. Destiny.

Ibrahim was gone. Hatto was silent. The image was silent, inscrutable.

He looked at it and knew what Ibrahim had meant. He could not even hate it. It had done no more than it was wrought to do. It was no human creature, to care that its doing had been bought with death. It would serve him well, if he would let it. If he could bear it.

He shuddered. Not now, before God. But later . . .

He would use it. He had a destiny. He even had a geas to keep him honest. He could not laugh, even in bitterness. Perhaps he would never laugh again.

"Tomorrow," said Hatto, like a bell tolling, "we go to Rome."

Gerbert bowed his head. "Tomorrow," he said. For all that he could do, for all its weight of sorrow, his heart had leaped up and begun, however painfully, to sing.

Part Two

MAGISTER ARTIUM

Rheims, A.D. 989

8

The archbishop was dying. In the city they barely knew it. In the cathedral they had begun the preparations for his burial. The cantor was composing the hymn of mourning; in the vestry they had taken out the vestments reserved for the funeral mass of a great prelate, and begun to repair the depredations of time and the moth.

The school tried to go on as usual. But the mood was strange, and everyone knew it. Half grief, for his excellency had been well beloved; half anticipation, for no one doubted who would take his place. Or what would happen then.

"Jews," came a snarl among the older students. "Saracens. Witches and sorcerers. We'll be overrun."

Even as Richer paused, the dissenter was fallen upon and pummeled until he yelled for mercy. But having gained it, he proved a wretchedly slow learner. "You know it's true! You know what that man is. He has Saracens in his very household. He mutters spells before the altar of his chapel. He'll turn this city into a nest of witches."

This time they gagged him with his own cincture, and kicked him for good measure. "No one," said the strongest of his chastisers, "no one talks like that about Master Gerbert."

They saw Richer then, and fell abruptly silent. One stooped over the offender, hissing in his ear. Richer, whose ears were as quick as a cat's, caught what he was not meant to catch. "Now you're for it. That's the master's pet: his tame wizardling."

It was amazing, Richer thought, how open a secret it all was. Outside of these walls, the school of the cathedral of Rheims was only that: a school of the liberal arts, the best in Gaul and maybe in the world. But here, everyone knew what else it was; what other Art some few of its chosen pursued. Not publicly, not where the ignorant could watch, but all the young imps had spied on classes that did not officially exist—and been royally disappointed, most of them. But enough had seen a wonder or two, to keep the rest coming back; and occasionally one would do more than that. Would find in himself some spark of what made a master. Richer knew. He had been one of them.

He grinned amiably at the huddle of boys, knowing well how daft he could look when he wanted to. It had its effect. They remembered that they had obligations elsewhere. They conveniently forgot their prisoner, who needed Richer's hand to pull him up, and Richer's help to untangle him from his cincture. He was not grateful. Richer did not ask him his name. His kind were less common in Rheims than anyone had a right to expect; they did no more harm than they must, and less than they might.

That would change, when Gerbert was archbishop. Seventeen years, he had labored at it: coming first to Rheims from service to pope and German emperor, to study logic under its great master, in return for instruction in mathematics and music for which the logician had proved to have no talent; strengthening the lesser arts, brightening his name, bringing in the best among masters and students; and slowly, quietly, letting it be known that he had another Art to teach. More—he would welcome others who could both learn and instruct; who would join him in making order out of the age-old chaos that was the art magic. They had a school now within the school, an order, a system, a sequence of masteries. They even had the old archbishop's silent acceptance, leavened with the love he bore the master.

It was going to be hard for Gerbert to lose that best of friends. Richer climbed the familiar narrow stair with little of his accustomed lightness. The door it led to was never barred; it never needed to be. It recognized Richer, and opened to his touch.

The master had a house of his own just outside the cathedral close, and a household large enough for a lord. Which, after all, he was: friend and teacher to kings and princes, liege man of the Emperor of the Romans, certain to be Archbishop of Rheims. But all those were only trappings. His heart was here in this chamber tucked between the school and the cathedral.

It was small. It had a window, shuttered in the bitter winter, though in summer it looked over the canons' cloister. Books tended to find their way there, sacred as often as profane, and Richer had seen a Vulgate resting with all apparent equanimity atop a grimoire. There was a table, a stool, a lamp. The first magic Richer had learned, had been to light that lamp without fire.

He did it now, taking in what the light showed him. Gerbert was making a new sphere of the heavens for his friend Constantine in Fleury Abbey; bits of it were scattered on the table. The sphere itself, a half-clothed skeleton, leaned precariously on a stack of codices. None was the one Richer had come for. He turned toward the bookpress, and started.

The master's antique bronze was famous in the school. Wherever Gerbert went, the wags said, there went the necessities of life: his chest of books, his army of servants,

and his heathen idol. It had a place in his house, in the
room where he received guests. For a while it had occupied a niche in his office in the school, where it terrified
the youngest pupils and tempted the older ones to steal it
and hold it for ransom.

Some of them must have tried it, or come alarmingly
close: the image was here, set as if on guard over Gerbert's
books of magic. Richer shivered in spite of himself. It was
a beautiful thing, and valuable, but he had never been
easy in his mind about it. Sometimes it seemed almost
alive: watching, listening, brooding in its mantle of power.
Which, surely, was only what any work of the founder's
art would bear, if it belonged to a magus, and if he used it
to aid in focusing his magic. A particularly tenacious rumor had it that the image was an oracle; that, if asked a
direct question, it was bound by geas to reply either yes
or no. Richer had seen no proof of that. It was simply a
beloved possession, a remembrance of the master's years
in Spain.

Yet Richer was not immediately willing to move it,
even to find the book he needed. He folded his long body
in front of it and considered the blank bronze face. It was
female, he had almost decided. Some trick of the light, or
of the place, or of Richer's sight which was not of the best,
had kindled a spark in the graven eyes: a spark which
seemed, for a breathless moment, to betoken a living
intelligence.

He shook it off. Too much labor, too little sleep, and
the constant tension that thrummed about the death of a
great lord—he was beginning to start at shadows. He set
hands to the cold metal.

"Careful," it said.

He did not start. He did not fling the thing away. He
did not even drop his hands.

"Your fingers will freeze," said the image. It sounded

86

like his nurse when he was small. She had not been old, or dull-witted, or a fool. But she had taken her charge to heart, and she had been most firm about it.

"Set me on the table," the image said, "and master yourself. The book," it added, "is not here. The master took it this morning."

Richer set the image where he was bidden, and stood chafing his numbed fingers. He did not know why he should be astonished. He had seen greater wonders than a statue speaking.

"I am rather more than that," it said. "You may find what you need in the lesser grimoire, there, beneath Hippocrates."

"Hippocrates?" Richer had forgotten the grimoire. He snatched at the small heavy book, raising it with a peculiar mingling of greed and awe. "Sweet saints, it is! And here was I, only last autumn, riding all the way to Chartres for a glimpse of a half-ruined text; and all the while, he knew that this was here. I could kill him."

"Don't," said the image. "It came not long ago. He was caught up in the archbishop's sickness, or he would have told you."

Richer flushed. It was something, to suffer chastisement from a lump of bronze. Unconsciously he clutched the book to his chest, scowling at the image. "I owe you thanks, I suppose."

"Your attention will do," the image said. "*He* gives me none. I am an oracle; and will he let me serve him as I was ordained to serve? He will not. The present, he says, is enough. And my friendship. Friendship! What is that, if he will not suffer me to help him?"

"Why? What can you do?"

"Warn him. Guide him through these quicksands."

"Is it as bad as that?"

"Yes," said the image.

Richer moved a step closer. "Is it because of the magic?"

"No."

"No? But—" Richer stopped, shifted. "He's not going to get Rheims, is he?"

"Yes," said the image, "and no."

Richer's teeth ground together. "Are you playing with me?"

"No." And before he could erupt: "He was afraid of temptation; and there was a matter of . . . guilt. He set a binding on me. I may only prophesy if questioned directly."

"Therefore, unless someone asks the right question, you can foretell nothing clearly."

The image could not nod, but he felt its assent, and its frustration. He had never thought of oracular spirits as prey to any such sentiments. "You would think," said this one, "that he would consider what he was doing in stopping my tongue. But when has he ever taken thought for anything that has to do with himself? He is one of nature's fools."

"He is the greatest mind in Europe," Richer said stiffly.

"Did I deny it?" The image sighed like wind in a bell tower. "He seems to think that you have a little sense. I would question that, but never your loyalty."

"You—" Richer choked on it, coughing till the tears sprang. "What *are* you?"

"His servant, of my own choosing. His friend, once he got over certain unhappy consequences of our meeting. His counselor, when he will allow it."

"His gadfly," said Richer. His eyes narrowed. "Or are you trying to press me into that service?"

"You," said the image, "have legs." And when he did not speak: "He needs his friends, and he needs them both loyal and clearheaded. Me, he never listens to. He says I fret."

"You're female," said Richer with sudden certainty.

"I resent that," said the image, sharp as two blades clashing. "I am a prophet forbidden to prophesy."

"Are you asking me to pity you?"

"I am asking you to help me. Our mutual master would stride naked into the desert, trusting in God and in his own brilliance to shield him from the sun. But the desert knows only that it is. Neither gods nor cleverness mean anything to it."

"What can I do? I'm no oracle."

"You are a man; you are loyal; you know what I am. Stand by him. Be braced, and do what you may to brace him, for whatever comes. He thinks that he knows the worst of it. He is a babe at the breast."

"If he knew what you thought of him, he'd melt you down for a chamberpot."

"He tried that," said the image. "Once."

Richer bit his lip. He did not know if he dared laugh. He remembered the book in his hands, ran his thumb along the smooth leather of its spine. "You should have no illusions about me. He seems fond of me, but I'm nothing close to what he is. If he won't listen to his oracle, he's not likely to care what one of his many students is thinking."

The image was impervious to doubt. "He will listen. Only give him time, and use your wits. And," she added, "take the small grimoire when you go."

He opened his mouth, but no words came. What he had taken for an echo of her voice, was the tolling of bells. The death knell, stroke and stroke and somber stroke.

"Go," sang the image like an echo itself. "Go!"

He snatched the grimoire, bundled it inside his habit with Hippocrates. Hastily he crossed himself, muttering a prayer for the departed. Only when he was done did it strike him. Books first, then the prayer. He was his master's pupil.

His master stood by the great bed, gazing dry-eyed at the man who lay there. A frail body for the spirit that had been in it, flesh shrunk to bone now, as if death could not wait even this little while before it seized all that belonged to it. The spirit was gone. Gerbert had shriven it; he had watched it go. It was a saintly soul, when all was considered. It had gone singing, eager as a child on its way to something promised, something wonderful.

Gerbert closed the wide wondering eyes, and straightened. Behind him, someone gasped and began to sob. He darted a glance, quelled a sigh. Yes, it would be that one. Arnulf, the old king's bastard, pretty as a girl with his wide blue eyes and his yellow curls, and just enough wits about him to tell a penance from a paternoster.

If Gerbert put his mind to it, he could be fair. The boy was no great light of intellect, but it was difficult to dislike him. He did not parade his pedigree; he granted respect to the peasant's son who, everyone knew, would be his archbishop. His trouble was simple mediocrity, and a lightness of mind that inclined him all too often to forget such niceties as truth and fidelity. In time, no doubt, he would be given high office in the Church—it would be expected of him, for his father's sake. Gerbert hoped that, when that time came, his superiors would have the sense to supply him with a competent secretary. Then he could look magnificent in his vestments, and the secretary could run the see for him.

Gerbert's teeth clenched. Grief struck like that, without warning, without mercy. It could not fell him. He set a kiss on Adalberon's cold brow. Part of it was apology. This royal offspring too had had a secretary, and looked magnificent, and been thought a puppet; but the Archbishop of Rheims had never been that. Whatever Gerbert had advised, Adalberon had chosen or not chosen, as his heart moved him. Before they were friends, they were lord and servant, and neither ever forgot it.

Now the lord was gone. The servant, turning, saw in the crowding faces what princes must see when they became kings. The shifting, the choosing: to accept, or to refuse. The dawning of awareness that the king was dead, long live the king.

They would do nothing until he spoke. It was not joy, that awareness of power. It was terror. His voice when it came was quiet, but they listened; they obeyed.

When the bells began to toll, it was all in hand. Gerbert's hand, as always. He was going to have to train a clerk or two to assist him. Richer, perhaps. A good one, that: good with words, good with numbers, passable with magic. The good ones found their way here; the power knew where to find its like.

Yes. Work would drive out both grief and fear. Grief for what was gone. Fear of what would follow. The Greeks had had a word: *hubris*. Getting above oneself. Attracting the attention of the gods.

"You let him die."

Gerbert stopped in the eye of the storm, and saw his conscience. Small, ancient, swathed in a vast expanse of black habit. "You let him die," said the apparition. "You who have magic, who can master death, you let him die."

"No man may conquer death," Gerbert said.

The ancient—was it man or woman, or was it anything at all?—cackled with laughter. "Any man may, if he be mage, and strong, and armored with love. But you loved ambition more."

"I gave him all I had to give."

"Maybe," said the creature.

Someone called to Gerbert. When he looked back, the apparition was gone. He felt cold and strange, as sometimes he did when the magic ventured on paths that were more grey than light.

What would an old god look like, if all his worshippers were gone, his altars cold, his youth leached away in ages of unbelief? Beautiful, deadly Apollo of the prophecies—would he have deigned to toy with an archbishop's servant?

Perhaps he occupied an image of bronze, and sent messengers to trick his master into prudence.

People were pressing on Gerbert, vexing him with urgency. He made himself hear what they were saying. "The king. The king is here."

Gerbert wanted to groan aloud. The archbishop had sent the summons as soon as he knew that his sickness was mortal; but the king had not come quickly enough. Or slowly enough. "God in heaven," said Gerbert. "Even a day . . ."

He received a measure of sympathy. Arnulf was there still. He could weep, Gerbert noticed, without marring his prettiness. A woman would happily have killed to learn his secret. Gerbert gave him orders, twice, to be certain that he remembered them; then sent him with appropriate escort to welcome, and thereby delay, the royal company.

"Why did you send him?"

Gerbert still heard Richer's voice from the region of his elbow, though the boy was a man now, and not a small one: a great deal of length and very little width, knobkneed as a spring colt, his mop of wild russet curls barely daunted by the dignity of the tonsure. He had the face to go with the hair, long, bony, and copiously freckled, and gifted with a remarkably sweet smile. Which he knew well how to use.

Which he was not using now. But the question was pure Richer. The boy was no better than Gerbert at keeping his thoughts to himself, or at remembering to whom he owed respect. Richer at least could claim an excuse: he had been born a nobleman.

"Why did you send him?" he repeated with his own peculiar variety of patience.

"How else was I going to stop his sniveling?" Gerbert snapped. He had not meant to be so sharp; he shook his head, rubbing his aching eyes. "He was there. He has manners, which is more than I can say for some."

"He also has an uncle."

"Everyone has—" Gerbert broke off. He knew what Richer was saying. "What do you expect? An assassin's dagger under his gown?"

"I don't know," said Richer. "He's not as stupid as he looks; and if his father had married his mother, he could have been king. If certain great churchmen had not decided that the kingdom needed a change of dynasty, he would certainly have been the nephew of a king. He may yet be one, if he goes back to his old ways. You know what he did the last time anyone let him loose within reach of his uncle. Now that he's within reach of his uncle's supplanter, what could he not do?"

"Hugh is king by right of election and by the will of the lords of Gaul," said Gerbert. "As Arnulf himself has admitted. He's no rebel now, whatever he was once. I can trust him to know how to talk to a king, and to know when to stop. He's safe enough."

Richer did not look as if he believed it. But it was done; he shrugged, sighed, swallowed what might have been a spate of words, and found something useful to do. He stayed close, which did not surprise Gerbert. Richer seemed to labor under the conviction that Gerbert was his especial property. Since he was competent, and he was usually quiet, Gerbert allowed it.

He was there when the king came. Hugh Capet had

carried himself like a king before ever he claimed a crown; now that he was king, he seemed comfortable in it, accustomed to the splendor as to the cares with which he earned it. The result, to Gerbert's eye, was a sort of ornate simplicity.

The archbishop was laid out in seemly fashion, with incense burning to cover the reek of sickness and death, and a fine white candle illuminating his face. When the king had bidden farewell to the man who above all had made him king, they would bear the body away to the embalmers, and then to the cathedral where he would lie in state until he was laid in his tomb.

Gerbert did not try to press himself upon the king. Arnulf, he noted sourly, had attached himself like a limpet to the royal side. He also noted Richer's glance, which he did not choose to acknowledge. If Arnulf wanted to overwhelm the king with his loyalty, let him. Cursed as he was with an uncle who by birth should have been king and who by rebellion was doing his best to overturn the election, he needed all the help he could find.

The king prayed long over the archbishop's body. His attendants waited with the patience of courtiers. Not all were at ease in the fog of incense, among the black-robed priests. Old warrior stock, those, bowing to the power of holy Church yet subtly contemptuous of the men who wielded it. One kept glancing at Gerbert as if the priest had been a slumbering snake. Gerbert saw him shape a sign; felt the fear that lay beneath it.

Gerbert stifled a sigh. It was nothing he had not seen before. If it was not fear of magic, it was fear of learning itself. Yet here, in the presence of death and of the king, it did not seem so little a thing.

He shook himself. Any more of that and he would be fretting as endlessly as the Jinniyah.

The king crossed himself, rose. His cheeks were damp

but his eyes were hard. They paused on nothing in particular, nor did he speak, though Arnulf dithered, whispering in his ear. He walked past Gerbert without word or glance, and left the chamber.

Richer hardly waited for privacy before he burst out with it. "See? *See?*"

"It didn't look like assassination to me," said Gerbert with mildness that should have alarmed Richer, if he had not been past it.

"He's up to something. Have you ever seen him hang on anyone like that?"

"Yes," said Gerbert. "Me, when he wanted to learn a little magic."

Richer snapped erect. "You didn't!"

The master raised a brow. Richer would have liked to be able to do that. "Why not? Power is dangerous without training."

"That puppy doesn't have the power God gave a flea."

"So he discovered. It's best that way. If I'd told him, he would have hated me for it."

"How do you know he doesn't hate you? He's a Caroling. You helped to take the crown away from his kin."

"He has more reason to hate the king. Whom, on the contrary, he seems to be courting."

"Yes!" cried Richer. "And for what? Why wouldn't the king talk to you? He was avoiding you, I could see it. What poison has that little snake been pouring into his ear?"

Gerbert sighed. He looked worn to the bone. "The boy has something he wants. Now if ever is the time for him to get it."

"At what cost to you?"

Now at last Gerbert frowned. "You are fretting, Brother."

Richer flushed, but he would not back down. "When the old king's bastard starts making love to the new one, something smells of rat. When you add to that an archbishop dead, a rebellion smoldering, and a chestful of laws against the practice of magic, you have trouble. *You*, master."

"I'll talk to the king," said Gerbert. Not as if he were convinced. As if he had been going to do it for his own purposes, and now he wanted to quiet Richer's fretting with it. "It's my duty as the archbishop's secretary. I'll see that he has facts to go with the young pup's whisperings. Whatever they are."

"Sedition."

Gerbert laughed, and for a moment he looked as young as Richer. "To the king? Go on, lad, you're starting at shadows. Go and rest. I'll have plenty for you to do in the morning."

Richer resisted, but Gerbert's will was immovable and his magic incontestable. Gerbert could enspell him to sleep then and there; and something in his eye promised exactly that. With bitter reluctance, Richer yielded.

But he had the last word, from the door, just before he bolted. "Carolings may be shadows, but there's a little substance in them yet. Aren't they the children of Charlemagne?"

9

Gerbert did not find it easy to gain audience with the king. Not that he was slighted, precisely, but his majesty was much beset with business; or he was resting; or he would see the master later, but later never seemed to come.

Gerbert knew avoidance when he saw it; he needed no lessons from Richer. Greater kings than Hugh Capet had taught him that aspect of royal behavior. They had also taught him how to deal with it.

He was not afraid. He was barely apprehensive. Even knowing that Arnulf had access when he did not. He had Rheims, in fact if not yet in name; he had the old archbishop's formal blessing. He did not intend to lose what he had gained.

Therefore he forbore to force his way into the king's presence. Let Hugh remember what Gerbert was, and what he himself would be without Gerbert's help. Duke of the Franks was a handsome title, but King of the Franks was handsomer by far.

Cold thoughts for a priest of God. Gerbert shivered in the warmth of his sanctum. He had been trying to pray, but the world was too much with him. The chart of the hours over which he had been laboring was losing its power to engross him. Yesterday morning, Adalberon had gone to his tomb. At his funeral feast, Gerbert had had a place near the king, but not beside him. The king had been lost in thought, or else in converse with one or another of his lords.

He straightened his aching back. His eyes, lifting, met eyes of bronze.

The Jinniyah had been most commendably silent. He did not flatter himself that it was obedience to his will. She only ever obeyed him insofar as it suited her.

He could remember hating her, shrinking from her, abhorring the very thought of her presence. He was a good hater, he had discovered; a steadfast holder of grudges.

He had tried to destroy her. Once. Thinking by then, in part, to set her free, but thinking most of casting out the memory of grief. And discovered the fullness of the price which he had paid for her.

She was his oracle and his destiny. In that great stroke of pride and power which had felled Maryam, he had not only bought the Jinniyah; he had made her part of him. His magic was in her.

Not all of it; nor even, in the beginning, most. Enough, only, to mean that her destruction would weaken him to death. When he knew it, in the passion of his revulsion, in his grief that would not heal, he did two things. He swore anew the oath which he had sworn to Ibrahim, to work no magic save for the gaining or the teaching of knowledge, nor ever to advance himself by it in the world or in the Church. And, when he had sworn this vow upon the altar of God, he had set the seal on it, gathered all the power that was in him, all the terrible, beautiful, demon-seductive magic, and poured it into the enchanted bronze.

"You were mad," she said.

He heard her as much within as without, ringing in

his bones. He regarded her face that was more familiar even than his own. "Yes," he said. "I was mad. But sane enough in the heart of it. I took back only what I needed. The rest I left to you. Never again will the magic wield me. You will see to that."

"That's not Christian humility. That's pride; and cowardice. Do you think that investing your power in a creature outside of yourself, is going to bring you one jot closer to escaping it?"

"No. But it keeps me from temptation."

She refrained, eloquently, from comment.

"I don't know when I stopped dreading the sight of you," he said. "Or how."

"Of course you do. When you saw the use in a tame oracle. Even if you did bind and gag me."

"I had to keep us both honest."

Her lip curled. "One of us is too honest by far."

"I forgive you."

She laughed. Someday he would invent an instrument that sang so, with such purity of tone.

No. He did not loathe the sight of her. Nor had he, in years out of count. Either it was his damnation, or it was his salvation.

He touched her. She was cold, as bronze must be when it is winter, even in the warmth of a mage's chamber. She had gone still, as if neither life nor power dwelt in her. But she was alive with both, a fire beneath the cold, a pulse like blood within the shell that bound her essence.

"You were my penance," he said. "You became my friend."

"A perfect description of a wife. As I make a perfect wife for a priest. The one who enspelled me would be delighted."

He smiled, but briefly. "Would you like to be free?" he asked her.

"It would kill you if you tried," she said.

That was like her: not quite an answer, but sufficient for the purpose. "You're not prophesying," he said. "You're talking around the question."

"I don't need to prophesy. I know what I would feel in my bones, if I had any. You'd have to use all your magic, and that is bound up in me; the spell's breaking would tear you asunder. Freedom would be sweet, but not at that price."

"You aren't willing to pay as I paid?"

She could not move, but she seemed to draw herself up. "I am neither the fool nor the mage that you are. I am merely a very minor spirit. And," she said, "your servant."

"Always that," he said a little wryly. His hand was still on her cheek, going numb with the cold. He lowered it.

"Master?"

It was one of Gerbert's own, quiet Bruno who had been his servant since he came to Rheims. The man was no less quiet now, but his eyes were watchful.

"A message, *magister*. The king will see you as soon as it pleases you."

Gerbert did not leap up like an eager boy. He took his time: put away the chart, gathered together the bits of parchment, the pens, the inks in their bottles. Bruno had fetched his boots and his heaviest cloak; having seen Gerbert into them, the servant produced his own and stood ready to follow.

Almost, spitefully, Gerbert considered making it his pleasure to keep the king waiting for a day or three. But the king was the king. Gerbert snuffed the candle by which he had been working, and paused. The Jinniyah said nothing. Of course she would not, before this man who had no magic.

He shook himself. He trusted too much in her presence, nagging, exhorting, advising; he was forgetting to do his own thinking. As he was forgetting his vow, to wield no magic in matters of the world.

Bruno was waiting. Gerbert waved the man ahead of him, and left his oracle to her silence.

He caught his breath as the cold of the outer air smote his face. It was close to vespers, from the look of the sun; he realized that his stomach was empty. He had forgotten to eat.

The sooner he faced this, the sooner it would be over. And yet he paused. Seventeen years, and still it could catch in his throat: this city that was his, this island of humanity in the wilderness that still, for all the labors of kings and farmfolk and holy Church, was Gaul. There should be a wine like the light that fell on it even in winter's snow, pale gold, effervescing in the eye like wine upon the tongue. It was cooler than the honey-warmth of Aurillac, softer than the swordlight of Barcelona, cleaner than the mists and miasmas of Rome. From the moment he saw it he had loved it, and the city on which it lay. Saint Remigius' city at the crossing of the Roman roads, ancient and holy, where kings came to be crowned.

Where a king waited, while a mere and humble priest dallied in the cold. He ducked his head into the warmth of his cloak, drew a breath that bore only a slight edge of ice, and stretched his stride.

———————————

Rheims was a fief of the Church, therefore it had no secular lord. But the king kept a house by the gate that looked out over the cleared and rolling fields to the river, large enough to merit the name of palace, part of it built into the city's walls. From the school the walk was not long, but there was a crowd to fight: Rheims had barely begun to empty, yet, of those who had come to see the archbishop laid in his tomb, and others had come after, drawn by the king's presence. Gerbert began to regret not coming mounted, with escort.

He had been accused of keeping great state for a schoolmaster. His accusers would have been gratified to see him now. But instinct had bidden him do it, and he trusted instinct, which laired in the roots of his magic.

The king's guards recognized him. They showed him respect, of which he took due note. One of the two, taking Bruno's place at Gerbert's back, conducted him within and handed him over to a page, who bade him wait in an anteroom.

No one waited with him. The palace was far from empty: it was full of armed men, their servants, their women, their hounds and hawks, a jester or two, a dwarf with a gargoyle's face, even the odd child. Yet none came into the small cold cell in which Gerbert sat. It was a chapel of sorts: a crucifix hung on the wall above a reliquary in a niche, a shadow and a gleam in the flicker of a rushlight. Gerbert prayed briefly, though the relic was not genuine. That was a service he would offer when he had taught the world what magic was: to winnow the true relics from the false. Though perhaps he would not be thanked for that. A shrine that had built its fortune on a lie, would hardly be grateful for the unmasking.

He did not like to wait, but he had had long training in it. He settled in as much comfort as he could on the bench that faced the relic, wrapping himself well against the chill, and set his mind to the puzzling out of a spell. There was a certain ratio in the composition of the powder with which one warded the circle; if that ratio were altered, bearing in mind the combined and the individual efficacies of its components, and the effect of the incantation and of the fundamental magic, then . . .

He was almost sorry to be called into the king's presence. His body was grateful: it was a good strong body, as bodies went, but it was no longer young. It creaked as he rose, and protested with pain.

It was still his servant. He mastered it with force of will; it bore him where he was bidden to go. Into the solar, as it happened, behind a hall full of men fed, wined, and readying for the night's diversions.

The king had eaten, from the evidence of the cup and the bowl, and the wolfhound worrying a bone at his feet. He was alone but for a servant or two, which was not usual.

Having done proper reverence, Gerbert sat where the king indicated, on a stool near the fire. One of the servants offered wine heated with spices, which Gerbert was glad to accept. He wrapped his hands about the cup to warm them, and sipped cautiously, savoring richness: cinnamon, cloves, the bite of pepper. He murmured a compliment.

"The spices were gifts," the king said, "from the Empress Theophano."

The Lady of the Romans, wedded to the Saxon emperor who had died all untimely, regent for the child who had taken the throne. She reckoned herself Roman truly: she was a princess from Byzantium which called itself the only proper heir of old Rome, kin to emperors of the east. She was very beautiful. She was also very capable, and strong-minded as any man. And she was, by oaths sworn first to her husband's father when Gerbert was a youth in Rome, Gerbert's liege lady.

"May God bless her generosity," Gerbert said. "She will be grieved to hear that my lord Adalberon is dead."

"She is not alone." The king took off the circlet that

bound his brows, and rubbed the deep furrow where it had been. He sighed deeply. "I know that God has a proven fondness for taking His bishops when their great tasks are done, but I could wish that He had seen fit to let us keep Adalberon for a little longer."

"Perhaps He has other purposes which none of us yet knows."

Hugh's glance was sharp. "Time only will tell us that. Unless . . . ?"

"My lord knows," said Gerbert with careful calm, "that a godly man does not vex the Divinity with questions as to what will be."

"Even if he has the . . . wherewithal to do so?"

This was perilous ground. Hugh fought well in the field, he could not have won his vassals' respect else, but the war of words and wits was more properly his element. Gerbert did not set down his cup: that would have been a betrayal. But he drank more slowly, and feigned more often than he sipped. He took his time in responding to the question. "A man who has the wherewithal to do murder, does not in wisdom choose to do so."

"No, *magister*? What if the murder is necessary?"

"No murder is necessary, sire. The taking of life for justice's sake is execution."

"Even in war?"

"That depends upon the motives of the murderer."

"So: and why not in prophecy as well?"

"Life and death are given into man's hands, to wield as God wills. Prophecy is the province of God."

"What then of the prophets?"

"God chose them. I," said Gerbert, "have not been so chosen, greatly though your majesty honors me in suggesting it. If you wish your fortune told, there are plenty in the realm who claim that power. Or shall I cast a horoscope? That, I can do. The stars are written in patterns for any educated man to read."

"And so any educated man seems moved to do." The king spoke sharply, impatient. "You are not any educated man, Master Gerbert. You are something beyond that."

"So I am," Gerbert said. "I have arts dead in Gaul since Rome became Byzantium. I've taught them to any who can understand. Twenty years ago I was something to marvel at. Now I'm simply the first of many."

"I sent my son to you," said the king. "He wasn't the best of your pupils."

"Nor was he the worst. He was and is a bright lad; you can be proud to be his father."

"You didn't teach him all that you have to teach."

"I taught him all that he needed to be either prince or king."

"A king doesn't need magic?"

There: it was out. Gerbert almost smiled. "No one *needs* magic. Magic needs us. A king . . . if it were given to him, he would bear a greater burden even than kingship. Power; possibility. Temptation. To use what he has, all of it, to work his will in his kingdom. How easy then to lose proportion; to equate his will with God's."

"Not if he has wisdom."

Gerbert straightened on the stool. "My lord, your son has wisdom—as much of it as is granted any man so young. What he has not, and that you may be glad of, is magic. It's a rare gift, that, and dangerous. There's danger enough for him in kingship. Would you wish more on him?"

"No," said the king. "No. He's a good pupil: he told me much the same. You taught him, at least, not to fear what he can't see. He's an alarmingly rational young man."

For a prince, Gerbert thought but did not say. His highness' rationality did not extend to women. Aloud he said, "I gather your majesty is satisfied with his son's education. Despite its omissions."

"Satisfied, yes. I know what you have here. I'd like to see it continue."

Gerbert tensed infinitesimally. "So it shall, my lord. The foundations are laid. We only have to build on them."

The king nodded. He, too, had tensed. He was coming to it. And none too soon, Gerbert thought. Until the king said, "You know that my crown is a matter of contention. I hold it by election. Another claims it by right of blood."

"Charles," said Gerbert with strained patience. "Duke of Lower Lorraine under the Saxon imperium. Brother of your late predecessor." Uncle of a certain clerk of the cathedral of Rheims, but he did not say that. "May God teach him the error of his ways."

Hugh was no fool. He knew irony when he heard it. He bared his teeth in a wolf's smile. "God, or the king in God's name. If you were king, *magister*, and Charles were offered to you on a platter, would you take him?"

"I might," said Gerbert, "inquire as to the price of the merchandise."

The king laughed. "A wise bargainer! What price would you reckon too high?"

"My soul," Gerbert answered promptly.

"Ah," said the king, sobering. "Yes. That would be high." He paused. "What of an archbishopric?"

Gerbert looked into the king's eyes, though they tried to slide away, and knew. He was not surprised. He did not, as yet, know what he felt. His voice came easily: he was proud of that. "So. Arnulf has become a loyal man. That's worth the price, if he can pay it."

"He promises that he can. Charles the pretender, delivered into my hands. And in return—"

"And in return, Rheims." Gerbert's wine had gone

cold. He sipped it regardless, wanting to drain it in a gulp. "It's a fair exchange."

"You think so?"

The king honestly seemed to care what he thought. He, who understood much that he had been refusing to understand, was oddly touched.

"You'll keep your place," the king said. "Unless, of course, you would prefer to go elsewhere."

Gerbert's shoulders tightened. "Rheims is home. My work is here. Where else would I want to go?"

The king seemed relieved; even pleased. "The boy needs you. He's young; he has no experience in ruling a great domain. And," Hugh added, "he may need an eye kept on him. Not that I mistrust him. He's agreed to swear fealty on the Eucharist, to become my man in soul as in body. But he's still young enough to be . . . impressionable."

"I see," said Gerbert. As he did. He was not to have what was his by right of labor and of ability, but he would be set on watch over the young intriguer who had it. For the kingdom's peace. For a king's ease of mind.

Now he knew what he felt. Anger; bitter disappointment. And black amusement. So much for his pride and his high ambition. He was forty-four at Candlemas. Arnulf was twenty years younger. He could guess which of them would outlive the other.

The king shifted uncomfortably. "You know how little I like this. You also know how little choice I have. I offered him another see, when one should become vacant; he wouldn't hear of it. Rheims is here, and now, and powerful enough to sway even Charles of Lorraine."

"I understand," said Gerbert. Clearly; not choking on it.

"You do," the king said. "Forgive me. I'm beset with

107

knaves and fools; I've forgotten what it's like to deal with plain good sense."

If he chose to see it as sense, that was his privilege. No doubt it salved his conscience. Gerbert rose and bowed as a schoolmaster should bow to a king. "I will do my lord's will as best I can. Does my lord give me leave to go about it?"

Hugh hesitated. His eyes met Gerbert's; he stiffened. "You may go."

It was not a good parting. But Gerbert dared not stay to mend it. He was a practical man; he was not likely to murder a king outright, even for such provocation. His magic was another matter. It recked nothing of oaths or of prudence. It knew only that its master was betrayed.

He could not go to his house. He could not face the school, or the cathedral, or—before God—the archbishop's palace. Night had fallen while the king cast down all that he had worked for, and trampled on the shards. The cold seared his lungs; but he was warm to burning.

His servant did not take kindly to dismissal, but he knew Gerbert's mood, and feared it. He obeyed.

Walls were no bar to a mage; gates, even locked gates, yielded before him. Gerbert strode away from Rheims under stars like chips of ice, seeing and not seeing them, knowing and not knowing the road beneath his feet, the wind in his cloak, the city falling ever more swiftly behind him. His body was but the mount he rode; he spurred it without mercy.

At the river he checked. The bridge arched over the ice, clad in snow that glittered in starlight. His boots thudded on the hewn timbers. It was not true, what the tales said, that a wizard could not cross running water; but the magic turned strange over it or on it or in it: wanted to flow as water flowed, as in the presence of fire it burned the brighter. Magic was the fifth essence that was all the elements and none; that, without them, could not be.

He was not cooling from the fire of anger, to tell over old lessons. He was ruling the magic by sheer, grim will. It could blast the king, or the interloper, or the city itself. Or if he would not have that, turn subtle: sway minds to a new will. He was Adalberon's chosen successor, groomed for it, trained for it, meant for it. Who was Arnulf, to lay claim to it? Who was Hugh Capet, to take it from him?

On the empty road, amid the fields that rolled snow-whitened into the night, Gerbert flung out his arms and roared aloud.

Richer found him a little before dawn, crouched by a fire in a shepherd's hut. The shepherd had abandoned it in one of the last wars; its roof was half fallen in and one wall broken down, but the rest were solid enough.

Gerbert greeted his pupil with a glance and a grunt. In this place, in this light, he seemed to have shed his priestly dignity. He looked as if indeed he had been born in such a place, raised to till the earth, to tend the sheep.

But power knew power, and Richer knew his master. He tethered the mule he had ridden and the mule he had led, and approached the fire, saddlebag in hand. He had bread, cheese, ale; he had a napkinful of hazelnuts.

Gerbert did not refuse his share. Richer nearly wept with relief. They ate in silence, warmed by the fire, the only sound the cracking of nutshells. Gerbert watched one of the mules uncover a patch of grass and crop it. Richer watched Gerbert.

After a very long while Gerbert said, "That's the archbishop's mule."

"She wanted to come," said Richer.

Gerbert's glance was sharp.

"You know she detests Brother Goldilocks," Richer said.

"That will be Archbishop Goldilocks to you, sir."

"Will it?"

Richer braced for wrath. None came. Gerbert dropped a handful of nutshells into the fire and watched them flare and crackle, his brows knit, but not in anger. "Yes," he said. "It will."

Incredulity tangled Richer's tongue. "But he—you— the king—"

"The king," said Gerbert, "is the king. The choice of archbishop is his. He has chosen. I abide by his choice."

Not easily. Not willingly: it showed in every line of him. "But it's *wrong!*" cried Richer.

"How do you know that? Arnulf brings something of great value to the kingdom: the ending of civil war. I can offer nothing but experience. It's not," said Gerbert, "as if I had any fundamental right to the office. What I can do for it, I can continue to do in my present capacity."

"Arnulf is a snake."

"Arnulf is a king's son."

Richer spat. "*That* for kings' sons. He's a bastard to the marrow. Do you know he's been wooing Rheims while he woos the king? The clergy have the illusion of election, after all. He's making sure he wins it."

"He will. The king expects it."

"How can you be so saints-beblessed calm?"

Gerbert almost smiled. Perhaps it was only a trick of the firelight. "Practice. And practicality. And a long cold night to think in. Maybe I'm simply not meant to hold higher office than this. A schoolmaster I am, and a school-master I remain. Others will take the great titles.

"But I," he said with some satisfaction, "still keep a

little of the power. That's where a mage belongs, Richer. In the shadows, shaping what passes in the light."

Richer did not want to believe it. "You've been cheated. You should rise up and fight it."

"And add another war to this one which Arnulf has promised to stop? No. I grit my teeth and swallow it."

"Go away, then. Take your school somewhere that appreciates you. Leave Arnulf to do his own drudgework."

"I admit," said Gerbert, "I've considered it. But I have my pride. I won't run like a whipped dog. Nor will I let that puppy ruin my work here. I'll outlast him, Brother."

"Or die trying." Richer glared at the fire until it cowered in terror. "My family has served the Carolings since they were servants themselves, bowing at the feet of the long-haired kings. But now, I tell you, I could wish to God that all of them were dead."

"As long as you don't do more than wish," Gerbert said. "Sore though the temptation may be. I'm no worse off than I ever was. I'm simply . . . disappointed. Men have been disappointed before. They haven't died of it."

"Haven't they?" muttered Richer. He was, oddly and unexpectedly, comforted. No less angry; no less outraged. Yet Gerbert was proving himself master of this adversity as of every other.

Gerbert rose, stretching. "Look: the dawn. We have a day to face, and a city. And a new archbishop."

He sounded almost cheerful. Richer shook his head, rising with considerably less grace, gathering up his bag and his bottle and the remnants of bread and cheese and nuts. Gerbert had taken a crust for tribute to the white mule.

Richer's smile took on an edge of malice. Whatever else Arnulf might have taken, Alba at least he would not get. She had made her feelings known, emphatically. His new excellency would not be sitting down in any great comfort for a day or six.

Richer did not even have to feel guilty. Alba had let fly entirely of her own accord. With Gerbert, now: with Gerbert she was her dignified self, accepting tribute, allowing him to mount. *She* knew who was her rightful master.

10

Arnulf was so ungracious as to gloat over his victory. "You know what you do best," he said to Gerbert when it was over. The election, without Gerbert's rivalry to slow it, had been a simple thing; less simple the task of transforming a clerk into an archbishop. He was still rubbing his new tonsure when he spoke to Gerbert, ruefully, for as a clerk he had not been as scrupulous in maintaining it as a priest and an archbishop must be; and he had been vain of his yellow curls. "What you've done, by all means, go on doing. I'll not meddle except as I must."

Nor had he, as spring bloomed into summer, and as the king's war with Charles showed no sign of abating for any of Arnulf's doing. Little as he could do, with an archdiocese to settle. He was not doing badly, Gerbert judged, though he was learning that wide blue eyes and an air of invincible innocence were of little use in contending with fractious underlings.

Now they were all here in the mellow gold of harvest time, gathered in council by their archbishop's command. Gerbert, absorbed in the complexities of housing, feeding, and entertaining all the bishops and half the lords of the see, hardly noticed that Arnulf was making himself scarce.

He did notice that the inner school had gone rather abruptly out of session.

"The archbishop ordered it." Richer was still there, but clearly that was his own choice. "What with the council and the uproar and the scarcity of lodgings, his excellency has given us all a holiday."

Gerbert had thought that his anger was long since cooled. It startled him with sudden, searing heat. "His excellency? His excellency, was it? Who is the master of this school? He or I?"

Richer was quite unfrightened. If anything, he looked as if he were enjoying himself. "He said that you were occupied completely in setting up the council; you didn't need to fret yourself with other matters, when he could take them so well in hand."

Gerbert half rose from his worktable. But behind the flare of temper was cold logic, and cold logic reminded him that Arnulf was, after all, archbishop. There would be time enough later to teach him where not to trespass.

Richer poked his long nose into the letter which Gerbert had been reading. Gerbert forbore to snatch it away. "So," the monk said. "You've still got friends at the imperial court."

"To little enough purpose," Gerbert muttered.

"Yet." Richer picked through the books on the table. "Will the empress offer you a place in her following, do you think?"

"Why should she? She has troubles enough of her own, without fretting over a single very minor servant who happens to have fallen into a trap of his own making."

Gerbert made little effort to hide his bitterness. Richer stopped fidgeting and regarded him steadily. "You could leave."

"No," said Gerbert. "I'll go only if I go to something

better. Arnulf hasn't meddled with me before this; I'm not so wretched as you might think."

"I never thought you were." Richer paused. "Is it true, what they say of her? That she's mastered the Greek magic?"

"Mastered it," Gerbert said, "no. She married too young; she centered too much of herself on being queen. But she has magic, and some little wisdom in its ways. Once it seemed that she might want to learn from me. Now . . . who knows? An empire is as demanding a master as any on this earth."

"As demanding as you?"

Gerbert glared; then, unwillingly, he laughed. "Almost. Do you have something useful to do here, or are you trying to waste my time?"

The boy did not even trouble to blush. "I'm wasting your time, of course. You forgot dinner again, did you know that?"

"Bruno remembered," said Gerbert, rising. "Since you have time on your hands, you can spare a little of it, surely, in aid of your education. When did you last trouble your head with astronomy?"

Richer managed to look both eager and dismayed. Music and medicine were his first loves. Astronomy, he had no great talent for. He tended to fall asleep. Still, he said, "I haven't forgotten too much of it."

"Good," said Gerbert. "You can do my calculations for me."

By a shielded lantern, on the roof, while Gerbert compared the sky to his charts and added new figures to his old ones. Richer did not mind. He had the abacus to play with, that miracle of the Moors which Gerbert had brought back with him from Spain. The stars were singing

115

their high cold song. The roofs of Rheims spread below, and beyond them the walls, and the darkness of field and river and wood. It was a fine warm night. Almost too warm for a woolen habit. Richer rolled up the sleeves and bared his knobby knees and an inch or so of linen trews, letting the soft air cool him.

Gerbert seemed not to notice. *He* was never anything but properly covered, winter or summer. The students liked to wonder what was under it. Maybe he had a tail, like an Englishman; or a cloven hoof. Though Richer had seen his feet in sandals, and they were perfectly ordinary feet.

"Asleep already?" Gerbert asked a little sharply.

He started, blushing fiercely in the dark. "No! My mind was wandering."

"So it was," said Gerbert. "There, now. Where did you leave off?"

Richer began to tell him, paused.

Gerbert was on his feet. The city, the wall, the field: all lay wrapped in night. On the field, something glittered; something rang, far and faint. Like metal on metal.

Like a gate opened that should have been locked fast; like armed men let into the sleeping city. Like—very like treachery.

Gerbert's face in the starlight was white and shocked. Not that it had happened. That he had had no warning at all.

Richer rifled his memory for an idea, a spell, anything. He found only emptiness.

Armed feet rang on the stone of the stair. The trapdoor was open in all good faith; it belched forth helmets, armor, drawn swords. Gerbert made no sound as they seized him. Richer fought, and got a drubbing for his pains. Gerbert was wiser. The one man who raised a fist against him, met his eyes and drew back muttering.

———————————

They were all penned in the archbishop's hall: a fine catch of notables in every stage of dress and undress. One young lord was as naked as he was born, and loudly furious. A lissome figure clung to him, darting glances through a veil of hair. If she was frightened, she had it well in hand, and her lover with it, and the cloak which slipped just far enough to bare a white curve of shoulder. Richer would remember that afterward: the bold brown eyes, the soft white skin amid the bobbing tonsures.

Arnulf was in the middle of it, as ruffled and seemingly as astonished as anyone, in his habit but without cincture or pectoral cross. He had, Richer observed, taken time to put on his ring of office. Or perhaps he slept in it. The amethyst glowed as he threw up his hands. His high voice rang over the tumult. "In heaven's name, brothers, I know no more than you."

"Indeed." Gerbert's voice, a soft growl. People clamored at him; he ignored them. "Look to your archbishop," was all he would say.

The uproar muted abruptly. A man entered under armed escort as had they all, but this one was armed himself, his helmet under his arm, his mail-coif pushed back on his shoulders. A wind seemed to pass through the hall: a long sigh.

Arnulf favored his mother for looks. Charles the duke, who called himself Charles the king, was a truer Caroling. Like Lothair his brother, he was a sand-colored man, long-faced, mild and almost scholarly to look at, even in armor. Even crowned.

Richer's knees had been bred to bend to men of that line. Even angry and betrayed, he was hard put not to bow. It was Gerbert who showed him sanity. The master seemed calm enough, but he did not move.

"Sir!" Arnulf strode from among his bishops in a fine fire of outrage, and faced his uncle. "Sir, what is this? What right have you to stand in this hall?"

"As much right as you," Charles answered him, "nephew. How is it that I find you running like a hound at the usurper's heel?"

Arnulf raised his chin. "He is the duly elected king of the Franks."

"Not here," said Charles coolly, "and not now. Rheims is mine."

"Yours by treachery!" Arnulf cried. "Who has done it? Tell me!"

"You don't know?" Charles beckoned. A man in a priest's robe emerged slowly from the shelter of guards. "Come, Father Alger. Show these men what loyalty is."

Defiant, Richer judged, and afraid. The man kept darting glances at Arnulf, who disdained to acknowledge his existence. Others, less haughty, snarled like dogs. Alger retreated to safety.

Charles shrugged, smiling. As well he could afford to. Had he not snatched this jewel from the very hand of the King of the Franks? To his nephew he said, "Will you submit?"

"Never," said Arnulf.

"You grieve me." Charles did not sound as if he would die of it. He raised his voice slightly, to be heard in the hall. "Any who will bow and swear fealty to me, may go free."

No one moved; no one spoke. Richer could admire that kind of courage. Though perhaps it was plain paralysis.

"So, then," said the duke. "Is it prison you choose?"

Still, silence. One or two, perhaps, would have spoken, but the others quelled them.

"Take them," said the duke.

Richer had to get a grip on Gerbert's habit and refuse to let go, but he had his way: he was locked with his master in a single cell. It had belonged to one of the archbishop's servants; it had a pallet spread on the floor, a box of oddments, even a bottle of appallingly bad wine. A slit of window let in a little air and a great deal of uproar.

"They're sacking the city," Richer said. He did not know why he should be surprised.

Gerbert had refused the wine, for which Richer could hardly blame him. He sat against the wall, clasping his knees, and seemed content to drowse. When Richer spoke, he opened an eye. "Of course they are. How do you think a commander pays his troops?"

"But it's the *city*," Richer repeated, like an idiot.

Gerbert sighed. "It always is."

Richer spun about, fists clenching and unclenching, eyes darting. "We can get out. We can call up the magic. We can blast them all."

"Try it," said Gerbert.

His tone stung Richer almost to madness: half resigned, half mocking. Richer snatched at fire, at magic, at the roots of his rage.

At nothing. It was there. He could not grasp it. When he tried, it turned to air and scattered.

"Yes," Gerbert said as if he had spoken. "He came prepared for us. There's a warding on his army; there's a mage sustaining it. Otric, I think: an old rival of mine from the emperor's court; or a pupil of his. He was always a master of windy emptiness."

Richer dropped down in an untidy tangle of limbs. "*Damn* them."

Gerbert did not rebuke him, which was as good as agreement. After a little while the master stretched out on the pallet and went peacefully to sleep.

Richer was no such master of his fears. He paced

until his feet ached. He tried the door, which would not budge. It had an iron bar, a cold bite on the edge of his magic. He peered out of the window, which granted a view only of a wall and a sliver of paling sky. He crouched in a corner and twitched, and tried to find some shadow of his master's patience.

Gerbert was biding his time. There was nothing else that he could do. He slept a little, less than he needed. Mostly he waited. None of the others had been taken away alone. As alone, at least, as Richer would allow. He could not help but conclude that he was wanted for something in particular. Not his magic, surely, if Charles had his own tame magus. Though even as a young mage not yet raised to mastery, Gerbert had managed to best Otric on his own chosen ground.

He could only wait, and hoard his power and his body's strength, and rest as best he might. His dreams were dim and troubled. He kept hearing a sound like shaken bronze, or like the Jinniyah's voice; but he could not understand the words. Only their urgency.

He started awake. By the light, it was full morning. Richer had fallen asleep propped against the wall; he snored softly. For all his gangling length and the bristle of stubble on his chin, he looked like a child. Gerbert eased him down to the pallet, waking him not at all, except to a dreamy murmur and a drawing together on the mat. His snoring had stopped, which was a mercy.

Gerbert stretched the stiffness out of his bones, rubbing eyes that felt sandy with tiredness. Thus far he had resisted the temptation to castigate himself for seven different kinds of fool. He should have known that this would happen. He should have planned for it; guarded against it.

How was he to know that, when it came, it would not come from Arnulf?

Had it not?

His mind saw again the scene in the hall. A drama worthy of Seneca. The uncle, triumphant. The nephew, betrayed. The audience, deceived.

Alger had not played his part as well as he might. He had not looked to the duke; he had looked to Arnulf. He should have known what he would get for his pains. No gratitude, and precious little silver. Traitors were not cherished even by those who bought them.

Gerbert was ready when the guards came to fetch him. They barely woke Richer, and Gerbert did not try. He staggered as he rose; the guards had to hold him up. They were not unkind. He would remember that.

The new master of Rheims had had the grace, at least, not to claim the archbishop's palace. The king's high house was more suited to the scope of his ambition. The road between was paved with ruin.

They were not killing people yet. But there were other horrors than killing. Women raped. Men beaten for defending what was theirs. Doors broken down, houses ransacked, belongings both precious and common scattered in the streets. Gerbert saw a soldier with his breeks undone and a great silver chain about his neck, guzzling ale out of a cookpot. He saw men pouring out grain like gold and trampling it. He saw real gold flung about like offal, the moneyers' stock turned to a plaything for drunken robbers. He saw a broken city and a bitter winter; he saw a white clarity of wrath.

That wrath brought him into the conqueror's presence. Charles was taking what seemed to be his ease among his vassals, dandling the woman who, only the night before, had clung so touchingly to her young lord. She seemed quite content with the change.

Gerbert, whose eyes were bitterly clear, could not see cause to despise her. She was merely surviving.

An art which he might do well to learn. He stood in front of the duke and held up his head, and said, "You are destroying this city."

He had shocked the rest, but not Charles of Lorraine. "I am chastising it. It turned away from the true line of kingship to a shabby pretender."

"Much the same was said of your ancestors when they displaced the long-haired kings."

"Ah," said Charles with a curl of his lip. "An old argument, and weak. I had thought better of you, sir— what shall I call you? Father? *Magister?* Lord magus?"

"Whatever you name me, I remain myself. The city remains, and it is suffering. That is its winter store which your men are dissipating in the gutters. That is its gold which they take, the gold which might preserve its people from starvation."

"Armies hunger also," Charles said. "Armies eat. Armies die unless they are fed."

"Armies burn or trample whatever they themselves cannot eat."

Charles sat up, dislodging the woman, who retreated with an angry glance at Gerbert. "Some excess is inevitable. That will be seen to. You may hang an offender or two yourself, if it will appease you."

"Why do you care to appease me?"

"I need you." The simplicity of that brought Gerbert up short. Charles smiled faintly. "You make a career out of that, it seems. The indispensable man. Hugh the Monk was hard put to it to conceive of Rheims without you. My nephew had to promise to make you his secretary and to give you anything you asked for, before his pretended majesty would begin to consider handing over the miter."

"It was my impression that you were part of the bargain."

Charles' smile widened. "And so I was: but not as any of you had imagined. What ever made you think that my dear brother's son would turn on his own family?"

"Where is he now?"

"With all the rest of Hugh's loyal fools. In my prison in Laon."

Gerbert shook his head. "Why does he trouble? An idiot could deduce who plotted this."

"No one but an idiot would have given him the archbishopric while I live to command his loyalty. Hugh Capet will bow to me yet, Master Gerbert. Then Arnulf will rule Rheims as Hugh himself gave him leave to do, and as the Church has chosen."

"The Church chose a lie."

"It chose," said Charles. "You bowed to it."

"I bowed to necessity," Gerbert said.

The duke nodded. "They say that you are a practical man. This city will need practicality if it wishes to survive intact until spring. You can defy me, sir, and take the city with you. Or you can serve the city by accepting the necessity of my presence in it."

Gerbert's jaw tightened. Beautiful Maryam who had only been in the way—Maryam had died for his anger. This sacker of cities, this wielder of traitors, would live unsmitten. Because Gerbert had sworn oaths which he was not prepared, even yet, to break. And because, even if he would, he had no power to break them.

"There will, of course, be conditions," said Charles. "You will not attempt to escape. Nor will you communicate with our enemies. You will be guarded, for your safety as much as for mine."

"And if I refuse?"

"I throw Rheims to the dogs."

"What profit in that for you? You need a kingdom intact, if you hope to rule it."

"I need an example to prove that I am not to be trifled with. Rheims will do—better than most. It is large enough to matter."

He meant it. Gerbert was no stranger to ruthlessness, in others or in himself. But this was his city. His labor had helped to make it. His love had gone into it. His lord and friend was buried in it.

He would not bow his head. He would not go that far. But he said, "I will do as I must. Will you stop the looting?"

"When it is time," said Charles.

"Now."

They stood eye to eye. Charles looked away first. "As soon as I may."

Gerbert nodded sharply. "See to it." He turned on his heel. His two guards followed, close as shadows, but they did not try to stop him.

His first concern was for the city. One night's rape had wounded it bitterly; the pillagers were slow to come to heel, drunk even more with license than with wine. They had set fire to the coiners' street and well-nigh burned down the whole of the quarter. The granaries were ransacked, the cattle stolen or slaughtered. If there was a chicken alive in Rheims, it was no thanks to the duke's marauders.

God Himself seemed minded to punish the city for its stupidity. When the reapers crept out to gather what was left of the harvest, morning sun darkened to a cold and driving rain that turned the fields to mire and rotted the grain in the ear; struck the apple from the bough; smote the vineyards with destroying hail.

Gerbert could not even raise his magic to defend the fields. The guard which Charles had laid on him was more than the pair who were by him waking and sleeping, never the same pair for long lest he charm them into disloyalty. If charm was a word anyone would care to use of a mage without magic.

Not that it was gone. It was there, but muted, quenched, shrunken and feeble. It was, as it were, bound in chains. Chains of air and iron. The simplest working taxed him to the edge of his endurance: the lighting of a lamp, even the reading of the stars that demanded more of the mathematician than of the magician. The great magics, he could not do at all. Not within his self; not with the tools of the mage. His chamber of power was barred against him and sealed with iron. His books were all taken away. And greatest of all, his Jinniyah enspelled in bronze, in whom was the fullest portion of his power—even she was taken away from him. It was her voice which he had heard on the night of Rheims' betrayal, crying treachery to his deaf ears. Now he could not find her. He had no strength even to look for her.

He never saw Charles' mage. The trap might have set itself for all he could learn of it. The touch that bespoke Otric grew less like him the longer Gerbert lay under it. It was subtler, slipperier, more secret. It had an odor of dark and hidden places.

It was eating him slowly. He could not stop it. He could barely stop the dissolution of his city. No more could he stop fighting with every ounce of skill and cunning and sheer cold anger. He would conquer this evil, or it would kill him. There was no middle ground. No yielding. No quarter.

11

Sunlight took Gerbert by surprise. He blinked at
it and tried to remember where it had come from. It
had been grey afternoon; he had been overseeing the
dole of grain, trying to hasten it before the early dark.
He had been a little unsteady on his feet, a little warmer
than the air called for. But between that and this,
nothing.

He tried to sit up, fell reeling back. An exclamation
escaped him; it broke in coughing. The coughing nearly
broke him in two.

Cool hands held him. They were strong. He struggled to see. Something touched his lips; he drank before
he thought: coolness, bitterness that caught at the throat
through the mellowing of honey. He gasped, gagged.

"Here," said a voice both sharp and gentle. "Don't
fight."

He could barely want to. He peered through swim-
ming eyes at Richer's face. It looked odd. Owlish. He
seemed to be trying to grow a beard.

Slowly his scattered self crept together. He was in his
own bed, as he should be, though not as far into the
morning as the sun's angle proclaimed. There was no
strength in him at all, but a weight like a world in his

lungs, and a smithy clanging behind his eyes. "I'm sick," he said.

Richer greeted that stroke of genius with admirable forbearance. "So you are." He stopped. He was, Gerbert realized, exhausted: corpse-white under the crowding freckles, unshaven, hollow-eyed, and dismayingly slow in the wits. His face lit like a lamp. "*Magister!* You're awake."

"I should hope so," said Gerbert sourly.

Richer mopped at his eyes, which had chosen that moment to overflow. "Thanks be to God and all the saints."

"That bad, was it?"

"Not if you're alive and growling at me." Richer grinned through the tears. "And I, for once, can growl straight back."

"How long?"

Richer did not want to answer. Gerbert glared at him until he did. "Not so long. Only a fortnight."

"A fortnight!"

The boy held him down with both hands, which was kindness of a sort. One hand would have been more than adequate. "Stop it. The city's taken care of. My lord Arnulf himself is back, brazen as he ever was, but this I'll say for him: he's properly appalled. He's been doing well enough where you left off. Gave his uncle a proper tongue-lashing, too. I'm sorry you couldn't have been there to hear that. You'd have found it gratifying."

"Arnulf." Gerbert bit off the name. He did not try to say more than that.

Richer spooned gruel into him. He took it without grace, but he did not resist. He needed strength, and he needed it quickly. He could not at the moment remember why. Something he had dreamed, amid the long dimness of his fever. Something true.

He was not even as well as Richer tried to pretend.

Sleep wanted to take him and keep him. When he was awake, it took most of his strength simply to stay so.

It maddened him. Even as a child he had never been sick. He tried to get up, though Richer raged at him, though he prostrated himself the longer for trying too much too soon. He had a city to look after.

"Arnulf is looking after it," Richer said over and over, with ever-lessening patience.

"Arnulf is why I have to look after it!"

The spasm of coughing crested and passed. No blood. There had been blood before. Perhaps, after all, Gerbert was beginning to heal.

The name, it seemed, had power to bring the man. Gerbert woke from a doze to a face that was not Richer's, and eyes that tightened the skin between his shoulderblades. Narrow, sharp, almost cunning. Then, with a flicker of lids, they widened and softened. "*Magister*," said the Archbishop of Rheims.

"Excellency." Gerbert could not see or hear Richer. Had they bound and gagged him and carried him away?

Arnulf sat by the bed, smoothing his gown. He looked splendid in episcopal violet. "I rejoice to see you recovering," he said. "Your illness has grieved us all."

"Has it?"

Arnulf smiled as if Gerbert's insolence honestly pleased him. "You sound like your old self. When you spoke gently to us at the height of the fever, we feared the worst. It's good to hear you bark again."

Gerbert set his teeth. "Where is Brother Richer?"

"Resting. Have no fear, he's close by; but we can't risk the physician's taking sick before the patient is cured. He has orders to stay away until he has slept."

"What did you enforce them with? Chains?"

Arnulf laughed as sweetly as a woman. "Not quite! His oath of obedience seems to have sufficed."

"Amazing." Gerbert was thirsty, and he needed the chamberpot. He did not want to ask this man for anything. "Are you nursing me in his place?"

"Alas," said Arnulf, "no. My uncle expects me to dine with him. I simply wished to assure myself that you are, indeed, mending."

"Why? Is there trouble?"

"Not at all."

He sat smiling, looking as innocent as a painted angel. Hard to credit that he had sworn fealty to a king by the most holy of all oaths, and handed that king's city to an army of rebels. That he had committed that treason under the very nose of a master of magic, and never . . . once . . .

Gerbert lay still.

No. Treason was an earthly art, and Gerbert had not been troubling himself to look for it. This that he was thinking, that he had dreamed in his delirium, was not possible. Arnulf had no magic. Gerbert had proven that by every test he knew. Arnulf could not have done what the hidden mage had done. Gerbert would have known.

So he had. Late, when all his guards were broken down, but truly.

"You," he said. "You did this to me."

Arnulf seemed shocked. "Why, master! How can you say that?"

"You lured me away from the makings of my magic. You weakened me; you opened the way for the fever. Were you hoping it would kill me?"

"Come," said Arnulf, "be calm. You'll sicken again."

"No. You don't want me dead. You simply want me in your power. Who trained you? Otric?"

Arnulf drew breath as if to protest, stopped, sighed, shrugged. "I see that there is no deceiving you, *magister*.

Yes, Otric taught me when I was very young, and again after I left you."

"You spied for him."

"I tested my power on you. Or it tested itself. It never wanted to uncover itself to you."

"Remarkable," said Gerbert. "Power that renders itself invisible. Can you do anything with it but that?"

"A little." Arnulf was not being modest. Gerbert doubted that he knew how. "It tends to negate itself. A pity, I've always thought. Else the possibilities would be endless."

"Thank God they're not."

"Perhaps. Too much power is dangerous. I do regret that I could do so little for you. I only meant to keep you from working spells to set yourself free. I didn't know that so much of your self was bound up in the workings."

"Now that you do, why not give them back?"

Arnulf looked regretful. "Alas, I can't. I need you here, lending your name, however reluctantly, to our cause. I can't let you escape. But I can take more care to preserve your strength." He frowned slightly. "It wasn't wise, you know, to entrust so much of your magic to anything outside of yourself."

"What makes you think I had a choice?"

"Ah," said Arnulf, as if he understood. "It's the way your power runs. Unfortunate for you. Most fortunate for us, now that I see you'll live."

In that instant, Gerbert hated him with a perfect hate. A monster, one could comprehend, and even forgive: one could see that a devil had possessed him. This flawless selfishness was beyond endurance.

Gerbert did not know what he would do if Arnulf lingered much longer. He let his eyelids fall over the burning of rage, let his body slacken as if in weariness.

As he had hoped, Arnulf tired soon enough of his own

unaided company. When he was well gone, Gerbert lay with his eyes closed, but his mind was as clear as it had ever been. It had much to ponder. And one comfort. Arnulf did not, it seemed, know the whole of what he had done to Gerbert's magic. While he thought that it resided in a chest of books and oddments, there might be some hope of winning free.

Then, thought Gerbert, there would be a reckoning.

Richer had not been idle while Gerbert worked himself into a fever. His magic was as useless as Gerbert's own, but he had bled none of it into another vessel; he was sound enough in body. Nor had his mind suffered for the time to think. He had marked Arnulf some while since for what he was.

He did not brag about it. "I'm not worth noticing. Therefore I'm given more chances to notice things."

Gerbert snorted. "You're also a shade brighter than you look. Have you happened to notice whether his excellency is collecting antique bronzes?"

Richer's cheeks were flushed. Logically enough: he was turning the mattress while Gerbert lay on the floor in a nest of blankets. He smoothed a lump in the ticking, reached for a sheet. "Actually," he said, "I have. He's keeping it next to his bed."

Gerbert laughed himself into a coughing fit.

When he could speak again, he was in his clean bed, in a clean shirt, grinning like an idiot. "God's bones! I needed that." Richer was scowling at him. He yielded to compunction. "That particular bronze, my friend, is rather more than it seems. And Arnulf is rather less a mage than he thinks, or he would now better than to keep it where he does."

Richer bit his lip. He was struggling, Gerbert realized, not to succumb to laughter. He gave up the fight, for a moment, before he sobered. "Your magic is in it."

Gerbert nodded.

"Why?"

It was the inevitable question. Gerbert did not want to answer. But to Richer, he owed at least as much as he had given Arnulf. "It was a price I paid for the way in which I acquired the image. I killed with magic to gain it. Therefore my magic surrendered its freedom. It became a part of what I had taken. I . . . encouraged it."

"We have to get it back," said Richer.

He looked ready to stride straight into the archbishop's bedchamber and seize the image. Gerbert caught his sleeve. "No. We know where it is. He doesn't know what it is. Let it be for a while. When I'm back on my feet, have no fear, we'll act."

That was sensible. Richer yielded to it, not happily. If he had heard Gerbert's confession of murder, he had not let it trouble him. Gerbert could envy such serenity.

Richer was hardly serene. Guilt was eating at him. This, he reflected, must be how adulterers felt when they faced the men they had cuckolded. He could not bring himself to confess that he knew what the bronze was. All of it. Oracle, ensorceled spirit, friend.

She would be frantic, trapped where she was. Unless she had turned traitor. Arnulf was very good to look at; and she would have seen all there was to see. A female, even a bodiless spirit, would be vulnerable to such things.

Arnulf endowed with an oracle was an appalling prospect. Richer could only hope that he fretted for nothing. Gerbert would recover, they would steal back the image, they would escape from this trap.

He put on his bravest face, and schooled himself not to see what sickness had made of his master. Gerbert had not, mercifully, asked for a mirror; he seemed untroubled by the gauntness of his body. "I've been rather thicker in the middle than a good ascetic should be," he said. "Now I look more as I ought."

Richer swallowed his objections. Gerbert ate, and ate well, which was what mattered. He seemed to have made up his mind to be sensible.

He worked at it with commendable zeal. He no longer tried to push himself past the edge of endurance. He slept as he was told, ate all that he was fed, and rose when Richer would let him, easing himself back into the labor of living.

Richer had schooled himself too well. He forgot that Gerbert would not know what he could not see. They both paid for that as Richer should have known they would, once Gerbert was well enough to leave his house and sit in the garden. He had always let the young imps of the town amuse themselves in its pear tree, if they broke none of its branches and left a little of its fruit for its master. On warm days, even in winter, they liked to come in through a gap in the wall which Gerbert, conveniently, kept forgetting to mend, and wage mock battles round the tree.

Richer had left Gerbert sitting on a bench in the sun with a volume of Cicero to keep him company, and gone to do some things that needed doing. When he came back, Gerbert was still there, and with him two or three children. Richer smiled. Trust the master to gain a youthful following wherever he went, even in his own garden.

Then Richer heard what one of them was asking. "Where's the teacher?"

"Silly," his sister said with all the scorn of superior age. "This is the teacher."

But the child was not to be deflected. "He's not, either. He's someone else. He's *old*."

Richer was on them before they could have known he was there. Whether it was his size or his wrath or his habit flapping in the wind of his speed, they broke and fled.

Leaving Richer breathless and trembling, and Gerbert motionless in the sunlight. The master seemed unperturbed, even amused. Then he said, "You could have broken it to me gently."

Richer did not know what to say.

"Let me see," said Gerbert.

There was no point in refusing him. Richer dragged his feet a little in hunting for the mirror, but not too much. The one he found was a good one: silver, and old. It looked Roman.

Gerbert did not look long at what it showed him. He let the mirror fall into his lap, and sighed.

"It's not so bad," said Richer.

Gerbert laughed, which was startling. "What's bad? I'm alive. These bones will pad themselves soon enough—amply enough, too, if I know this body of mine. I never had any beauty to lose. This . . ." He ran fingers through his hair. Nature had lent a hand with the tonsure, but the rest was thick still, its old unmemorable brown gone silver in his sickness. "I look venerable. I. Who'd have thought it?"

"Not venerable," Richer said. "Distinguished." And he did. His face had never been anything but plain, but it seemed cleaner carved, the eyes larger, more brilliant. They had always been Gerbert's best feature, wide and clear, neither brown nor grey nor green but a mingling of all three. Now they were like water, both deep and clear, flecked with gold like a dazzle of sunlight.

Richer shivered, not with cold, and not with fear. Not exactly. There was magic in those eyes, chained though it might be, by wisdom and priesthood as much as by Arnulf's treachery.

They glinted, wicked as a boy's. "Venerable," Gerbert repeated. "August. Feeble. Unthreatening. I haven't been under guard since I took sick. Have I?"

"No." Richer said it slowly, as he began to understand. "You are devious."

"I learn from example." Gerbert let Richer help him up, though he insisted on walking back into the house, leaning on Richer no more than he must and rather less than he should.

"Do you know what I'd like to do?" he asked when he was in his bed again. "When this is over, when I've dealt with the wreckage that little serpent and his damnable uncle have made of my city, I'd like to go away. Become a pilgrim. To Spain, maybe. To Egypt, where the magic is oldest of all, and where they say it lives still in the hidden places. And in the end, when I'm ready for peace, to Jerusalem."

Richer smiled, though his heart was cold. "That's something to look forward to."

Gerbert shot him a glance. "It's moonshine. It keeps me going when I'd like to lie down and die."

"You can't. You have too much to do."

"Exactly." Gerbert drew a long breath, let it go again. "And first, I have to get my magic back. I have . . . to . . ."

He was asleep. Richer drew the blanket over him and tried not to cry. Idiot, he mocked himself. Now that Gerbert was out of danger, now he broke down and bawled like a baby.

And why not? cried the child in him. He buried his face in the blankets and let his heart wash itself clean.

12

Poor, frail, broken Gerbert won much pity when he hobbled back to his duties. Even Richer, who knew what he was doing, was almost taken in by it. But Gerbert was too honest to lie to one who knew him well. People who believed him, saw the gaunt face and the whitened hair and the frequent pauses to rest, and looked no further. They did not see what Richer saw: that his eyes were the color of thunder.

Gerbert was angry; the more so, the more he saw of what winter and a standing army were doing to Rheims. It was anger that gave him strength to do a strong man's work; for without him the city had floundered, sinking into confusion and despair. He whipped it to life again.

His guards had not come back. He was watched, but not with endless vigilance.

As soon as winter broke, staggering, starving Rheims won a reprieve: Charles divided his army and took two parts of the three to harry the king's lands. Gerbert put the remainder to work repairing what they and their fellows had broken. They did not like it, but Arnulf was giving Gerbert a free hand, and Arnulf was their lord's kinsman. They began, in some small measure at least, to earn their keep.

"And where's the king through all of this?" Richer wanted to know, querulously.

Gerbert looked up from a packet of letters. "Senlis," he answered.

Richer blinked, diverted from his complaint. "What?"

"The king is in Senlis," Gerbert said with remarkable patience. "Convoking his bishops. Discussing this predicament of ours."

"Discussing! All he needs is cold steel."

"Not quite. Charles, he's dealing with as a king may. Arnulf is another matter. They've excommunicated Alger, and a baron or two who helped him. His excellency, they don't seem to know of yet; or else they have no evidence. He could be acting under duress, after all; as am I."

"Arnulf never did anything he didn't want to do." Richer peered at the letter which had told Gerbert all of this. "Who wrote that? Ah—Archbishop Ascelin. So he's managed to get out of Laon, Carolingian captors or no. Far be it from me to speak ill of my lord Adalberon's favorite nephew, but sometimes I think that man is as slippery as Arnulf himself."

"He is. He also knows the significance of a solemn oath, which Arnulf all too plainly does not. You won't catch him swearing on the body of Christ when he fully intends to break his oath."

"No: he'd find a way to get out of it." Richer paused. "Maybe Arnulf meant it when he swore it."

"He broke it." Gerbert's voice was iron. "Are you done with that letter? Here, take this packet to the cathedral; tell Father Infirmarer it's the best I can do, he knows what the roads have been like since last autumn."

Full of Carolingian brigands, Gerbert meant. Richer tucked the packet into his sleeve, catching its pungent herbal scent. It was not one he recalled offhand.

Father Martin the infirmarer would tell him what it

was. At length, no doubt, and on the run. There had been no lack of sickness in the city, much of it born of hunger and fear.

Things were quieter now. He could almost imagine that Rheims was at peace under its proper lord, lean from a hard winter but looking to the summer with hope and gladness.

Then he remembered Gerbert and shivered. Gerbert had changed as he mended. He spoke less; he smiled seldom. With Arnulf he was icily, flawlessly correct.

Richer did not want to be in the way when Gerbert's temper slipped its chain. That calm of his when the archbishopric went to Arnulf, that was hard won and harder kept. Arnulf's oathbreaking had won that young idiot an enemy, and a bad one.

Did he even know? Gerbert had been acting like a beaten man, at least to Arnulf's face: quiet, obedient, humble. But that was the quiet of the storm building. Magic or no magic, it would break.

Soon, Richer suspected. He had seen Gerbert's face in the cathedral at the Easter Mass. It had been transfigured; and not, for all its pallor, with light. His eyes had fixed on Arnulf's hands elevating the Host, and they had blazed.

Richer hesitated, stumbling on the cathedral steps, and almost went down. Light and color flamed above the door: the mosaic wrought by artists from Ravenna, Christ enthroned in judgment, with the souls of the blessed shining white and gold on his right hand, and the damned black as soot beneath his heel. Their faces filled Richer's vision, contorted with terror.

The grimoire. The book of magic which Richer had taken the day he spoke with the Jinniyah, because she bade him; which he had laid in his clothing chest and forgotten. Forgotten, that is, until looking for help and hope in the midst of Gerbert's sickness he had hunted out the copy of Hippocrates and brought the other with it. He had remembered it again in the deeps of the winter, and because he found it comforting, had told Gerbert where it was.

Gerbert had seemed barely interested. He was still weak then, working less hard than he liked but much too hard for Richer's peace of mind. He had said what he said of the image which Arnulf had stolen: "Let be. It's not time. When Rheims has won through the winter, then we think of breaking free."

Now he had somewhere to go: Senlis, and the synod, and the king. He had a long grievance that had festered into something appallingly like madness, and as much of his old strength as he was likely to gain. In that grimoire were spells of the white magic, good ones, strong ones. But in it also were spells which shaded to grey. Dark grey, some of them, and deadly dangerous.

The herbs which Richer carried were not all that Gerbert had bought.

Richer staggered up the steps. He barely remembered finding the canons' cloister, the infirmary, the infirmarer. He flung the packet in Father Martin's astonished face and bolted like a hare.

Hippocrates was where he belonged. The grimoire was gone.

Richer whirled to run. Halted. Collapsed in a tangle. If Arnulf had taken the book, then that was that. If it had been Gerbert, then had he not the right? It was his book. The Jinniyah had foreseen that he would need it. With its aid he might be able to work a white enchantment, an escape from this prison. He would not try for revenge. The bishops in Senlis would give him that. The king might even give him Arnulf's head into the bargain.

Richer wound his fingers in his hair and pulled it

until it hurt. When had Gerbert ever relied on anyone else to pay his debts for him?

Inspiration struck like an arrow in the brain. The Jinniyah. She could talk sense into Gerbert. Richer knew she could. And she had his magic. If he had it back, it would heal him; it would make him remember his wisdom. Then they could fly from Rheims and cast their troubles into the lap of Mother Church.

And how was Richer going to win her? Walk up to Arnulf and ask him for her? Buy her from him? Steal her?

Steal her, indeed. No doubt Richer could find an excuse to wander into the archbishop's bedchamber. But the bronze was quite as large as life, and correspondingly difficult to hide even under a monk's voluminous habit. If he tucked it under his arm and walked blithely out . . .

He lowered his hands from his tormented hair, and stared at them as if he had never seen them before. Big, rawboned, ruddy-furred and copiously freckled: a perfect clown's.

Suppose, just suppose, he carried it off. In all senses. He was the master's dog, everyone knew that. If they noticed him at all, they looked at his gangling awkwardness and laughed. Poor, feeble Gerbert and his tame fool. Who would expect either of them to turn dangerous?

He had to do it in broad daylight. Night was no good, with Arnulf sleeping there, and half the episcopal army camped in the corridor. He was going to need all his courage and most of his store of lunacy. Then he had to hope that Gerbert would not have acted before Richer could.

"No buts," he said aloud. "No wobbles. Just do it."

Today he could not. It was too late. Tomorrow was Sunday. Arnulf would sing the high mass, and most of Rheims would be there to hear him. Even Gerbert. Arnulf liked people to see that his rival was now his faithful servant. He was not likely to care where his servant's servant was, or what he was up to.

Which left one final dilemma. Could a thief pray that his theft might succeed?

No matter. He would pray. Let God decide whether He would listen.

Gerbert suspected that he had gone a little mad. Maybe more than a little. It was the whole of it together. Losing the archbishopric, then seeing it betrayed; enduring servitude to its betrayer; fighting for his city. And all of it with half of him torn away, the rest groping in the dark, seeking blindly to be whole again.

He should not have waited—first for the city, then for his sickness, then again for the city's sake. He should have snatched his Jinniyah and run, the moment Arnulf became archbishop of Rheims.

Such wisdom, one had, when one could look back on one's follies. If he had been wise at all, he would never have left Aurillac.

He knew where the grimoire was. It was like a fire in the darkness. Most of it was no use without the spark of magic; but there were a few spells that needed little more than strength of will and strength of voice, and all the makings in their proper order. Not that they were simple, but because they needed so little of true magic, they were perilous. Any man with discipline and determination and a little learning could avail himself of them. And, thereby, gain a new kind of power.

It was not quite the black art. But neither was it the high white magic which grew out of true power. It partook of compulsion; of the pact arcane.

Of which, Master Ibrahim had had little good to say. "The pact," he had taught his apprentice, "is a sign of weakness. A true mage has no need of it. Either his magic suffices to work his will, or if he be of the darkness that makes slaves of men and spirits, he can compel obedience without need of bargaining. He who chaffers like a merchant with the beings of the greater or the lesser worlds, is merchant indeed, and no magus."

True enough, Gerbert thought. But a man bereft of magic must take power where he might. Once he had his Jinniyah back, then he could forsake this shame and be again the master of magic.

There was one great advantage in this kind of spell. Since it called power from without, it did not tax the body's strength as true power did. He need not wait until he was all healed, if indeed he ever would be. Something had broken in him; he was beginning to suspect that it would never wholly be mended.

He wasted no time in feeling sorry for himself. He knew who had done this. He would see that Arnulf paid, and paid high.

He had, to be sure, sworn oaths. But this was no matter of power in the world or in the Church; only of magic that had been taken away. And he would not harm Arnulf. Not he; not his own, inborn power. Arnulf himself had seen to that.

Arnulf, in whom he had centered all his hate. Arnulf, who had broken him in body and in power.

Carefully, in secret even from Richer—especially from Richer—he had gathered what he needed. Now he had all of it, both what he could buy and what he must make. The virgin parchment had not been easy, nor the athame: the dagger forged of silver under the moon. That had cost him somewhat of his recovery, and some suspicion from Richer, who had needed a potion or two to make him sleep.

Tonight Gerbert would do it. The day was quiet, its

only labor the ordeal of the mass, which Arnulf made him serve like an acolyte. He suffered it because he must, and begged off from dinner afterward. Richer would not have been so easy to dispose of, but the boy had taken a well-earned holiday. He would have gone to St.-Rémi to be among his brothers, one of blood and the rest of the cloth. Alone and fasting, dreading what he must do yet fixed upon it, Gerbert missed that endless, faithful, frequently exasperating presence.

Best that he be out of it. This sin would be Gerbert's, and Gerbert's alone.

Richer had been thinking much the same, but turned about. He had not exactly lied regarding his reasons for disappearing after matins; he had simply let people decide that they knew where he was going. He helped them by setting out in the direction of the abbey. But, having diverted anyone who might see through as bad a liar as Richer was, he drew up his cowl and slouched to lessen his height and became simply another anonymous monk in a city full of them.

It was natural enough that he should hang about the archbishop's palace. The prayers he muttered, audibly lest anyone try to question him, were quite real, and quite heartfelt. The beads were cool in his hands, comforting.

For a terrible few moments, he knew that he had failed. Arnulf had not yet gone to the cathedral. He was late, and much displeased, berating the sluggard who had overslept and omitted to wake him. His servants scurried, flustered. Richer found himself pressed into fetching his excellency's bath, along with another stalwart and a train of lesser luminaries with steaming buckets.

His excellency was waiting in his shirt and in no good temper, being shaved by a tight-lipped barber. Once the razor slipped. Richer wondered if Arnulf had acquired his vocabulary from his uncle's soldiers.

Richer was maliciously tempted to linger and see if the rest of Arnulf matched his face, but his better nature prevailed. What with the confusion in the outer room, no one noticed one black habit edging toward the inner door.

Someone was behind it, fussing about the bed. Richer froze on the threshold. Not that the room was occupied by anything mortal. That something else was there.

As if a man going blind slowly, had noticed it only because a miracle gave him back all that he had lost. As if his ears, dulled by imperceptible degrees, found again the keenness of his youth. Richer had not known how much of his magic was gone, until it flooded back fullfold, staggering him where he stood.

It was there where report had placed it, on a table by the bed, where Arnulf could lie and gaze at its antique beauty. No doubt it pleased him to have such visible evidence of his rival's submission. Or else he simply liked to look at it. It was even prettier than he was.

Richer's heart sank. There was no way in the world that Arnulf could fail to know what the image was, and what was in it. Even if Richer could steal it, it was no good to him if it betrayed him to its new master.

His jaw set. He had to try.

With a great deal of flurry and temper, Arnulf finished his toilet and set out for the cathedral. Most of his servants went with him. Richer ducked into the bedchamber before he could be pressed into service with the bath. He heard the others curse him for escaping, but none thought to look within rather than without. It took them an unconscionably long time to clear away the debris, and themselves with it.

At last he could draw a free breath. He turned toward his quarry, and stopped.

Judith Tarr

An old gammer of a monk had finished tidying the bed. As Richer turned, he turned also, mumbling to himself. He blinked at Richer, clearly none too quick in the wits, or he would not have said, "Here, here, it's all done, what are you hanging about for?"

Richer could think of any number of things to say. In the end he said nothing, simply walked to the table and set hands on the bronze. The magic roared and flamed in him. There were wards upon it. They had no more substance than shadows.

The old monk was babbling. "What are you doing? Put that down. Put it down, I say!"

The bronze rang like a bell. Richer started and almost dropped it. The old monk's mouth opened and closed. It was mildly comical, like a fish gasping, and no sound in it at all.

"Now," said the Jinniyah. "I'm holding the wards and the man. Take me; be quick. I can't hold much longer."

Richer could not move. The man was outside. Richer was within. The wards were between: a sphere of silence, a wall like finest glass, ringing on the utmost edge of hearing. It made him dizzy; it reft him of his wits.

The beautiful inhuman voice soared to the point of pain. *"Take me!"*

He lurched forward. The old monk stared, eyes half starting from his head. He was staring, Richer realized, at something well beyond the stumbling thief.

Richer tucked the Jinniyah under his arm as he had half-jestingly said he would, and essayed another step. It was rather steadier than the last. He could walk, after a fashion. He giggled as it struck him. He was royally drunk; and no wine anywhere near. It was all magic.

No one either stopped or questioned him. There was magic in that as in all the rest of it, trembling now with effort, but holding fast. He seemed to have no power over

146

his feet. They carried him out of the palace by a back way, through its burgeoning garden, into a dark stone-scented passageway and down a stair. With a small shock, he recognized the crypt of the cathedral. There was the undercroft with its flickering candles, there the tomb of an archbishop who had lacked the pride or the influence to be buried in the upper reaches. Richer set the image on the lid and grinned at it.

It stared levelly back. Its eyes were as disturbing as ever, both lifeless and intensely alive. A smile seemed to curve the graven lips.

"Well?" he said. "What now?"

"You ask me?"

He giggled again. Once he had started, he could not stop. He dropped to the cold floor, shaking with it, helpless as any drunkard.

"You are worthless."

The Jinniyah's scorn sobered him. Somewhat. He kept erupting into new fits. "But you see—I can't—it's so *strong*!"

For a moment he went blind. He clutched at air, stone, sanity. Slowly the light came back. The sweet madness was gone: the splendor that had been his master's magic. He leaned against the tomb and remembered how to think. "God in heaven! I've always known what he is, but to *be* it . . ." He drew a steadying breath. "It's too much for the likes of me."

The Jinniyah spoke above him, clear and cold. "When you have finished babbling, you might see fit to tell me what you intend to do with me."

"Take you back to Master Gerbert."

"Under Arnulf's nose?"

"What do you think I just did?"

"*You* did nothing. I found us a hiding place in which he may not think to search."

The last of Richer's drunkenness withered and died. "He knows what you are."

"He has been using me as my geas will allow."

"Dear God." Richer lowered his head into his hands. "He'll raise heaven and hell to get you back."

"He will. But perhaps," she said, "not for a while. The monk will remember nothing but a moment's confusion, and nothing that should not be there—and everything that should. We have perhaps a day and a night before the magic fades: before Arnulf sees that his table is empty. Unless, of course, he questions his oracle. My power falls short of illusions that speak when spoken to."

"Then let's pray he doesn't."

"Amen to that," said the Jinniyah, which widened his eyes. She laughed briefly. "What, did you think I'm a demon? Iblis is my forefather, I confess it, but my family has made amends. I was a good Muslim before I fell among the infidels."

Richer crossed himself without thinking, which made her laugh again. He scowled at her. "How do I know you haven't betrayed us all?"

"I told him nothing beyond yes or no, and those when he invoked my geas. I must prophesy. Nothing and no one has ordained that I must also tell what I am and what I bear."

"You're free enough with me."

"I choose to be."

Richer drew a long sigh. He knew he should be more wary, but he believed her. That was one of his magics, to know truth from falsehood. It was pleasure like pain, to have it back again.

He shook himself. He was dallying, and the day was running on. "I have to find a place to hide you while I ready our escape. If you hadn't led me here—"

"Here is safe," she said. "Under the altar cloth is a loose stone. Lift it out."

There was indeed, and behind it a space, a hollow in the great carved table. Perhaps it had been meant for a relic which had never come; perhaps some forgotten priest or builder had meant it for a hiding place.

Richer hesitated. "This feels like sacrilege."

"If I can bear it, surely the altar can."

Slowly Richer set the image in the niche. It was a close fit. He blessed bronze and stone alike, at which the Jinniyah mercifully kept silent. He could not bring himself to cover her face with the stone.

"Let be," she said. "The cloth will cover me."

He hid the stone behind the tomb, and stood with the cloth in his hand, staring at the glimmer of bronze. "Are you sure you'll be safe here?"

"As safe as I can ever be." That was hardly comforting. "Go now, look to our escape."

Richer let the cloth fall, smoothed it carefully. He was shakier now than he had been in Arnulf's chamber. Reaction, some of it, and fear that he had missed some crucial and damning detail.

"God," he said to the altar. "God, guard us both."

"Amen," said the voice of air and bronze.

13

For a moment as the day waned, Gerbert dreamed that he had his magic back again. It was glorious; it was intoxicating. Then it was gone. The world was all the darker in its wake, his madness all the stronger. If his courage could have faltered, now it was unshakable. He would do this. He would win back what Arnulf had taken away.

When compline was sung, Gerbert was ready. He had sent his servants away; the house was silent, empty but for the murmur of the wind that had risen with the evening. He shuttered the largest chamber against it, and cleared the space of encumbrances: the table on its trestles, the benches, the cabinet in which reposed his treasure of linen and plate. That was no easy labor for a man on the far side of sickness, and fasting besides. He had to pause after, sweating, battling darkness that came and went.

At last it left him. He sent fear after it, and guilt. His hand on the knife's hilt as he drew the circle of power was perfectly steady, his voice unwavering in the words which he must say. Words quite like them sealed wards major in workings of the high magic; but these wrought patterns that needed no sealing of power. Their cadences lulled him. He firmed his will to remain their master. It was like singing in choir. A hesitation, a stumble, and all the patterns would collapse.

Yet as it lengthened, it took on its own power. It shaped itself; it twisted, seeking escape from his will.

The circle closed, sealed with the signs of the elements: earth and water, fire and air. Earth from consecrated ground, water of baptism, fire burning atop a white candle, air embodied in sheerest silk. Gerbert stood within, in the center, with his book and his athame and his parchment, his lighted candle and his bowl of virgin silver and his box of costly essences. One by one he set them in the bowl and kindled them. As the first burned, he spread his parchment on the floor. The second purified his blade. The third—myrrh, that was for mortality—saw the blood spring red into the bowl, quenching the flame, raising a strong sweet smoke. He dipped his quill in it and began to write. Prayer, invocation, prayer. Wòrd by word in ink that was the stuff of life. All his being centered on that shaping: each letter clear, distinct, begetting its rightful successor.

And then there were no more. He knew a mighty sadness, as at a line of kings that had ended in silence and the grave. Almost he saw their faces, mortal blood and mortal bone.

Ink, parchment, crabbed and ancient words.

What the hand had written, the tongue encompassed. His voice was strong enough to startle him, fine trained cantor's voice that rang as in vast and empty spaces.

"By the body of Christ, by the blood of the Crucified, by Father, Son, and Holy Spirit, by the great names, the mighty names, the names of the Lord of lords, Adonai, Jehovah, Tetragrammaton, Hagios, Ischyros, Athanatos, Adonai, Adonai . . ."

Thunder gathered. The hairs of his body rose and

trembled. Sweat sprang burning cold. But his voice was free of all of it, borne with will and hand and heart, in white fire of power.

"Come, thou spirit of air and darkness, power of night, power of endless silences, thou whom I name in the name that is God's; come to me in shape that is fair to mortal eyes; come swift, come silent, come all obedient to my command. Bring thou no ally, bear thou no malice, lest the Angel of the Sword smite thee down to deepest hell. Come!" And he spoke the name that in itself was power, the name which he had chosen out of all that he had learned only that he might forget; and when it was spoken it was fled, forgotten truly, gone, save for an empty word in blood upon a parchment.

And then was silence. Gerbert stood in the circle in the reek of drugged smoke, and all about was only stillness. Deep in his center, he knew the dawning of despair.

Shadow stirred. He dared not move, even to stare, lest it be empty hope. Even when the whisper came, softer than wind in leaves, he stood still. "What would you, mage? I wait upon your will."

He shuddered—even he, whose power had mastered mightier spirits than this. Then he had had power. Now he had only words.

They were enough. "Show yourself to me," he said.

The shadow drew closer. He saw eyes: a shadow and a gleam. Shape drew itself below them. Face, body, no garment but a cloak of dark and lustrous hair. No sweeter body had ever been. Dark face, white smile, eyes that for a moment—for a piercing moment—

Gerbert cried aloud. "You are not she!"

"I could be," the spirit said in her own remembered voice. Even yet it could wound him to the heart.

"You will not." Gerbert was cold in the memory of grief, his mind clear at last and almost too late. "Put off that shape, in God's name, or I will flay you with whips of fire."

The spirit laughed, mocking, but it blurred and shrank. This semblance too he knew, with a small cold shock: the ancient monk who had accused him of allowing Adalberon to die. Had this being known even then that he would summon it? Or was this another of its mockeries?

If the spirit had hoped to betray him further into weakness, it was disappointed. He faced it steadily. "So, then," he said. "I did not dream that other meeting."

"Perhaps you did," the spirit said. "Perhaps I am no demon at all, but the conjuring of your own mad brain."

"What care I, if only you obey me?" Gerbert raised the athame. The spirit flinched from the gleam of it. "Hear me now, by the bonds which I have laid upon you. Fulfill this charge for which I have summoned you. Bring to me that which is mine, whole and complete, and do not tarry, nor seek to deceive me."

The spirit wavered like smoke in a gale. "I cannot."

"You will."

"I cannot," the spirit repeated. If it laughed behind its eyes, still its fear was real enough. "It is gone; taken where I cannot touch it."

Gerbert rose up in wrath. "How dare you lie to me?"

Before the fear now was anger. "I am not the Liar's get. I speak truth, O son of Eve. The thing you seek is beyond my power to take."

"Where?"

The withered face grew crafty. "What will you pay for the knowledge?"

"What need I pay? You are bound until I free you."

"Bound only to the task for which you summoned me. That, I cannot fulfill. I do no more without due payment. It is the law, O my master."

Gerbert's teeth clicked together. Of all the chances

which might befall the working, this was one which he had never thought to see. That the Jinniyah should be gone. That the spirit would not obey him. It watched him warily, but its fear had faded. A long pale tongue flicked over its lips. No demon, that one, not precisely, but no angel, either. Its kind craved mortal blood, the rich and transient sweetness of fleshly life. He felt the bonds weakening; on the parchment at his feet, the letters of blood had begun to fade. Words alone could not hold that will so long or so fruitlessly.

Darkness unfolded in Gerbert's mind. Anger had begotten it. Madness fed it. He smiled slowly; and the spirit quivered. Even it could fear him still, powerless though his folly had left him. "Suppose," he said, "that I give you leave to harry a man at your will. Will you tell me where my servant has gone?"

"I may harry him?" the spirit asked. "You set no limits on it?"

"This only: that you harm no other, save only him. He is a traitor, a breaker of his most sacred word. He is yours by my gift, if you tell me what I would know."

"Bold," said the spirit, "to offer another's soul and not your own."

Gerbert's anger sent the spirit reeling back. "His soul is no part of it! I give you his body and his will. All else belongs to God alone."

"You are proud," said the spirit. "Have a care, or your people will make a prince of you."

"An archbishop will suffice." The athame shaped the sign of the cross. "In the name of the Father, and the Son, and the Holy Spirit: tell me what I would know!"

"For the harrying of an archbishop," said the spirit, "I do more. See where your magic lies."

Gerbert's eyes were full of it; his soul wept to be apart from it. He reached in will-less yearning.

The vision frayed and scattered. His circle was broken, his foot across its border. The spirit's laughter filled his reeling brain. "Go!" he shrieked at it. *"Begone!"*

Gerbert stumbled bruisingly to his knees. The spirit was gone. He had not dismissed it properly. He had railed at it like a harridan. And the bargain he had struck with it . . .

His mind eluded that clarity, lest it stop him. He would do what he would do. This, first: the scouring of the chamber with clean smoke and pure water. The clearing away of the elements of the spell. The parchment was tattered as if with great age and hard use, the letters of blood faded to shadows. When he touched it, it crumbled, and with it the spirit's name. The name without which he could not master it.

When he had his magic back, it would not matter. He laid the athame with the grimoire in a box, shivering a little as the hilt left his hand. For a moment it seemed to cling, to beg him to keep it with him. He closed the lid upon it and thrust the box into the breast of his habit.

Discipline, he willed himself. Restraint. Those were a mage's virtues.

The chamber was empty. His heart was hardly more. His magic waited, hidden where nothing of shadow could touch it. He let his yearning lead him to it.

"You fool."

He knew that voice. He had forgotten how eerie it was: life without breath, will without substance. He stood on sanctified stone and stared, and almost—almost—remembered sanity.

"You fool," said the Jinniyah from beneath the altar. "You babbling, bumbling idiot. What have you loosed upon us all?"

Gerbert scrabbled at the cloth which covered her. It slipped and fell. The Jinniyah glared out of the niche. His magic throbbed about them both. His soul opened to draw it in; and her with it, cold bronze as familiar as flesh. He cradled her like a lover.

She sighed as if in spite of herself, echoing his own heart-deep gladness. They were whole again, both of them. His blood flowed molten with magic.

Something stirred behind him. A presence trembled on the edges of his power. He looked without surprise into a lamplit face, a pair of cold blue eyes. Arnulf's smile was wide and meaningless beneath them. "Ah, *magister*. Have you sunk even to theft?"

"I take back what is mine," Gerbert said.

Arnulf laughed. There was no mirth in it. "I see now how blind I was. So much, so well hidden, and in plain sight. You are subtle, master magus."

"Peasant cunning," said Gerbert. He drew a breath that caught on splendor. His magic, all his magic, roared and flamed in him. One flick of the will, and Arnulf would be his, blood and soul. It was sweet, that prospect.

The lamp in Arnulf's hand guttered and dimmed. With sublime contempt, Gerbert kindled the light of his power. Its clarity was merciless in that place.

Darkness swelled within it. A shape in black, wearing the face of mortal antiquity, seized the light and swallowed it. Gerbert staggered. Power knew power; and this spirit was strong. In magic's absence he had known nothing but that he had need, and that this being could fulfill it.

It stretched out a hand as thin and twisted as a claw. Arnulf stared at it as if he had not comprehended, yet, what truly had brought him here, or why. His lips moved: incantation, or prayer, or simple disbelief.

The spirit mocked him with a yapping like a dog's. "You are mine," it said, "by my master's will. Come, be brave. Pain suffered soon is soonest over."

Arnulf's eyes turned to Gerbert. Gerbert should have rejoiced to see that proud prince sunk even as low as this: pale, baffled, waking to fear. "You hate me so much?" Arnulf whispered.

"More," said the spirit. It stroked Arnulf's cheek with appalling tenderness. "Mine," it crooned. "Mine."

The archbishop gasped and shuddered. "In God's name!"

"Adonai!" howled the spirit. "Adonai!" The air was cold with horror. The light had fled. Gerbert saw with the eyes of his power, dim and shadowed sight: the spirit a shape of darkness, Arnulf a candle that flickered low. Clawed hands stretched to take him.

"No!"

Gerbert started and nearly dropped the Jinniyah. Richer burst into their circle, a storm of limbs and flapping skirts and flaring magelight, falling on man and spirit with all the ferocity of his warrior kin. Arnulf went down with a gasping cry. The spirit reared up. Richer smote it with a bolt of power.

It quivered as if with pleasure, and smiled at Gerbert. Its teeth were like a wolf's. "Two of them, master? You are generous."

Gerbert shuddered. Something was struggling outward from his heart. A word. A thought.

"Sathanas!" cried Richer, thin and shaking. "Go, thou spirit accursed, spawn of darkness, denizen of the nether pit. I conjure thee, I constrain and command thee, I will thee begone, and all thy foulness with thee!"

The spirit did not even waver. It was no devil. It was

a lesser thing, and more terrible. A shape of madness given substance. Revenge with will and wit and power. It seized Arnulf. It seized Richer, and drew them to itself.

Gerbert raised his hand. He had summoned the spirit, and he was a master of magic. It paused, astonished. "Let them go," said Gerbert.

The spirit was unwilling, but his power was unbending. Richer fell like a rag, discarded. Arnulf, the spirit kept. "He is mine," it said. "He belongs to me."

So he was. Gerbert gathered to consent; heard a voice say, "No." He glared down at the enchanted bronze. "What! Do even you betray me?"

"You damn yourself," she said, "in this that you will do."

"He is damned already."

"But not by you."

Gerbert raised her as if to dash her to the floor. She flexed in his hands, slipping about. Her eyes met his. They did not beg. They willed him to see as she saw. Madness; sanity. Damnation and salvation, the swearing of oaths, and the bartering of lives for one man's anger.

He wanted that anger. He cherished it.

"Let him destroy himself," the Jinniyah said.

"And you with him," said the spirit. Its humanity had fallen from it. Its robe rippled, unfurling. Wings fanned the stone-cold air. "Do you know what you hold, master? That is the Liar's daughter. Death is her price."

She rang between Gerbert's palms. "Death is cleaner than what that one takes. I am paid for. Will you burden yourself with that other price?"

Gerbert's throat burned with bile. His mind was a roil. His magic clenched in his center.

He looked at Arnulf and knew the burning sweetness that was hate. Arnulf pawed feebly at the claw that clutched his throat. Power saw him for what he was: a hollow thing, a shape of air, a mind fixed immovably upon itself. And yet, for all its shoddiness, it remained a man. The soul that glimmered in it was as immortal as any other.

"I will not take his soul," said the spirit of Gerbert's summoning.

It spoke truth; yet it did not. What it would take was never Gerbert's to give. "Let him go," Gerbert said.

He was master. The spirit struggled, but his power bound it. It let its captive fall. It bared its white wolf-teeth and flexed its talons. "You will regret your charity," it said.

"So be it," said Gerbert. "Now, go, and trouble him no more."

The spirit paused, as if it would speak. Gerbert raised his hands and his power. The black wings boomed; the spirit shrieked as if in agony—or in laughter. It whirled away into the dark.

"You've not seen the last of it," said the Jinniyah, cool and incongruously serene in the spirit's wake.

Gerbert wanted to lie down and sleep until Judgment Day. Or, if he could not do that, to burst into a storm of weeping. As it was, he did neither. Richer had dragged himself up. Arnulf lay crumpled where the spirit had dropped him. He breathed; there was no wound on him. His mind, taxed to its limit, had simply and sanely taken refuge in unconsciousness. He was a very sane man, was Arnulf Oathbreaker.

Gerbert's sanity was ensorceled in bronze. "You will yet pay the price of your summoning," she said.

He surprised himself with the beginnings of a smile. "At least it will be I who pay it." He gathered her in a fold of his mantle and held out his hand to Richer. "Come, lad. It's time we went to Senlis."

Richer looked from Gerbert to Arnulf and back. "You've forgiven him?"

Gerbert's teeth set. "What makes you think that?" He pulled Richer with him toward the outer door. "Come, don't dally. There's little enough left of the night, and we've a long ride before us."

Richer swallowed protests audibly, choking on them. The Jinniyah was quieter. Gerbert led them both into the free air.

14

I, Arnulf, once by the grace of God Archbishop of Rheims, acknowledging my frailty and the burden of my sins, in the presence of my judges and my confessors the lord bishops Seguin, Darbert, Arnulf, Godesmann, Hervé, Ratbod, Walter, Bruno, Milo, Ascelin, Odo, Wido, and Heribert, grant them judgment of my transgressions, and confess to them without deception. From them I seek the reparation of penitence and the salvation of my soul, wherefore I yield up the duty and office of archbishop, for which I acknowledge myself unworthy, and from which I have alienated myself through those crimes which I have confessed to these my lords in secret and which I have proclaimed in public tribunal. Thus let them bear witness, and let them have the power to set and to consecrate another in my place, who may rule worthily and serve usefully that church over which I have so unworthily presided. And that henceforward I might have no power in law either to seek or to seize what I have surrendered, by my own hand I affirm these oaths. I, Arnulf, once Archbishop of Rheims, have read and understood; I set herewith my hand and my seal.

Richer had to give him credit. He read the text of his own deposition in a clear and steady voice, calm before the gathered bishops, calm even before the king whom he had betrayed. There was no humility in him. He had a certain air, a little defiant, a little subdued, like a boy whose sins have found him out. Richer wondered if, in the end, they meant any more to him than that. He could have had the grace at least to pretend to be a broken man.

The bishops seemed grimly satisfied. Ascelin of Laon, as supple a serpent as Arnulf but rather more clever, looked as if he might have been tempted to smile. Gerbert's escape and his testimony had given the synod of Senlis the evidence it needed, but Ascelin had netted the fish. Not Arnulf alone had come to his lure of alliance and his bait of the best cook in Gaul, but Charles himself and all Charles' sons. Their fault and their folly that they had come to the feast and found, at the end of it, men with drawn swords. They were well and truly secured in the fortress of Orleans; they would, it was hoped, die there. Ascelin's cook, Richer had heard, had been given to the fallen rebel to console him in his captivity. Richer wondered if Charles had any taste left for the dainties of the table.

Arnulf, as a prince of the Church, had fallen under the Church's justice. It was no harsher than he deserved. Barely harsh enough, some muttered. He was stripped of his office but not of his priesthood; he would return to Rheims as a clerk of the cathedral.

They were taking his marks of rank one by one, with ceremony: the miter, the cope, the pallium that was his mark of authority from Rome, the ring of which he had seemed so fond. He was a lonely figure amid the grim and glittering bishops, bereft of his splendor, shivering in his thin linen shirt. An acolyte clothed him in plain Benedictine black, not looking at him, handling him as if he were a lifeless thing.

That pricked him. His lips thinned; his eyes flashed down the nave of Senlis' cathedral. It was full to bursting; eyes stared back, avid or accusing or merely curious.

Monks in his own habit surrounded him. He stiffened, but he neither resisted nor spoke. He let them lead him away.

Richer's breath left him slowly. He had not known that he was holding it. It all seemed tawdry somehow: so much pain and so much labor, so many lies and deaths and betrayals, and at the end of it, only this. A man in a black habit, led back to the life which he should never have left.

Richer glanced at Gerbert who stood beside him. Freedom and the restoration of his magic had made the master strong again. He looked almost as he always had. Thinner, still, and grey, but no longer transparent, as if he would turn to mist and melt away. If he had pursued Arnulf's deposition with a passion once reserved for his beloved books, Richer could hardly blame him. Gerbert was, before all else, an honest man. Lies and treachery revolted him. And Arnulf had taken his magic. That, even the most Christian magus might not forgive.

Gerbert was hardly thinking of Arnulf, whom once he had hated. Hate had died in the crypt of Rheims' cathedral, when he saw the liar fallen and the spirit stooping over him. Anger had lingered yet a while, and he had tended it with care, for he needed it to face the bishops and the king, and to speak for his city. It was for Rheims that he had done what he had done. Escaped captivity in a mantle of magic, ridden until his barely mended body was like to break, faced the synod exactly as he was: unshaven, filthy, staggering with exhaustion. But even at the edge of endurance he was eloquent. Their shock at the sight of him had turned to wrath at the tale he told. They had declared Arnulf anathema; then they had summoned him to trial; then, when he took refuge with his uncle in Laon, loosed on him the one of them all who was more treacherous than he.

That was none of Gerbert's doing. But he had not risen to oppose it. The last of his anger had kept him silent.

Now it was gone, and justice done. Yet he was not at peace. He had sinned in wrath, and he had sinned in pride. What he had done was not undone. His oath to Ibrahim was broken in spirit if not, precisely, in truth. He had watched with sleepless vigilance, and no shadow had stirred where he could see, no claws stretched to rend either his enemy or his friend. The spirit might truly have been driven out. Gerbert's bones knew that it had not.

Part of him was always on guard. The rest turned now to memory, and to comfort. The king's hall in Senlis; the king's face. The king's voice admitting with grace enough, "Yes, *magister*. I erred. I should never have made that man Archbishop of Rheims."

Gerbert had said nothing.

Hugh looked at him and shook his head. "You've paid high for my mistake."

"Rheims has paid higher," Gerbert said.

The king's brow darkened, but he did not rebuke the insolence. "I shall redress you both as I may. I'll give you what I should have given in the beginning."

It was a royal apology. Gerbert bowed low, accepting it. So would he bow on the morrow when the bishops held their formal election. For form's sake he would have to protest his unworthiness.

And was he?

That there were better men in the world, he had no doubt at all. That any of them was as well suited to be the shepherd of Rheims . . . he did not know. Was it hubris, to suspect that none of them was?

The rite of deposition was ending, the throng beginning to disperse. He felt eyes on him. He should linger: it was known what the morrow would bring, and he would need friends if he was to rule Rheims in peace. The pope, who had blessed Arnulf's accession but not his deposition, was not going to bear easily this action of the bishops. Rumor had it that he was sending a legate, and that the man was armed in Arnulf's defense. In Rome, it was all very simple. Liar and traitor to his king, Arnulf might have been, but he held his see by the pope's will. The pope had not willed that he be cast out of it. King and bishops had done that of their own accord.

The Holy Father would surely learn to see the justice in it; but there would be a battle. Gerbert was braced for it, and he meant to win it.

But now he was weary. He had taken no joy in his victory. It was too hard won. He was numb; he wanted only to rest, to sleep, to be free of all this clamor. He wrapped himself in shadows and slipped away.

He was growing old indeed: now when he would go hunting his heart's ease, he relied not on his own legs but on those of the mule that had been Adalberon's. Alba was indulgent of his follies. Wiser than a mare, she went at her own pace, and left him in peace to confront himself.

He was no saint, nor ever would be. Since he had never hoped to be one, he was not unduly distressed. He had faith, to be sure. He was as good a Christian as he could be, and still be both scholar and mage. He tried to be a good priest, a good shepherd to his people.

What he had done in illness and in anger, God might

forgive. Weakness had driven him to it, and love for his city. But whether he could forgive himself . . .

He still could not make himself regret that he had wanted Arnulf dead. Even yet he suspected that the viper might strike again. Its back was broken, but no one had troubled to draw its fangs.

I could do it.

Shadow dimmed the sunlight, whispering in his ear. His magic shuddered like Alba's hide beneath a stinging fly.

Every step of that conjuring was ill taken. Richer excused him with sickness, madness, desperation. Gerbert had no such charity. Madness, yes, and pride, the pride of despair. Not for him Richer's clean simplicity: to walk in, take the Jinniyah, hide her in an altar until he could make his escape. No. Gerbert had had to do it in the worst of all ways: by sorcery. He had wanted the world—and Arnulf most prominent in it—to know beyond all doubting that, even without power, he remained a master of magic.

The callowest apprentice would have known that that was folly. Richer had known it, and Richer was hardly noted for his prudence. If Gerbert had waited but a night, he would not have needed the spell at all; he would have been free and sinless, a mage in power as in name.

But he had not waited, and he had botched the working. He had let his temper master him. He had made bargains which he could not fulfill; he had forgotten the words that would have dismissed the spirit beyond its power to return. And he had lost its name, by which even then he could have mastered it.

Now it was free in the world, and it was hungry. By the law of its kind, it could not return to its own realm until it was sated; but it could not be sated save by human life, and that life, Gerbert must give. And he would not. Could not. He had forbidden it Arnulf. He could not offer it an innocent, or even a criminal condemned to death. That was murder, and his soul rebelled.

Therefore it was stalemate. The spirit could touch nothing while his power stood on guard. He could not relax that guard lest the spirit take what it must take.

It haunted his dreams. It shadowed his waking. It hovered, it whispered, it tempted. *Feed me and I go. One small life. One worthless soul. Then you are free of me.*

It wanted him to break and rage and set it on the prey which he had promised it. Gerbert would not. If he destroyed any man who wronged him, he would do it by mortal means; in justice, not in rancor.

But his strength was waning slowly. He could not be Archbishop of Rheims, and master of magic, and servant of king and emperor, and still hold off this demon which he had summoned. Raw power was not enough. Formal magic could not expel it without its name.

He could bind it. Not easily, not eternally, but long enough perhaps to discover its name. Then he could bid it begone.

The guilt and the shame, he would never lose. He knew no one to whom he could confess it. Mages were not often priests: the Church and the power were an uneasy mating. Gerbert knew how wary the bishops were of that side of his self; he had had to labor hard and long to convince them that it had not tainted his priesthood. This would seem to prove the opposite, though in his mind it stained not the priest but the mage. The priest was true to his vows. It was the mage who had sinned against his oath; who was forsworn as utterly as ever Arnulf had been.

No. Not quite. He had willed the breaking, but he had stopped short of acting on it. That much comfort, cold as it was, he could take. It might give him strength to do what he must do.

He blinked. With all his mind turned inward, he had not noticed where the mule was carrying him. The sun was low, dazzling his eyes. He shaded them with his hand.

The road stretched before and behind, Roman-straight beneath the mould of years. The sun slanted down it. On either side rose a scattering of trees. They were thin, but they veiled the way behind, the clearing in the great wood of the north that was Senlis.

Even a mage could be uneasy to find himself alone and weaponless in a wood at sunset. Beasts lurked in woods, and not all of them ran on four feet. Poor prey as he made in his priestly habit, his mule was fine, and her caparisons were worth a penny or two. He had been too preoccupied to notice that the lad had put on the best bridle with its inlay of gold, and the saddle with the cloth of Byzantine silk.

His magic sensed no threat but the one that never left him. He eased a little, but he gathered the reins to turn the mule about.

She resisted. She had her eye on a succulent bit of browsing just ahead, and a babble and sparkle beyond that betokened a stream. Gerbert sighed, shrugged. A moment more could make no difference. He let Alba have her head.

Beyond the stream a path wound up among the trees. It was neither wide nor high enough for a mounted man, but for one on foot it was ample. As Alba dipped her head to drink, Gerbert slid from her back, moved by what impulse he hardly knew. He tethered her loosely to a branch and laid a word of guard and binding on her, at which she gave him a look of reproach. "It's not that I don't trust you," he said. "But someone might find you too tempting to resist."

She snorted, unmollified. But there was grazing enough

within her tether's reach, and she was a wise mule. She did not try to argue.

Gerbert kilted up his habit and eyed the path. An odd excitement quivered in him. He had forgotten how strong and hale a body could feel. He paused only long enough to sling the saddlebags over his shoulder—no need to tempt a thief more than he could help—and set foot on the path.

It was an easy ascent, no tax on his strength; it wound a little as the trees ordained. After a time it found again the stream which crossed it below, and followed that. He stopped once to drink and to bathe his face, and to wonder briefly what he was doing. But only briefly. When the magic beckoned so, a mage was wise to heed it. He crossed himself, to hallow what he did, and blessed the stream. It laughed at his caution. He smiled back, shifted his burden, went on.

He knew it when he came to it. It was older than any living thing about it: an oak that seemed as broad as a tower. Beneath its tangled roots the stream sprang, sparking like fire; for the last rays of the sun, piercing the dimming wood, fell full upon the face of tree and spring.

A little below the source, the water filled a shallow basin of stone, then brimmed and overflowed into its narrow channel. Gerbert sank down beside the pool, suddenly exhausted. For a little while he had been young again. Now age had taken him back.

As by maddening degrees his breathing quieted, he saw what the sun was showing him. The spring rose under the roots of the oak, in a hollow like a cave, its roof a vault of living wood. There beyond the bubble of water stood a figure. It was carved, he suspected, of oakwood, dark now with age and furred with moss, but its shape was clear to see. A woman; a maiden in a gown that did little to obscure her shapely young body.

No; no maiden. Her belly rounded in a way that even a priest, if he remembered mother and sisters, could recognize. One hand guarded that fruitful curve; the other held, incongruously, a cross.

Someone had been careful to make this seem a Christian shrine. But the power in it was older by far.

Gerbert shivered, yet not—strangely—with revulsion. The dark goddess, or Blessed Virgin if it pleased her to be reckoned so, bore no evil in her. Power, yes, great enough to be perilous, and not all of the light; but darkness had no great part in it. Before she bore a cross, he knew in his bones, she had borne a blossom. A dark rose?

She seemed to smile as the sun faded. *See*, she seemed to say. *See what I keep for you.*

Gifts lay at her feet. Whoever brought them, brought them often, for what purpose Gerbert could not guess. For luck? For the bearing of a child? He saw a withered garland, a cake much nibbled by mice. But most notably a small still shape that, not so very long ago, had been alive. It glimmered in the dimness: a white dove with the snare still on its neck, its body barely stiffened in death. The one who had left it, must have heard Gerbert and fled.

Gerbert's shadow quivered, drawn to the scent of new blood.

And he knew.

He could not sing hosannas. He could not even, yet, thank the power that had led him to this place. He moved with great care, as if the image and the bird were nothing more to him than curiosity. He set the saddlebags on the ground by the pool and took the packet of bread and cheese, and as if on a whim, carried it into the shrine and laid it at the feet of the image. The prayer he murmured was genuine. He crossed himself, bowed, let his hand find the dove. "A pity to waste tender meat," he said to the air.

It trembled with hunger.

Sunset blazed in his face. Above his head, trapped amid the branches of the oak, shone a single star. The moon glowed above it, pale still but brightening as the light faded. It was waning, but it was strong enough yet for what he intended.

This was not a magic that came easily to a man, still less to a priest of the God Who denied all divinity but His own. But that priesthood gave Gerbert one small edge of strength. Given to the monks in childhood, sworn to the threefold vows before his blood began to burn with the beginnings of manhood, he had never known a woman. He did not reckon it truly purity—that was for angels, and for saints whose faith freed them from any bodily temptation. But to the moon and the old magic, it was enough.

It was as heady as wine. He firmed his will against the madness in it, focused his mind on the cool and ordered paths of his mastery. The wild magic struggled, but he was strong, and skilled in his strength. For a moment he remembered a Sabbat over Aurillac, a choice made, a path taken; he smiled.

He took from his bag the four white candles for the four corners of heaven; the white stole with which he would sanctify his working; and, slowly, the athame in its wrappings of dark wool. The shadow took no notice. It yearned toward the dove which he had laid beside the pool.

He kissed the stole and laid it over his shoulders, bowing for a moment under the weight of sanctity. He set each candle in its place about the pool, naming it as it must be named. Michael of the flaming sword at the gates of the south; Gabriel the trumpeter in the vaults of the west; Raphael whose healing power warded the east; and Uriel the watchman of the north. As he spoke each name, its candle burst into flame, round and white and steady though a little wind had come to whisper in the branches.

The water was dark, still as a mirror. Gerbert bent over it. Deep within, something glimmered. His hand slipped through numbing cold to close about a hard round smoothness. A stone a little smaller than an egg, shaped like an egg, white as the moon, polished smooth. It was heavy in his hand. With as much care as if truly it had been an egg, he laid it on the moss by the pool's edge.

He took up the body of the bird. In one swift, encompassing motion, he gathered his power, freed the athame, opened the limp white throat. Blood trickled from it onto the stone.

The shadow swooped. The athame glittered athwart its path. It reared back. Eyes pale as moons fixed on the falling blood. But the whisper of its voice said, "No."

Gerbert said nothing. The dove's body emptied slowly. The stone lost its last glimmer of whiteness. He laid the bird down; he raised the stone. In the pool's center, like an eye, glowed the moon. Gerbert's hand eclipsed it. Where the moon had been was the shadow of the stone. He trembled. The power was like the surge of the tide, pulling at him, straining the bonds of his mastery.

"Come," he said. "Drink."

The spirit stretched toward the bird. Again the athame halted it. It hissed. The bloodstone drank the moon. Deep in its heart, a red light grew.

"Drink," said Gerbert. "Drink deep."

The spirit mantled like a hawk. Its eyes raged.

"Come," said the mage, soft and deep. "Drink."

The spirit howled. Gerbert stiffened, but his hand did not move. The stone glowed like a coal, beat like a heart. Moon and madness filled it; life pulsed in it. The spirit swayed as by no will of its own. Its wings fluttered wildly, now driving it back, now casting it forward. Its claws raked toward Gerbert's face. He did not flinch.

With a cry of anguish and of resistless desire, the spirit fell upon the stone. It flared with heat more terrible than any fire. It swelled; it bloomed; it engulfed the shadow that had seized it.

Gerbert knelt by the pool's edge, gasping, cradling his hand. Before him, between his knees and the water, lay the stone. A carbuncle a little smaller than an egg, red as blood, luminous as a coal, with a darkness in its heart.

His shadow was free under the moon. He turned his face to the cold light; and for all the agony of his charred and blistered hand, his heart swelled with purest joy. "Now," he said. "Now I shall be healed."

Part Three

PONTIFEX MAGICUS

Rome, A.D. 996

15

His Holiness, Gregory, fifth of that name, Bishop of Rome, *Pontifex Maximus*, servant of the servants of God, shifted on the cushions of his throne and throttled the urge to yawn. The tiara was an aching burden on his brow; the vestments were a torment in this ghastly Roman heat. Briefly he considered hating his royal cousin for condemning him to it. He might have had a blessed, simple, unvexing bishopric in a climate suited to human habitation. Hungary, perhaps. Poland. Even the people there . . . a horde of heathen Magyars, man for man, was rather more genteel than the populace of Rome.

For a gratifying moment, he considered the prospect of a match, Roman against Magyar, bare-handed. He would wager on the Roman. Magyars drank mere bull's blood. Romans imbibed sedition with their mothers' milk.

He was not, God be thanked, a Roman. He was a royal Saxon; and he was, at the moment, displeased.

Rheims again. It was always Rheims. The Franks were as quarrelsome as Romans, and as stubborn in their rebellion. He had the tale of it from his predecessor's chancery, which it had vexed to no perceptible end. A man of dubious lineage and uncertain loyalty, but duly elected and duly endowed with the pallium, that bit of linen embroidered with crosses and blessed by his properly ordained superior, that was sign and seal of his right to hold his office: that was Arnulf whose partisans clamored in the curia. A man of no lineage at all and proven loyalty to the imperial dynasty, but elected in dubious circumstances and unsanctioned with the pallium: that was Gerbert who had displaced him. The Frankish king—himself an interloper with no blood right to the crown—and the bishops convened in synod without papal sanction, had presumed to resolve the matter to their own satisfaction, despite protests from Rome. The papal legate himself, Abbot Leo of legendary probity and monumental obstinacy, had interdicted all who took part in that second election, and removed the interloper from his see. To no visible effect. Arnulf had not been permitted to take back his place. Gerbert had continued in it, administering it with—of that, Gregory had been assured—exceptional competence.

Damn the man, thought Gregory, regardless of his sacred office. Which man he meant, he hardly cared.

The one in front of him was voluble if hardly eloquent. "And so you see," said Herluin, "when my lord Rothard died, unworthy though I am, the bishops elected me to succeed him in the see of Cambrai. But I feared, Holy Father, to accept consecration from hands themselves unconsecrated by the approbation of the Holy See. Hands that—if I dare say it—"

He floundered to a halt. The man with him took up the gauntlet. Notker, his name was, Bishop of Liège. His eyes glittered; he fairly foamed at the mouth. "Yes, brother, dare to say it!" He faced the pope. "The man, Holy Father, is a liar and an interloper, a lowborn grasper after power. *Any* power, Holy Father. The whole world knows that he sojourned in Spain in his youth; half the world knows what he studied there. Sorcery, Holy Father. Necromancy. All the black arts."

"Well," said Herluin, fluttering. "I wouldn't go so far as to say—"

Notker rode over him. "The man is a sorcerer. He practices his arts in the very cathedral of Rheims. He frequents the company of Jews and Saracens, and worse than that, Holy Father, worse by far—he teaches the arts of the devil to the youths of his school, and he does so openly, flagrantly, with no vestige of shame."

Gregory straightened on his throne. He had heard the charge before.

"Simon," the bishop of Liège was thundering. "Simon Magus is born again. The devil—the Antichrist—"

What, Gregory wondered, had Gerbert done to earn such detestation?

"Really," Herluin babbled. "Really, Notker, just because he's blunter than you like—"

It was past time to put an end to this. Gregory's guards restrained Notker before he could do murder; a chamberlain saw to Herluin, who was almost weeping with distress.

"I shall," said Gregory in the echoing silence, "give thought to this matter."

This audience was considerably quieter, and although summer was considerably more advanced, rather cooler. Gregory had set it for the morning, before the day's heat was at its fullest. Unfortunately, it was no more pleasant than its predecessor had been.

Not that he disliked the man who stood in front of him. Herluin was a weakling and Notker a bully. Gerbert was neither. A little brusque, a little impatient with the demands of ceremony, but honestly respectful of the office and of the man who held it. He had not insulted Gregory with archiepiscopal regalia. He looked well in the simplicity of a priest's gown, not a handsome man but a distinguished one, with his strong blunt face and his clear grey eyes—or were they brown, or green?—and his silvered hair. He had a beautiful voice, which he knew how to use. Once, when he smiled, his face lit like a lamp; and for a moment Gregory was dazzled.

But all the charm and all the eloquence and all the competence in the world could not alter one essential fact. "You hold your see without sanction from Rome," said Gregory. "You have held it in defiance of your vow of obedience. I cannot confirm you in what was never rightly yours."

Gerbert's anger was plain to see: his eyes went pale, his lips tightened. Yet he spoke softly. "Holy Father, I believe that I am the rightful archbishop of Rheims. My lord Adalberon chose me to be his successor. My king, though for a while he went awry, came in the end and through suffering to the same conclusion. Arnulf is and was an invader and a breaker of his oath."

"He was," said Gregory, "duly elected. Rome granted him the pallium. Rome never stripped him of it."

"Rome was suborned by the serpents in his pay!" Gerbert controlled himself with a visible effort. "My lord, we did what we had to do. He had laid waste to his see; he had handed it over to the enemies of the king, in defiance of the vow he swore on the Eucharist itself."

"Still," said the pope, "he was judged by those who had no right or power to judge him."

Gerbert was speechless. Gregory almost pitied him. He could not but know that he was in the wrong, and yet he had done it out of the conviction that he must. There was a dilemma for an honest man.

This honest man had made and broken kings. And no

kingly blood in him; none at all. Gregory, who was the kinsman of emperors, stiffened his back and his will. "I see one recourse," he said. "I will judge your case, in full." Gerbert stood rigidly still; in his eyes was a dawning of hope. "On one condition. You will restore Arnulf to his see."

Gerbert's mouth opened.

Gregory went on, implacable. "Restore him, and I will judge him. If I determine that his crimes merit his deposition, then I will depose him."

"And if not?" Gerbert demanded. "If you decide that he is more convenient mitered than unmitered? What then? Shall I see my people torn again out of the few years' peace which I have won for them? Must my king fear anew the threat to his crown?"

"The pretender is dead," said Gregory. "His sons are dead or powerless. There is only Arnulf to consider. He can claim no kingship. If he has sinned as grievously as you allege, then he will lose the archbishopric. What have you lost but a few months' uncertainty?"

"Rheims," said Gerbert, as if he could not help himself.

Gregory set his teeth and straightened his back. "It has been said that you are ambitious; that you abetted Arnulf in his treachery until you saw greater advantage in the king's cause." Gerbert erupted in protest; Gregory silenced him with a lifted hand. "This is not a trial. I simply warn. Your friends are many and your fame great. Yet, like any man who would dwell in high places, you have enemies; and men who are neither, but who strive to perceive you for what you are. Some might propose that the petty treachery of your rival is as nothing to the multiplicity of your sins."

"One of those accusers being, perhaps, the Bishop of Liège?"

Gregory had smiled before he thought, a swift, mirthless grin. "You are, by all accounts, an honest man. Surely you can understand what force constrains me. I am the Vicar of Christ. I must administer the laws which I and my predecessors have made. To begin this trial, I must demand that Arnulf be restored. Then and only then may I judge him."

Gerbert's head bowed, but not in submission. "Holy Father—"

"No," said Gregory.

It was flat, and it was final. Gerbert made obeisance with excruciating correctness, and left.

Gregory took off the tiara and rubbed his aching brow, and glared. Servants scattered. He barely noticed. He rose. "Enough of this," he said. "By God, enough!"

One brave idiot dared to remonstrate. "Holy Father, the Margrave of—"

"A plague on the margrave!" Gregory cast off his cope in the face of assembled shock, and bared his teeth, shocking them further. Why they should be so appalled, after the godless fools who had gone before him, he could not imagine. He turned his back on them all and went in search of a moment's peace.

"May God preserve us from an honest pope." Gerbert had been pacing for a good hour, simmering. The words burst out of him all at once. He stopped, spun to face the Jinniyah.

She met his glare with a level stare. "He's in the right, as he sees it. How can he help but refuse you?"

"He refuses to see what stares him in the face."

"How can he see it? He wasn't there. All he knows is that the king and the bishops of Gaul are contesting his power to sanction a bishop's election. That's striking at the heart of the papacy itself."

"Since when," gritted Gerbert, "have you been an authority on papal politics?"

"Since my master involved himself in them."

He snarled and went back to his pacing. It was his privilege as an archbishop from Gaul—however hotly contested his right to that title—to lodge in a room of his own in a hostelry not excessively far from the papal palace. It was a tiny cell of a room, airless and indifferently clean, but its door was solid. He could be reasonably certain that no one heard his colloquy with his antique bronze.

At the moment he did not care if the entire papal curia knew that he had a heathen spirit for a familiar. "Everything," he said. "Everything I do withers on the branch. First Rheims is snatched from me by a king's misguided policy. Then I win it at no little cost to body and soul; but can I keep it? Arnulf and his allies spew their poison wherever they go. They turn my bishops against me. They hiss in the ear of the pope himself. They smite me with the cold hammer of the law; they teach my people to hate me. No one in Rheims will dine with me or attend my mass. I am sick of it, I tell you. Sick, sick, sick!"

He broke in a torrent of coughing, cursing through it, until the room filled with frightened servants. He could not even drive them out; he had no voice left. They put him to bed, hovering and fluttering, maddening him with their worry.

He had to feign sleep before they would leave him. Then in truth, for a little while, he did sleep. He dreamed that Richer was there, fretting but being bearable about it.

He woke with a start. He was alone. Richer was in Rheims, looking after the inner school and writing a history of the Franks. The two went together with an odd logic. Gerbert, as Richer liked to say, was in both. They had not kept the idiot from all but packing himself in Gerbert's baggage. Gerbert had had to trap him with a threat: to set over the school of the Art no less a master than Arnulf himself. That was a low blow; but it won Richer's submission.

Gerbert would never admit that he had misjudged. He had been ill at intervals since the year began. He had seemed to be better when he left in haste for Rome, hoping against hope to arrive before Herluin could win his case and his pallium. Now the sickness was back and Herluin had his sanction from the pope's own hand, untainted by Gerbert's intercession; and Gregory would not hear Gerbert's defense unless he surrendered his see.

"And that," he said into the airless dark, "I will not do. Rheims belongs to me. I have paid for it. I will not give it up."

16

Gerbert clung to the saddle of his mule and tried to peer through the dazzle of sunlight. His eyes were full of water; his ears rang; his lungs labored against the weight of sickness. He thought he saw walls, towers, a blurred banner. "Rheims?" he tried to ask.

"Pavia," someone said. And in a different tone, which perhaps he was not meant to hear: "Can we move any faster? He's about to drop."

"Better not," said someone else. "Stubborn old bastard. If he'd let us put him in a litter . . ."

"No," Gerbert said clearly. Or he thought he said it clearly. Of course this was not Rheims. This was the royal city, Pavia that was queen of Lombardy, set like a jewel in the richness of the plain, and far away on the edge of the world, the march of mountains. The Alps that had defeated Hannibal would hardly slow Gerbert, sickness or no. His city was beyond them, his school of the arts and of the Art, his poor beleaguered archbishopric which he did not intend to give up.

Alba, scenting a stable, speeded her amble slightly. As long as he could cling to her back, he was not a useless old man. He drew himself up. The pope had not guessed that he was ill. He would be damned if Pavia would.

Someday magic would find a way to banish fever. One or two of the students in Rheims had a gift in that direction. Richer—

Richer was not going to learn that his master had needed his potions and his power. Else Gerbert would never hear the end of it.

"You won't tell him," said Gerbert earnestly. "Promise me."

"I promise," said the shadow at Alba's head. Sometimes it had Bruno's face. Sometimes it had wolf's teeth; or its cloak unfurled into wings. Then it would grin, and Gerbert would know where his sickness had come from.

His servants turned on him. They faced him to a man, and refused to leave Pavia until the doctors judged him well. "Quacks!" he raged. "Charlatans!" And, to his traitor servants: "Mutiny!"

His body, alas, rebelled most treacherously of all. It could barely stand. When he drove it toward the stable, it fell and lay prostrate until the rebels laid him in bed again.

In the end, perforce, he yielded. He lay and seethed, but he did not try to get up. Often.

He was not grateful to discover how quickly he mended, once he gave his body time to rest. It had simply been worn out. The spirit's malice had been a dream, a delusion of his fever. It was safe in its prison, trapped and powerless.

While he lay ill but not unconscious, he learned that he had indeed seen a banner over the city: the golden eagle of the emperor. Otto, third of that name, was in residence, though likely soon to forsake the fogs and fevers of Italy for the cleaner air beyond the mountains. Outland blood never prospered in this pestilential country.

Some part of Gerbert that was not lost to sickness,

recalled that he had hoped to find the emperor here. At first he could hardly care. But as his body began, too slowly, to mend, his mind shook itself free of the fogs that beset it. It was awake again, and thinking—scheming, his enemies would say. It focused on this young emperor with the fixity of a mind that had little else to occupy it; it gathered all that it might, of what Otto was, and who, and what he might portend to a mage who had been an archbishop and who was now little more than carrion. But carrion with a flicker of life in it yet.

Otto would be out of boyhood now, and into youth. His father had died, leaving him the empire, when he was barely out of infancy; his mother, who had been a princess in Byzantium, had ruled as regent until she died, not so long ago. Italy had killed them both. The boy was interesting, people said, half a Greek and half a Saxon, but all a Roman.

Gerbert had known his mother and his father, and his grandfather whom people called the Great. This third Otto, Gerbert had never seen. He was pious, rumor had it; he had the family fondness for men of learning, and not a little of that himself. Remarkable in a youth who had been emperor at three, who had led armies to war at seven.

Remarkable enough, perhaps, to be of use to a desperate man. Gerbert had sworn oaths of fealty to the German emperors; and he had been loyal to them, whatever the cost, in all the years since he left Hatto's guardianship to serve that first, great Otto. Surely this latest of that line owed him something. A hearing, at the least. And, perhaps, a word to his cousin the pope, a suggestion that his holiness might do well to judge in Gerbert's favor. Gerbert would ask no more than that.

When he was well enough to walk about a little with a stick to lean on, he sent his message. It was simple. *The* magister *of Rheims begs leave to look upon his imperial majesty.*

"Only to look?" the Jinniyah mocked him, but gently.

He was recovering his temper with his strength: he merely glared at her. Some fool, thinking to indulge his master's eccentricity, had set her by the bed, which Gerbert in his right mind would never have allowed. Even in the exigencies of travel, when there was no place for her but beside him, he had always kept her covered when modesty required it.

"Not," he muttered, "that you could have seen anything to tempt you."

"No?"

She was laughing at him. A harlot without a body, an elderly priest who had never had one to brag of—a fine pair, they made.

Before he lay down, he turned her face to the wall.

Much more quickly than he would have expected, his message received an answer. It was as brief as his own. *The* magister *of Rheims may attend his majesty on the morrow after the daymeal.*

Gerbert came perilously close to refusing. It was too soon. He was too weak. Worse than that: he looked like a sick man. He did not want a young man's pity.

That Gerbert did not refuse, had nothing to do with what one did and did not say to emperors. He was stubborn, and he had had enough of lying about, feeling sorry for himself. He called for a bath, though the servants— good Franks all—cried that he was sealing his death warrant; he called for a barber. He would go as a simple priest, but his habit was new, his linen clean. If he could not look either young or hale, at least he would not look as if he were about to give up the ghost.

The barber had a mirror. Gerbert was not appalled by what he saw there. A certain transparency did not go ill with the habit and the tonsure. His eyes were grey today, almost silver.

"Lead us not," sang the Jinniyah, softly, softly, "into temptation."

He flung his nightrobe over her and dismissed the barber, who was looking sorely puzzled.

There was, then, the matter of getting to the palace. Alba's saddle was as yet an unscalable eminence. A litter, therefore, it had to be.

Gerbert did not have to like it. It was not only pride. That a mage would not willingly cross water, the world well knew. What the world did not know was that a mage could not in comfort contemplate the rocking, swaying progress of a litter.

It was that or nothing. He set his teeth and let himself be helped into the infernal conveyance.

It cast him up, green and shaking, in the first courtyard of the palace. Servants were there to look after him, dismissing his own anxious escort. Well trained, these: their service was subtle, their assistance unobtrusive. They expressed neither pity nor dismay. Nor did they hurry him. He had time to calm his heaving stomach, to find his land legs. They offered wine; he discovered that he could swallow a little, and that it steadied him.

At a pace that seemed less labored than stately, his guides led him through the palace. They did not press him to hasten; they paused at intervals that he might rest. Later, when he could spare thought for aught but breathing, he would be interested to note their destination. Had it been an older Otto who summoned him, he would have been profoundly honored.

The small chamber had not changed. It was still an oddity in a fortress: a place of light and air for all its smallness, one wall an open portico that looked upon a bit of garden, the others painted in an ancient style to seem a sunlit hillside. The floor was its anchor: myriad tiles laid in a pattern of perfect simplicity, the cross and crook of the *Chi-Rho*, gold on white.

There were attendants, as there must be; some would be lofty indeed. Gerbert did not see them. On the low cushioned chair—its cushion faded now, and somewhat worn—where an Otto had always sat, was Otto.

He looked like his mother. That, for a moment, was all that Gerbert saw. He had her great eyes like an icon's, her pale oval face, her long elegant nose. His hair was lighter, with a suggestion of his father's ruddiness; the down that was trying to become a beard was reddish fair. He was slender, almost frail; for a Saxon, he was not tall, though he would still be taller than Gerbert.

Their eyes met.

This was what it was to fall in love. The shock that ran through the body, that had nothing to do with desire. The certainty, sure and absolute. *This was made for me. This is the other half of myself.*

He was aware of absurdity. A priest who at fifty had grown old. A boy who at sixteen was barely yet a man. A peasant's brat and an emperor. A magus and—

Theophano had had power, little use though she made of it. Her son had inherited it. All of it. And more. How much more, Gerbert could only begin to guess.

They must have spoken words of greeting, words that were no more than empty air. The attendants seemed to notice nothing amiss. There was a chair for Gerbert, with back and arms, and cushions blessedly soft. The emperor insisted that he sit in it, though Otto stood himself, bending over Gerbert. "If I had known you were ill," he said, "I would never have made you come here."

Gerbert stiffened. But it was not pity with which the emperor regarded him, or even dismay.

"Next time," said Otto, "I'll come to you."

It was as simple as that. There would be a next time.

Otto, Emperor of the Romans, dropped down at Gerbert's feet and smiled at him. "I'm sorry I made you come when you were sick, but I'm glad you came. It's been a long wait."

"You've been expecting me?"

Otto did not laugh at his stupidity. "All my life. Mother told me, you see. When I was ready for you, you'd come."

"What am I, that the emperor should wait for me?"

"*Magister.*" It was both title and answer. The strong brows knit. "Do I presume? I'm not worthy, I know, but—"

"My emperor is worthy of anything he pleases."

Otto tossed his head, impatient. "Oh, do stop that! I get a bellyful of it from the court." He stopped, clapped his hand to his mouth. "*Magister!* I didn't mean—"

Gerbert laughed. He could not help it. "I know what you meant. So you want a teacher. Haven't you had enough of that as of flattery?"

"Not what you can teach."

"And what do you think I can teach?"

"Whatever you think I can learn."

Gerbert knew that he should be wise. A man in love was the worst of fools. No matter what kind of love it was.

Was this what Ibrahim had felt when he saw Gerbert?

Gerbert's heart contracted. There would be a price for this. This was an emperor. A good one, people said, though young. So had Nero been. And Gerbert knew what had become of Nero's teacher, who had been the wisest man of his age.

Cold thoughts before those clear brown eyes, that look of hopeful expectation. Otto would not go the way of the tyrant. Theophano had been no Agrippina. This was no raddled, Godless Rome.

"Do you know," asked Otto softly, "what I dream of? Rome; but not the tattered shadow that the years have made of it. Rome reborn, the high laws, the ordered peace under a single lord. Am I arrogant, *magister*? Do I presume too much, in wanting to be Constantine?"

Gerbert's breath caught. Audacious, indeed. And yet . . . "You have the power," he said.

The boy's eyes shone. "Do you think so? Do you really think so?"

Careful, Gerbert warned himself. This was not simply the eager boy he seemed to be, leaning on Gerbert's knee, charming him with adoration. That narrow hand could sway an empire. That mind—bright, yes, and quick, and perhaps it had the seeds of brilliance—could will whatever it pleased, and see it done.

So prudence warned. Gerbert's heart was beating. Here was power indeed. Tense, braced, waiting for one to aim it. What every teacher dreamed of: a pupil worthy of his teaching. An heir who could be all that he was, and infinitely more.

Old fool, his head said. His heart surged over it and drowned it. "Tomorrow," he said, "we begin."

Gerbert would lodge in the palace. Otto would not hear of anything else. With miraculous dispatch, Gerbert's baggage and his servants appeared and were installed in a suite of rooms that, when last Gerbert had been there, had belonged to the empress herself. "Of course," said

Otto. "I have to be emperor, but whenever I can, I'll be your scholar. Why make it difficult by putting you where I can't get at you?"

It was excellent logic. It was also somewhat disconcerting. Gerbert wondered if Aristotle had felt like this when he came to be tutor to Alexander: as if he had been caught up in a whirlwind.

The emperor's physician was part of the amenities, and he was not to be put off by rudeness or temper or outright rejection. A Greek, he, and—Gerbert stilled under his hands—a mage. The man smiled faintly, nodded more faintly still. Recognition; acceptance. And warning. Some things, even here, were not spoken of lightly.

Gerbert bowed his head a fraction. That was wisdom. He had learned it in Barcelona. People, even priests, could accept much; but only if it was broken to them gently. One taught not by proclamation, or by blasts of magefire, but by example. By pursuing one's purposes without fanfare; by hiding in plain sight.

It was evening before he remembered what he had come for. In the light of Otto's eyes, he had forgotten even Rheims.

Where Gerbert had thought to find only frustration, the barring of his way to his city and his archbishopric, there, suddenly, was his heart's center. There in a moment the world had shifted. What he had taken for his destiny, seemed now but a hollow thing, a bitter tax on mind and body.

But Gerbert was nothing if not a stubborn man. He had begun this battle. He meant to finish it.

He waited his time—longer, perhaps, than he needed, simply to be with Otto in unstained amity. Time that had dulled the splendor of the old true things—numbers, music, the stars in their courses—now brought them back untarnished. He was like a boy again, discovering with Otto the manifold wonder that was the world. Otto did not ask him to partake in the drudgeries of empire. He wrote a letter or two now and then, to seem useful.

Otto laughed at that. "You are the most useful man in the world."

"But that's pure pleasure," said Gerbert. "Too pure for an old plowhorse."

"Plowhorse!" Otto snorted. "Well then, you've earned your clover. Why not savor it in peace?"

"Peace." Gerbert rolled the word on his tongue. "Is that what it is? I'd been calling it happiness."

They were in the chamber of the garden, now accoutered as a schoolroom, Otto where he most liked to be, at Gerbert's feet with his arm around the master's knees. He was always one for touching, perhaps because an emperor was so seldom granted that familiarity. He looked up at Gerbert, and his eyes were shining. "Are you happy?"

Gerbert nodded slowly. "Improbable, isn't it? All out of time and place, sick and desperate and like to go mad, suddenly I'm happy. If I'd stayed in Rome as some thought I should—if I'd never left Rheims at all—"

Otto shivered. "Don't talk of horrors."

But once he had begun, Gerbert could not help himself. "You know this can't go on. I'd be your teacher my life long, and take naught but joy in it. But—"

"But," said Otto, and his eyes had gone dark, "the world is calling you back. What if I forbid you? What if I command you to stay with me?"

"Would you do that?"

Otto held his gaze for a long moment before giving way. "You never stop fighting, do you?"

"Never while the cause is just."

"You know it's not my judgment," said the emperor. "If it were . . ."

"If it were?"

"I'd have to hear both sides."

Otto said it quietly, but there was no diffidence in it. Gerbert throttled sudden, irrational rage. Here—even here, Arnulf's poison festered.

Reason rose trembling to its feet. Not poison. Justice.

"Cousin Bruno," said Otto, meaning the pope, "is a very upright man. A bit of a stick, we used to say. He's not to be bought, and he's not to be threatened. He'll judge as his conscience bids him. If he rules against you, I won't try to force him to recant."

"So," said Gerbert bitterly. "Even you believe the liar."

Otto shook his head vehemently. "It's not that he lied. It's that he was archbishop, and still may be. And between the two of you, you've thrown Rheims into confusion. Is that wise, *magister*? Is it fair to your people?"

"Would you have me flee with my tail between my legs, and leave him to ravage my city?"

"You can't tell me that you haven't prepared for that very contingency. Who rules Rheims now?"

"Men who know how to rule it."

"Friends?"

Gerbert shut his mouth with a snap. "What does friendship have to do with competence?"

Otto grinned as if he had won a point. "If I know their kind, and you, they'll hang on, and they'll prosper. They won't let a fool teach them their trade."

"Rheims is mine by right, my lord," said Gerbert, stiff and cold. "I will not surrender it unless and until the Holy Father has judged us both."

"But for that, you know where Arnulf must be."

Gerbert's teeth gritted. "And once he's there, do you think he'll budge for anyone, king, pope, or God Himself?"

"Then, if he's condemned, you'll win all you could desire; and he'll have the wrath of the Holy See to contend with."

"No," said Gerbert. "I can't allow it. I'm sorry, my lord, but I can't."

"Why?" Otto asked him.

"Because—" Gerbert's voice died.

"Because he miscalculated once, and proved somewhat too easy in his virtue. Because he has done to you no more than you, in fighting for the see, have done to him." Otto's voice was as gentle as it was relentless. "*Magister*, has it struck you that you are obsessed?"

"I am fighting for what I believe is mine."

"Just so," said the emperor.

Gerbert was silent. He could think of nothing to say that would not make matters worse.

Nor, it seemed, could Otto. He was not angry, that Gerbert could perceive; merely perplexed. In a little while, without a word, he rose and went away.

17

The news from Rheims was bad. One of Gerbert's own masters brought it, master of magic from the inner school, Rabbi Ephraim ha-Levi looking as harmless as ever: an old man, frail and translucent, peering about with an expression of perpetual, amiable befuddlement.

That, as Gerbert well knew, was eyesight that stopped just short of blindness, and long prudence. The old man looked about him sharply enough once they were alone. He would not, as ever, drink Christian wine; he had, as ever, his own small flask, with which he kept Gerbert company.

He came directly to it, which was another of his virtues. "The inner school has voted in conclave, from novice to master, to disband itself until peace should return. The masters from Spain have returned there; there is, they tell us, a school of the Art in Toledo that may profit from what we taught in Rheims. The Christians have gone back to their kin or their cloisters, or, if they had none, to St.-Rémi with Brother Richer. The abbot is not amused, but he acquiesces."

Gerbert allowed himself a grim smile. Milord abbot owed Gerbert rather more favors than he liked to contemplate; and he had a deep fear of magic. Fine purgatory it must be, to be compelled to give sanctuary to a nest of mages.

"We scattered none too soon," said Ephraim. "There had been talk of a harrowing; of rooting out, at least, the Jews and the Saracens. But before those, and worse in most minds, the women."

Gerbert's brow went up. "Women?"

Ephraim scowled. He looked remarkably formidable. "Women. No doubt you were preoccupied, between your sickness and the growing trouble, or you would remember. You know how God has tried my soul. A tribe of strapping sons, and never a one with a brain in his head, still less a grain of magic. One late, unlooked-for daughter; and what should she be but mageborn enough for all the rest of them. Was I to waste such a gift?"

Many men might. Or might have taken care at most to mate her to a mage and breed a clan of magelings.

Ephraim, as blissfully unmindful of nature and gender and propriety as ever Ibrahim had been, went on with his tale. "She could hardly sit in classes with the novices; yet she insisted that she should. Was she not as much a mage as they? And that was not at all, as I told her, but she never heard me.

"A little after you left for Rome, God answered her prayers. He brought Sister Hathumoda and her cousin who was a new widow, and they were mages of some little accomplishment, taught by a wisewoman in their childhood but desirous of high learning. We took them in and made a class of them, women all and gifted much alike. We were circumspect, but the cousin is young and not too ill-favored, and young men will talk. It became apparent in the city that the heathen sorcerers were holding hostage a nun and her beauteous kinswoman. That, together with the quarrel against your right to the see . . ."

Gerbert saw it. Gerbert saw it very well indeed. On

the other side of anger, he knew that if it had not been the women, it would have been the heathen sorcerers. Arnulf had honed Rheims to a nest of blades; now they had risen to hew Gerbert.

"Best you not go back," said Ephraim. "There is that, as well: some would see you dead. Poison in the chalice, a knife in your bed—you are not safe anywhere in your see. Your enemies have cried interdict against you should you attempt to reclaim what is yours; any who aids you, comforts you, gives you meat or drink, is outcast from holy Church."

"That much was true before I left," Gerbert said, though his throat was raw with pain.

"Now they enforce it. Your palace is empty of servants. Your priests and monks have fled. The outer school," Ephraim admitted, "goes on, if a little diminished; the chancery continues as chanceries will, taking no account of the man who holds the title. Whatever can thrive without you, is thriving handily."

Bitter words to hear, spoken in Ephraim's way, without softening of the blow.

"My family and I," the old man said, "have a mind to try the air in Italy. Naples, they say, is full of witches. My daughter may find the teaching, and the peace, that she needs."

Gerbert's head bowed. Suddenly he wanted to weep, or rage, or fly to Rheims on the back of the wind, and raise the power, and smite his enemies into the dust.

Therefore he bent his head. He knotted his fists until they throbbed with pain, and drew long shuddering breaths. Gone, all gone. Broken, scattered, seared with anathema. All that he had made, hoped, ruled, was torn asunder. By a traitor. By a breaker of his most sacred oath.

Ephraim, having delivered his message, did not tarry. His wife and his sons and his splendid little witch of a

201

daughter were waiting down the river. They had never approved his practicing of his Art within the very cathedral of terrible, priestly Rheims. Royal Pavia would be little more to their liking.

"Am I a monster," Gerbert asked the air, in the sweet clarity behind madness, "for that I suffer the presence of him and his kind? Worse than that. I take pleasure in it. In seeing how a mind can work, when other ways and other gods have shaped it."

That was heretical. He retreated from it to the refuge of wrath. "Arnulf," he whispered. "Always Arnulf."

Somewhere in the black-red darkness, he found himself in his innermost chamber, sitting as if transfixed, in his scarred right hand a jewel like a coal. The shadow stirred in its heart, twisting slowly. The faintest whisper of a whisper tantalized his ears. *Free me,* it seemed to beseech him. *Feed me.*

Oh, indeed, at last. What were vows and pride and honor at the end of all that he had made? When he made this jewel he had thought this battle won, all but the final skirmish. And that had burgeoned into war.

Arnulf, dead, would put an end to it.

The jewel winked out. A narrow hand covered Gerbert's; the sleeve to which it was attached was stiff with gold.

Gerbert stared blankly at Otto. The emperor was, indeed, emperor. He was arrayed for high court: the stifling splendor of Byzantine imperial dress, from buskins to heavy layered vestments like a priest's to the crown with its pendant pearls. His face in that luminous frame was thin and sallow and very young, but his eyes were royal eyes, dark and burning. "No," he said.

The fingers over Gerbert's were cold but steady, and surprisingly strong. Gerbert watched them draw his hand over to the box with its sheathing of iron, and tip the jewel into it, letting fall the lid with a sharp, decisive click.

"I know that it is news to drive any man mad," said Otto, "but you will not go mad. I forbid it."

"That," Gerbert's tongue said for him, speaking of the spirit in the jewel, "that will feed; nor shall I ever have peace until it does. That peace is peace for Rheims. Yet . . . what profit if I gain the world, and lose my own soul?"

"Then why," asked Otto, "do you cling to Rheims?"

Even he could ask that; even Otto.

The emperor pressed harder. "There is another peace; mortal peace. Fair judgment for the see; end of this war by the pope's decree. Rheims is barred to you until the quarrel is settled. Stay with me, teach me, go where I go; wait with me for his holiness' decision."

Gerbert's head shook of its own accord. His hand fell on the box; the scar burned as it had when first he won it. "This will find another way. It will see that Arnulf wins my place; it will hone my hate. Then it will strike."

There was fear in Otto's eyes. Not of him or of the incubus; for him.

Otto had discarded the crown. His hair was tousled, boylike and vaguely comical above the glittering robe. He spoke, as it seemed, to the air. "How badly is he beset?"

The air answered in a voice of shaken bronze. "Badly. It lairs like a spider in his mind. It eats at his body's defenses."

That was Gerbert they were speaking of. He drew breath to rebuke their insolence.

The Jinniyah overran him. "I do what I can, but my power is hardly infinite. And the spirit is growing stronger."

"Surely it's not omnipotent," said Otto. "It couldn't have done all that he says it has."

"Arnulf is a mage," the Jinniyah said.

203

Otto stood still. His eyes were wide, comprehending. "He feeds it. But it can't . . . feed. And my master in the middle. Mother of God!"

As they spoke together, they seemed to forget that Gerbert was there. His hand darted. The carbuncle filled the hollow it had made for itself, the livid scar. It sang of freedom, of feeding, of peace.

"What shall I *do*?" cried Otto. His voice cracked and soared upward like a child's.

The Jinniyah said nothing, though the air was thick with frustration. His words, however indirectly, had invoked her geas.

He seemed to know. Which interested that minute fraction of Gerbert which was inclined to notice. Gerbert's familiar was keeping a secret or two; or failing to keep one.

Again Otto tugged at Gerbert's hand. This time Gerbert resisted. He would set the spirit free. He would win them peace. His soul was no great matter.

"Advise me," gasped Otto. "Help me!"

That was a soldier's mind, to think so clearly in the midst of a battle. "You have to free the spirit," the Jinniyah said, clear as a bell ringing. "Free it utterly; dismiss it. Ban it from this earth for all of time."

"How?"

Clear, that. Innocent. Gerbert almost laughed.

"Listen," said his devious Jinniyah, "and do as I shall tell you."

Now, she meant, Now, Otto quite obviously meant to do it. He called in his power, and it came, all the scattered faces of it. Gerbert had never known he had so much.

He was no callow novice. He knew what he did. He knew how to marshal that multitude; he gathered it as in a single hand, and held it, waiting.

The Jinniyah was silent for an endless moment. Had even she been astonished to find a master where she had expected an apprentice?

She was cool when she spoke, unstartled. "Now, mage. Break the stone."

Gerbert would do it for them. Easily. Simply.

"He must not," the Jinniyah cried, high and piercing, "or it has him! Quick, strike!"

Otto struck with all his force. Flame roared up. Night roared in its heart.

Two throats, one voice, flesh and bronze together, thundered words in no tongue that earth had ever known. Crying a name—ah, traitor, she had known!—crying it in tones that shook the sky.

The shadow trembled in that tempest, frayed and shredded and scattered. The power sang its paean. They had won; they had destroyed the enemy.

They had *not*. Gerbert smote with all the force of thwarted rage.

What caught the blow, what tore aside his madness in a bitter light of sanity, he never knew. Maybe a little good was left in him. Maybe the incubus had not mastered him as utterly as it had thought. He saw the Jinniyah whom he had purchased with death, to whom he had entrusted the treasure of his power; he saw the young mage who was an emperor, to whom he had sworn fealty, whom he loved. They were all caught up in gladness. They never knew what had risen up to shatter them.

What he had done to Maryam, he had done in ignorance, with the inescapable swiftness of instinct. This, he knew in its fullness. The power gathered, poised to fall. The black rage; the shadow with its avid eyes, rent asunder by the force of the spell, yet clinging, hungering. It had left enough of itself in Gerbert to gain a hold on mortal being; and the Jinniyah and the emperor had withdrawn their power before the spirit was all cast out.

Like Arnulf whose sins had begotten it, it was never defeated until it was truly dead.

No. It was hardly a word. It was pure will. Gerbert turned the whole of it to the turning of the stroke. Away from its targets. Toward what had roused it. It twisted, fighting. Grimly he held to it. It showed him treachery incarnate: Arnulf, Otto, the Jinniyah with her lying prophecies. It beckoned with the sweetness that was hate.

The shadow sang to him. *Free me, feed me, give me joy.* Joy that swelled in his own heart, soared and bloomed and sang.

He smote it down. "No," he said aloud. "Not again." The name that he had heard was heavy on his tongue. He set it free. "In the name of God, by the six names, by the nine names, by the ninety-nine names, by the Name of names that is hidden till the earth be made anew, I adjure and command thee, I enjoin thee, I ban thee. Go forth for all ages of ages. Go, thou spirit of the nether pit. Go, and trouble us no more."

The echoes rang. The shadow wailed, long and lost and all betrayed. *Mortal faith! Mortal faith!*

His hands swept the air of it, and cast it forth. "Begone!"

It scattered, melting, wailing into nothingness.

And then was silence.

The candle flickered low in its sconce. The Jinniyah glimmered, bodiless beauty staring blankly into the dark. Otto had fallen to his knees. His jewels flashed and flared as he struggled for breath, like a runner at the end of a race, like a warrior who comes alive from battle.

He barely flinched from Gerbert's hand. Under the glittering robes his shoulders were as thin as a bird's.

"Whelp," Gerbert growled. "Don't you know enough to hold on until the spirit is gone?"

Otto lifted his face. It was like parchment, bloodless, empty of aught but eyes. Deep within them, a single claw of shadow flexed and tore. Otto crumpled without a sound.

With a harsh, terrible cry, Gerbert lashed out. The last tenacious remnant of shadow flicked away, dwindling. As it dwindled, it laughed.

Gerbert clung to the lifeless body and cried like a child.

"Come," said Otto, struggling weakly. "Come, don't cry."

Gerbert's head flew up. His fists were knotted in silk. Otto's breast heaved under them; his eyes were open, aware. He looked as if he could not choose between a scowl and a smile.

"I've killed you," Gerbert said with the simplicity of despair.

Otto's lips quirked. "Not quite yet, I think." Gerbert's hand had loosened; Otto sat up. His breath caught. "*Ah!* I've the mother of all aching heads. You're strong, *magister*."

"You—" For once, Gerbert could find no words. His hands reached, touched. Warm flesh, life pulsing undiminished, weariness that was the aftermath of great magic. A wonder, a miracle, a blessing beyond hope.

Maryam had been caught off guard. Otto had been smitten in the midst of his power; and Gerbert had turned the blow. He was dizzy and sick and his head, he said, was like an anvil under a hammer, but he was very much alive. He suffered Gerbert's cry of gladness and his sudden, bruising embrace; he returned the latter with good enough will. "There," he said. "There. Don't you know I'm used to this? It's what a king does. He casts out devils."

"That is a figurative expression."

Otto laughed, though he winced. "Then I am a figurative king, with a figurative power."

Gerbert glared at him. "Power. Indeed. You told me you were a novice."

"I am," said Otto.

"You are not. You are a journeyman of some years' standing. You have glimmers of mastery."

The boy blinked. "I don't."

"Then what do you call what you just did?"

The force of it rocked Otto; he clapped his hands to his ears. "All I did was cast out a demon!"

"All," Gerbert said. "*All.*" He did not know whether he wanted to laugh or to howl. He seized Otto and pulled him close. "Naïf. Innocent. Idiot. You are not a novice. Believe me, you are not."

Otto's arms went round him. Emperor the whole of his life, and still he could trust as a child did, utterly. His voice was soft with wonder. "I never thought I was anything. But if you say so . . . Oh, *magister*! Shall I really be a mage?"

"You are one," said Gerbert.

Otto shivered. "No. I'm not ready. Let me get the feel of this, first: of being the beginnings of one."

Gerbert held him without speaking. After a little while he stiffened; Gerbert let him go. He rose shakily, catching himself on the table's edge. Gerbert, who was no more steady, clutched in fear; he waved away both fear and hands. "I'm well. Or will be, once I've slept. As you should, *magister*. We've taxed ourselves sorely with all this magic."

That was youth, to speak so lightly of such horrors. He smiled at Gerbert and accorded him a soldier's salute. "To victory, *magister*!"

He went under his own power. That was almost more than Gerbert could do. But pride had its uses. It brought

Gerbert to his bed, and laid him unhastily in it. He sighed once, for all that he had done, and not done, and almost done; for that Otto was alive, well, unwounded, and Gerbert, at last, was free.

On the edge of sleep, a shadow laughed.

18

Gerbert yielded to necessity and to his own treacherous heart. He followed his emperor to Germany. There in the country of his fathers, far from the mists and miasmas of the south, Otto thrived and grew strong. His pallor faded; he broadened a very little, flesh creeping to cover the sharp, fragile bones.

There were troubles. Winter, which was always cruel. War in the east. The cares of an empire that was still a frail and cobbled thing, more dream than solid fact.

"I've a whole long life to make it whole," Otto said. In the clear cold air of his northern forests, he was irrepressible. And he wanted, passionately, to learn; to *know*, as once Gerbert had done.

As Gerbert learned anew to do. He felt—by all that was holy and miraculous, he felt young again. His sickness passed unregarded. Striding behind his young emperor, riding with him, resting with him, teaching him, pausing on occasion to attend to the music of his chapel, Gerbert remembered what it was to be young and glad and tireless.

When Ephraim came to Pavia, he had brought some of Gerbert's cherished instruments: his spheres of the heavens, his globe of the earth, his abacus, his monochord with which he taught the mathematics of music. He had his books; he had a pupil worthy of them. He lacked for nothing that befitted a scholar; not even happiness.

The palace in Rheims was empty of an archbishop. Arnulf had not moved to claim it. He was practicing humility, people said; awaiting humbly the judgment of the Holy See. Gerbert called it playing for sympathy.

He astonished himself with his own coolness. The red hate was gone with the demon that had spawned it. What remained was little more than a lingering distaste. He would never forgive, but he was coming, a little, to forget.

"Suppose," said Otto one evening at the gates of summer, "that I asked you to give up the fight. Would you do it?"

Gerbert's lips tightened. He shook his head.

They were in an old and hallowed place: the palace at Aachen that had been Charlemagne's. Its walls breathed forth more damp than greatness, but its splendor, though tarnished, was still enough, now and then, to catch at the heart.

Neither noticed now, or cared, that Charlemagne had held audience in this chamber with its painted walls and its moldering bearskin flung incongruously on the floor. Otto's toe worked itself into a rent in the skin. He stared at it as if it belonged to someone else. "You are stubborn," he said without heat.

"It's mine." Otto did not look up, but Gerbert felt his keen attention. Gerbert drew a breath, not quite a sigh. "I was young when I came there, a scholar in search of new worlds to conquer. I grew into the school, and it grew into me. I learned to love the city, and its church, and its archbishop. When he made me master of the school, I thought that I had attained the summit of my life. I had found a respectable school as these things are reckoned in Gaul, a training ground for the priests of the parishes and the laborers in the archbishop's chancery, and such sons of kings and lords as had a hunger for learning. I made it more. Out of those scholars, and out of the cloisters in the see, I chose the best. I offered them the higher arts. For some, even, there was the Art, which I neither concealed nor revealed, simply offered in silence.

"All that, I made. And while I made it, I made my way in the world. There was my oath to your house, which I swore before ever I went to Rheims, and which on occasion I was called on to honor. My lord archbishop availed himself of me when he had need, coming in time to share his archbishopric with me, making me part of his inner counsels. He meant me to continue when he died, as he knew he must, for even when I met him he was not young, and he was never strong.

"When he died, I knew what I would be and do. Then the king's policy intervened. For a few months' peace of mind, he sold the archbishopric of Rheims. And Arnulf dealt with it as he had begun: in false coin, in treachery. I was his prisoner. I saw what he did to my city. I swore that I would free her.

"And I did," said Gerbert. "Whatever Rome may say, until Arnulf's partisans swayed the Holy See to contest my claim, I gave Rheims peace."

Otto nodded slowly. "You did," he said. "Have you thought that, like any good artisan, you might one day call it finished, and let it go?"

"Of course," Gerbert said. "When I die."

"What if . . ." Otto paused. "What if that time should come before then? What if you were called to something higher?"

"I—" Gerbert stopped. He had thought of that. Sometimes. Deep in the night, when his guard was down, and he could dream as any human creature may.

But, waking, he knew the measure of what he was. Excellence enough, surely, to rise as high as he wished—or as he dared. Yet beside that, cold truth. He was a peasant's son. No right of birth or lineage entitled him to any power in the world. Rheims . . . Rheims, he had loved. He had fought for her, and lost her, and gained her, and now perhaps lost her again. He could not let himself think in the daylight, of aught beyond her.

"Oh," said Otto, hastening to fill the silence. "I didn't mean this, here. This is only a rest between labors."

Gerbert swallowed. "What," he asked, "my lord, did you have in mind?"

Otto blinked and looked guilty. "Nothing. Really. I was just thinking."

"Yes?"

The boy blushed, but his eyes were angry. "Don't do that to me, *magister*. I was thinking that I love this, and you; I don't want it to end. But you are not meant to be a humble master of the chapel, even if it is the emperor's chapel. I'm keeping you caged like a singing bird, but you are an eagle."

"Have you ever heard an eagle's voice?" Gerbert asked dryly.

"You are mocking me," said the emperor.

"No," Gerbert said, "my dear lord. I'm no eagle. A lark, maybe, that sings as it soars into the sun, and sings when it falls. I've fallen to my own proper level. If it pleases God and the Holy Father to restore me to my old eminence, then so be it. If not . . ." That was hard to say, harder still to contemplate. "If not, so be it. I thought I had no life without Rheims. Now I have you. I am content."

Otto shook his head slightly, but he said nothing.

"Now," said Gerbert after a stretching pause, "on the subject of sesquiquartal numbers . . ."

From Aachen to the marches of the east was a royal progress. War was at the end of it, Otto's armies drawn up already, a thin and mortal wall against the wild tribes. But he who had ridden to war since he was a child, was in no haste to join in this one.

"An emperor should lead his army," he said on the road to Magdeburg. "But he should also know when to trust his ministers to lead it."

They had paused in the heat of noon, the whole long train of his court and his chancery, his household and his company of warriors that was half warband and half praetorian guard; for a little while they rested, ate, took what ease they could in a valley that was almost open. A fire had scoured it, and though it grew green again, it seemed more field than forest, pillared with the charred corpses of trees.

Otto had found a space that must have been a meadow even before the fire bared it to the sky. His horse cropped the rich grass, a peaceful sound, made musical by the jingle of the bit.

Gerbert was there, close as Otto wanted him, propped against a vine-grown stump. There were others: one or two of Otto's priests and holy women, his physician buried as always in a book, a courtier or six, and the odd, restless guardsman. Most were mages, or wanted to be. Power called to power, whether its possessors willed it or no.

It was never spoken of. There never seemed to be need.

That meant something. Gerbert was on the edge of understanding it. Power in magic, power in the world: they belonged together. And yet . . .

Otto's voice shook him from his reflection. "See what we become," he said. His hand took in them all, those who lived for war, those who lived for God, those who lived in and for the court. "My grandfather's father—the

Fowler, they called him, because of all things there were in the world he loved most to hunt with his falcons. He couldn't read; he couldn't write even his name. He was a warrior king, and he knew that he would die one. But he had dreams. He wanted more. He raised his son to be a king and not the leader of a warband: a ruler as well as a soldier. And my grandfather learned, and remembered, and knew what he wanted to be. He heard the name of Charles who found us heathen savages and made us a Christian people, Charles the Great, Charlemagne. Charles had been more than king; he had been emperor. The very pope in Rome had blessed his kingship.

"My grandfather wanted that. He wanted to be greater than any Saxon had been before him. He took scattered, warring Germany, and he won it, and he made it all one. Then at Aachen they crowned him with the crown of Charlemagne, and the pope in Rome blessed him. But he never learned to read until he was a grown man—and in that, too, he was like the great one who had gone before him.

"He raised my father to be an emperor. He had him taught by masters; he whose own father had been a rough soldier-king, made his son a civilized prince. He won for him a bride out of Byzantium that calls itself the true and only Roman Empire; he left him an empire in its own right, though feeble still, as any young thing is when it is born."

"Or," said Gerbert, "as Lazarus must have been when he was raised from the dead."

Otto favored him with a smile, though it died quickly. "Lazarus, yes, with the grave-clothes on him still. But life under them, and growing strong. Then, all untimely, he died. My mother ruled well, and held his empire together until I should be old enough to take it; and she dreamed his dream, the stronger for that she was true Roman, born

216

royal in the east and learned in all the arts of Byzantium. She raised me to be more than emperor. She raised me to be Roman."

"Nothing for the Saxons?"

That was a lordling whose blood was pure as far back as any could reckon; whose forebear, he was not ashamed to admit, was Wotan himself. It made him bold even in front of his emperor. Insufferable, Gerbert would have said, had the boy been a pupil of his: begging for a dose of the rod.

Otto regarded the lordling with calm dark eyes, until he blushed and began to fidget. But he was never one to heed the promptings of prudence. "Romans," he said angrily. "Romans, Romans, Romans. Have you forgotten where you came from? Saxony was good enough for Henry the Fowler. His son was half a Frank and all a fool. *His* son cast eyes east and south, and talked of Rome, Rome, Rome. And Rome killed him. He abandoned the good clean air of Saxony for the Roman fens; he ran barking at the pope's heel. And where is he now, and all his dreams of empire? Dead and gone."

One or two of the guards watched Otto, alert, like hounds on a scent. The courtiers had moved away from the young fool as if from a contagion. He stood red-faced, breathing hard, and perhaps his dim brain comprehended, at last, how far he had transgressed.

Otto smiled with honest sweetness. "Sit down, Liudolf," he said, "and share the wine. It's good: it's Falernian."

Liudolf reared up. "Even the wine is Italian! Look at you. Greek clothes, Greek manners, Greek face. Greeks sliding and slinking around you. Romans hissing in your ear. Where are the Saxons, I ask you? What do you leave for us?"

"My patience," said Otto, with an astonishing measure of it. "I remember what I am. I was born to more

217

than Saxony, queen of duchies though she be. She is but one of all the realms in the world. Think! What is a single duchy, if it knows nothing but war? War from without, from rival kings, from barbarians; war from within, as its lords do battle one against another. We of Saxony made Germany a kingdom, and taught it the first lessons of peace. Then we dared reach farther; we dared to dream. What Rome was, we could aim for. We could will it to be, we of Saxony. Therefore my grandfather looked eastward for the mother of his son's son, to that remnant which calls itself the heir of Rome. And it yielded to him. It would not, quite, grant him his title of Emperor of the West, but it acknowledged his power. It sent him a princess who also dared to dream."

"A sop," Liudolf said. "An emperor's by-blow."

Otto's eyes narrowed and began to glitter. "A princess, and royal. My mother, O son of Marburga. She brought the grace of the east into our rough west. She showed us how an empire is ruled."

"Why do we need an empire? The Franks have their own troubles: their old king is dead, their new one cares more for bedding his kinswoman than for ruling his kingdom. Italy is a sink of sedition. Spain is all Moors and sorcerers. Germany is enough. It should be enough."

"So would it be, if there were no one else in the world. Do you forget what we go to, and why? Have you forgotten how many outlanders hunger after our simple and sufficient country?" Otto's passion had risen; he quelled it with skill almost frightening in one so young. He shrugged with careful casualness, and mustered a smile. It was a very sweet smile; but this sweetness was neither honest nor simple. "And besides, Liudolf, friend of my childhood, *I* want more. I am the Emperor of the Romans. I am going to make that title mean something. In Gaul, in Italy, in Spain. Even," he said, "in Germany."

"It will kill you,"Liudolf said.

Gerbert looked into those earnest blue eyes and shivered. The boy did not know what he did. In old days they would have said that a god possessed him. Now . . .

"It will kill you," said Liudolf, "as it killed your father. Rome is dead. You are no Christ, to bring it back to life again."

The guards moved. Otto did not stop them. One raised an armored fist. He watched in silence, steadily.

"You'll die," said Liudolf with the persistence of the mad. "You'll die, and Rome will have your bones."

The guard struck.

Gerbert was there, with no memory of movement. Even with power he was barely a match for that raw, mortal strength. But surprise aided him, and astonishment, to meet such resistance from a man so old and seemingly so frail. He caught the blow and turned it, and sent the man reeling back. He did not trouble to watch him fall, but turned, and spoke to his emperor. "No," he said. "This is more than insolence. It wants blood."

Otto's brows went up. He was angry, but not beyond reason. "Is it . . . ?"

Gerbert tensed in sudden, heart-deep dread. Paused. Shook his head. No. It was not. There was more in the world than one mage's mistake.

And yet this was dangerous. That a mad fool prophesied Otto's death; that Otto's people heard it.

Liudolf, oblivious, glared at Gerbert. "And you! You feed it, you with your Gaulish wiles, your Moorish magics. They drove you out of your own country. Now you poison our king with lies and sleights and moonshine."

Gerbert spoke with utmost gentleness. "My vows and God's law forbid me to do murder. Execution but feeds what feeds on you. Therefore I let you live." He raised his hand. Liudolf's eyes followed it as if they had no power to do otherwise. Gerbert's fist snapped shut. Liudolf dropped without a sound.

Gerbert very nearly followed him. But there were eyes all about, and awe, and the tang of fear. A breath brought back a little of the strength that had flooded out of him. He sat down steadily enough, and addressed the soldier nearest the fallen boy. "Bundle him in a cart and let him sleep it off. He'll wake by evening with a head like a three-days' debauch, and a distinct disinclination to argue with his emperor."

The man was startled enough to obey. The others were taken aback. "Do you mean he isn't dead?"

"Weren't you listening?" Gerbert was more irritable than he might have liked, but he was tired, and they were being ridiculous. "Haven't you ever seen a jealous child before? He's been listening to the wrong masters; he's had his chastisement. He'll hold his tongue hereafter."

The awe did not abate, but the eyes found other things to stare at. When Gerbert went to retrieve his mule, the others were not long in following suit.

"I know what you did," Otto said.

Gerbert considered pretending that he had forgotten. It was days past now, and the talk had begun to fade. Otto was ready, in a day or three, to take the field with his armies. But for this hour they were master and pupil as always; Otto, having struggled through a thicket of figures to an answer Gerbert would accept, was taking a quiet revenge.

"What I did," said Gerbert, "was silence an envious infant. He's behaved himself since, I notice."

Otto laughed. "I doubt he'll ever dream of rebelling again. You put the fear of God in him." He sobered. "That's not all you did, *magister*. Do you believe in omens?"

Cold small feet walked down Gerbert's spine. He said, "I am a Christian and a priest."

"That's not an answer."

No; and Gerbert did not intend to give him one. "I believe that you have enemies who would gladly see you displaced by a weaker king, or by one more amenable to Saxon browbeating. I believe that these set Liudolf on you, knowing how far his folly would take him, hoping that you would have him disposed of. Then they would have had a martyr for their cause. Instead, they have a fool who suffered just and ignominious punishment, and who has become a conspicuously loyal servant."

Otto scowled. Gerbert would not give way. Otto sighed, sharp with frustration, and said, "Now they all forget what he said, and talk endlessly of what you did. Did you know that you called lightning out of a blue sky, and that a legion of angels came down to smite the idiot for his insolence?"

"Angels?" asked Gerbert. "I'd have thought it would be devils."

"Not where I can hear them. It's odd; now you're more popular instead of less. As if people were relieved to know for certain what everyone has always suspected. They'd rather an open and acknowledged mage than one who keeps it a secret."

"I never did. I didn't trumpet it from the rooftops, either."

"Exactly," Otto said. He paused, eyes on Gerbert, not quite smiling. His flash of temper was gone. Suddenly he looked very young, and almost mischievous; but solemn, too, as if he cherished a secret. "*Magister*, do you remember when we talked about Rheims?"

Gerbert could not help it. He always stiffened at that name; his eyes always darkened, his reason swayed and fell, and he remembered rage and loss and bitter humiliation. It was a dimmer memory than it had been. Otto's face kept getting in the way.

Its owner went on with quiet persistence. "I asked you if you would consider giving it up, if something higher were offered you."

"And I said no," said Gerbert, short and harsh.

"So you did," said Otto. He paused. "I'm asking you again."

"You know what I'll say."

"Suppose," Otto said, "that I had an alternative. Suppose . . . that an archbishopric was vacant, and no one would contest your claim to it."

Gerbert's breath caught in spite of himself. But he was too old for hope, or for games of what-if-there-were. "Am I such a trouble to you? Do I seem so badly to need a sop to my pride?"

"Why? Are you so proud that you would scorn Ravenna?"

The silence rang. Gerbert's ears were going. He had not heard that. Ravenna— "But only Rome is higher!"

"Just so," said Otto. His brows were knit. "I can't give you Rome. I'm sorry for that. I'd have liked . . ." He shook his head. "What am I saying? Bruno—Gregory—is my cousin. He's young, he's strong, he'll live long and rule well."

"Would he approve your setting me in the place second only to his?"

"He already has." Otto laughed at Gerbert's expression. "He doesn't hate you, *magister*. He believes in upholding the law, that's all. This resolves the problem of Rheims, gives you what you richly deserve—"

"Does it? What becomes of my city? Shall I hand it over after all to the one I've fought against for so long?"

Even to himself, Gerbert sounded less passionate than weary of it all. It was as clear in Otto's eyes as in his own. He had done all that he might to ward Rheims against incompetence. Without Charles and his sons to tempt him, perhaps Arnulf would refrain from treachery. He was not a bad man, merely weak.

Reasonableness hurt. Arnulf could have tried to kill Gerbert a dozen times over. Except once, inadvertently, in sundering Gerbert from his magic, he never had. He had simply wanted, and taken, and lost, and tried to take again. No malice in it, only selfishness.

Gerbert was no saint, either. And he who had thought only to be the lark in his cage, was offered the eagle's portion. Beautiful Ravenna of the Byzantines, queen consort of the west, in all her honor and her power. A whole new see that had never known him, that would learn to know him.

He stiffened his will. He would not give up the fight.

Otto met his eyes and spoke softly, but he did not speak as a simple man does, still less a boy who is barely a man. He was an emperor, and in that title was power beyond that of any mage. "Do you love Rheims, *magister*? Do you love it truly?"

"With all my heart," said Gerbert, though his voice shook.

"Enough to give it up?"

Gerbert sucked in his breath. It was like a blow to the vitals.

Otto struck again, gently, mercilessly. "Do you love Rheims enough to let her go in the name of her peace? Can you do that, *magister*?"

Gerbert opened his mouth to cry a denial. He was not strong enough, or pure enough, or selfless enough. All he knew was stubbornness. He wanted Rheims. Rheims, and no other.

Did he?

Arnulf in the place that was his. But he in another,

higher and prouder and stronger. Wise, these young Saxons, these boys raised to rule a world; and subtle; and cruel. To take away what he loved, to offer him power in its stead.

His head shook. That was not what tempted him past even pain. It was something much simpler, and much more complex. It was the gift, and the giver of the gift, and the love that shone in them both. For pride alone he would not do it. For Otto . . .

It was, in the end, hardly a choice. It made itself in the raising of his hands; in the bowing of his head. Otto's swift brilliant smile warmed him to the marrow: even in the dim, cold places that even yet could lament his poor lost Rheims.

19

The Archbishop of Ravenna contemplated the thousand small niggling nuisances of a see newly taken and long left to its own devices, and considered the consolations of the cloister. And grimaced, as much at himself as at his troubles. A week in the cloister and he would be bored to distraction. A month, and he would either have gone mad or set out to repair every small niggling nuisance in the abbey. There was no help for it. He was what he was, and that was an incorrigible meddler. Which, he reflected, was not an inadequate description of a mage.

He sighed and stretched. His secretaries were hard at work about him. Not all of them were delighted with their new master, but they had come to an accommodation. He did not tolerate laziness, nor did he punish it. He dismissed it. Preferably to a task more onerous by far. Mending the city's walls. Clearing its streets of refuse. Tending its sick and its poor.

This had been a mighty city once, seat of the exarch from the east, and not even Rome kept such splendor intact as glowed at every turning in Ravenna. Byzantium itself must be like this, he thought, raising his eyes to the glittering walls. A saint stared back in great-eyed serenity, not at all perturbed to see her city fallen into the hands of a Gaulish barbarian.

When he first came here, he had wondered if he would ever grow accustomed to the crowded walls, the colonnades with their inlays of precious stones, and everywhere the dark and staring eyes. The living people had seemed almost inconsequential amid the images: big blond Lombards like the people beyond the Alps, or, outnumbering them by far, the little people, thin and dark and quick, bred for intrigue. Now already the splendor was fading into familiarity, though the strangeness could still bring him up short, and twist his heart with longing for northern simplicity. The people . . .

The people were born wary and bred wary, and he was a foreigner. They trusted him no more than he trusted them. Yet they had chosen, for the moment, to obey him. They called him *lord magus* to his face, *signor' strego* behind his back; and he did not need to ask what that meant. Their tone implied fear but no hatred, and deep respect.

Here he would found anew the school which the struggle for Rheims had broken. It would fit; there would be no need to hide it, or to lie about it, or to pretend that it did not exist. The old power slept here, but it slept lightly.

He was dreaming again, old dreams: his school, his Art accepted openly, his Church coming to see it as he saw it, the old fearful laws struck from the canons. And when it was all settled, then he would be free. He would go where he had always yearned to go: Spain, Egypt, Greece and Byzantium. And then at last, when he would rest, to the city of peace; to Jerusalem.

But not while Ravenna needed his steadying hand. Not while his emperor had need of his strength and his teaching to raise up the new empire. Maybe they would go together, Gerbert in the evening of his life, Otto when his heir was old enough to rule as regent. An heir not even born, not even conceived; though he had sent an embassy east as his father had before him, to win for him a princess of Byzantium.

Gerbert shook himself. He was growing old for a fact, maundering when he should be wading through the morass that his predecessor had made of Ravenna's accounts. A man appeared in the corner of his eye, hanging about from the feel of him. "You," said Gerbert, sharp with reproof. "What are you dangling for? Go down to the chancery; fetch me the ledger for the year before last."

The idler was prompt to obey. Gerbert forgot him in the intricacies of an old feud between a very minor lord and a very contentious hermit.

The ledger appeared under his nose. For a moment he stared at it, annoyed. He raised his eyes to glare at the one who had thrust it at him so rudely, and met a broad and wicked grin.

He leaped up with a shout that scattered blots on every parchment in the room, and felt himself swept into a bruising embrace. "Richer, you rascal!" he kept saying. "Richer!"

His old pupil set him down with gentleness that was startling after the strength of his embrace, and held him, still grinning. His teeth were as crooked as ever, his freckles if anything more profuse, his hair as wild a thicket as it had ever been. Gerbert had forgotten how tall he was. The gangling colt had grown into a long-limbed racer, the awkwardness smoothed into rangy grace.

Gerbert, to whom the years had been less kind, looked at him and understood how fathers felt. He stared back—bless him, without either shock or pity, in welling gladness. "Master," he said. "Oh, master, you look splendid!"

He did, Richer was thinking, though he kept trying to deny it. Richer had been braced to find him cruelly aged. His youth was gone beyond recall, to be sure, but he looked as if he did not miss it. He was his old, irritable, capable self, only more so; there was a light in him, a strength and a purpose that outshone any mere vitality of few years and less wit. Tempered, that was it, like iron in the forge.

Richer would have effaced himself as a monk should in an archbishop's court, but Gerbert was having none of that. He freed his secretaries, to their enormous and poorly hidden relief. There were still duties to get through—an audience, a dinner, a messenger who must be received—but Gerbert disposed of them with facility that left Richer breathless.

Then he had freed himself, and Richer remembered how he had always had that art of winning time to be alone with his pupil or his friend. Though not so alone in this strange, glittering room with its big-eyed saints and, on a table, a familiar gleam of bronze. Her features were cool and austere and not quite alive; her eyes smiled.

"She likes it here," Gerbert said, a sort of explanation. She said nothing. Had she gone mute?

Richer sat by her, folding himself on a stool, leaving the cushioned chair for Gerbert. Who did not immediately take it. He stood in front of the table and did a strange, unconscious thing: he ran a finger down the molded cheek. He caught himself, stared at his hand. "I keep doing that," he said with no embarrassment that Richer could see, merely puzzlement, and perhaps a little self-mockery.

"Of course you do," said the Jinniyah, most unmute and most amused. "I'm beautiful, no? And bodiless. God mated us well, O my master."

Gerbert touched her again. It was not a caress. Not quite. He sat and folded his hands and smiled at Richer. Sharing the jest; being glad that he was here to share it. "Now, Brother. Tell me everything."

There was not much to tell, but somehow it made a great deal of telling. The outer school went on. The inner, of course, was gone. Arnulf had made a move or two in its direction, but he was not the mage that Gerbert was, nor ever the teacher. "He's lost his looks," Richer said. "He's thickened; his hair has thinned. He's had to learn to get by on more than prettiness."

"And has he?" Gerbert asked.

He seemed calm, interested, without malice. Richer shrugged. "He tries. I think he wants to do well. He's shallow, but he asks advice, and generally he takes it. He seems," Richer admitted grudgingly, "to have become a good enough archbishop."

"Amazing," mused Gerbert, "how little that hurts. Do you know how much I hated him?"

Richer nodded.

Gerbert shook his head and smiled. "Of course you do. You were closest of all. And now it's gone. Or mostly," he added, with an air of wanting to be fair. "I never was a very good Christian. A much better Ciceronian, I. Or Magian."

"You'll do for the purpose."

Gerbert laughed. He had always had a wonderful laugh, rich and free, as if he had not a care in the world. "Ah, lad! It's good to see you." He leaned toward Richer, still smiling. "Now tell me. What brings you all the way to Ravenna, in winter, without a word of warning?"

Richer squirmed a little. He had expected the question. He had prepared a fistful of answers. The truth slipped through them, irresistible as always, especially in front of the master. "I wanted to see you. My history is finished, or mostly; I wanted you to see it. Rheims isn't Rheims without you. And—and—'" He let it out. "I was hearing—I heard—you've found the other half of you."

There it was. Sea-green jealousy, naked and unlovely.

Gerbert did not laugh or scowl or even deny it. "That's a year and more old."

"It's taken me this long to face it." Richer glared down at his twining fingers. "I of all people ought to know what I am. I am your rough, stumbling Peter. He is your John, whom you love."

Gerbert was not appalled by words so close to blasphemy. He said, calm and unruffled, "I'd been about to send for you. My school won't be my school without you to teach in it."

" 'On this rock—' " Richer could not keep it up. Even envy sat badly on him. It kept showing him its backside, and making him want to laugh. "God's bones, *magister*! I was going to beg you."

"You know you'd never need to." That was love; Richer felt it. His stunted soul wanted to clutch it and whine, *Only for me. Say it's only for me.* His brain, wiser perforce, told him to be glad; to smile; to clasp the hand held out to him. It was only a hand, thin and dry, a little cold, an old man's hand; but the power in it rocked him to his foundations.

"Master," Richer whispered. "Master, you've grown strong."

Gerbert shrugged slightly. It was the Jinniyah who said, "Awed? You? Come now, be sensible. It's only Gerbert."

"Only!" Richer was outraged. "He is only the greatest mage in all the world."

"Maybe," she said, as if she pondered it. "There may be one or two . . . a master in Ch'in . . . an adept in Africa . . . Toledo, perhaps . . . Cairo . . ."

She did it to madden him. He growled at her, and she growled back, preposterously, like water in a sea-bell, and that made him laugh; and it was like old days again.

Richer found his place waiting as if Gerbert had been keeping it for him, close by, doing what needed doing, running his master's errands, beginning the labor that would flower, in a little while, into the new school of the Art. Otto's name was not mentioned, except where it must be, in matters that related to the empire.

Richer did not ask about him, though people were eager enough to tell. They all knew how much love was between their archbishop and their emperor. They fed on it, as lesser souls always did, snatching crumbs from the tables of the great.

Maybe Otto was the other half of Gerbert. Richer was here, and meant to stay; and no court or war or empire would call him away. Possession, as the Jinniyah would have told him, was nine points of the law.

Gerbert was Gerbert, which meant that if he ever slept, his servants did not know it. Perhaps it was a mage's malady. Richer, who was both mage and monk, would often find him in his library at improbable hours, fiddling with yet another of his odd and ingenious contraptions, or buried in a new book. There were many of the latter here; that most were Greek did not deter him. The Jinniyah could read them, and did, translating them into her Moorish-accented Latin.

"Arabic," Gerbert corrected absently, plucking the thought out of the air as he all too often could. "Her accent is Arabic."

"Is there a difference?" Richer bent to peer at the book. It was, indeed, Greek. He knew the letters and a word or two—less than Gerbert. "Where did you find this?"

"In a box in a lumber-room," Gerbert answered. "It's old." Which Richer could see, and smell, for himself. "It seems to have been written by a servant of the general Belisarius himself. A Secret History, see. It's full of scandals."

He should have looked censorious, venerable prelate that he was. He looked more nearly mischievous. "Some of it is even making my Jinniyah blush."

"I am incapable," she said with dignity, "of any such thing." She paused. "What I am, is envious. Even at my most wanton, I was barely a match for the Empress Theodora."

Richer's brows went up. "Am I supposed to be the voice of Christian chastity?"

"God forbid," said the Jinniyah. "Here, master. Turn the page. I want to know what she did *after* she—"

"Nothing, apparently." Gerbert had turned the page, which was blank. The next began a new heading. He puzzled it out for himself. " 'On the—On the Emperor Justinian's—Treasure'?"

"Treasure," agreed the Jinniyah. "Symbolic, surely. A little closer, if you please." Her lips moved as she read, but silently. Her brow raised. Richer had not known that she could do that. Probably she had learned it from Gerbert.

"Well?" they asked, both at once.

"Well." She sounded richly satisfied. "Listen, my masters. Listen very well indeed."

———————

Richer did not know whether to feel furtive or absurd. Here he was at high noon as near the equinox as curiosity would let him come, trying to look like a portion of the ramparts of Ravenna. Behind him lay the grey and lonely marshes that stretched to the sea; in front and below, a tiny littered square like a cul-de-sac. It was not at all a logical place for either a square or a statue, but statue there was, so marred and scarred by age and human hands that he could not even tell whether it was wrought of bronze or of iron.

"Iron," said the bulge under his cloak. She could see through it, she had told him. It was not magic, unless it was a magic of every veiled woman in Islam.

Now that she had spoken, his scattered wits came together; the throb in his power, not quite pain, that he had taken for a warning against the guards who walked the walls, centered on the image below. Its shape was that of a man with arm uplifted, finger pointing toward the wall on which Richer huddled. Someone had striven nobly to strike off the head, or perhaps only its crown or helmet, but the iron had withstood the blows.

The square was empty but for a lone stooped figure in black, doing something indistinguishable just beyond the statue's shadow. There was nothing in it to mark it as the spiritual lord of Ravenna.

Gerbert seemed unmoved by so much iron, so close. Just as the sun came to its zenith, he set his stake in the earth where the shadow's finger pointed, measuring a careful distance with plumbline and string. Richer felt the tug of the spell that both warded and concealed the mark. The iron twisted it, but Gerbert was its master. He sealed it with a sign of the cross and without ado, and made his cowled and anonymous way across the square.

Richer met him at the joining of alley and wider street, one monk meeting another for a slow progress toward the cathedral. "No one saw from above," said Richer, "and none that I could detect, from below."

"Good," said Gerbert. His voice was sharp. Richer,

jostled against him as a troop of bravos swaggered past, felt his weariness.

"Damned iron," Gerbert muttered. "They knew what they were doing, those old pagans."

"Then should you even try to—"

"How can I not?"

Indeed, thought Richer. It was not greed for treasure that moved Gerbert. It was another avarice altogether. Richer had his fair share of it. Simply to know what was worth hiding in such fashion, so subtly and yet so blatantly, with so much iron forged so clearly to twist magic into uselessness.

"The moon is full tonight," said Gerbert. "The better for us. A transformation of the eye: iron into silver, power's converse into an illusion of power. I'll confuse the iron till it hardly knows what it is."

Richer grinned in his cowl. Now there was sophistry. A mage was a perilous beast, but a mage who was also a logician and a theologian was deadly enough to outface the devil himself.

Who would not, Richer devoutly hoped, put in an appearance tonight. He was not in the mood for high magical heroics. He was simply and insatiably curious.

The stake was there, unmolested as far as Richer could tell. The moon was coy, now staring down, now veiling herself in cloud. Gerbert, refreshed by an hour's prayer and an hour's sleep after a day of ruling Ravenna, moved lightly in his mantle, like a shadow himself. The walls about the square were blank, blind. If anyone lived there, he slept deep, and kept no dogs to cry the alarm. A shadow flitted across Richer's feet, startling him nigh into a fit; it mewed its contempt round a mouthful of mouse and went to consume its prey in peace.

Gerbert approached the statue and the stake, silent, his power drawn close about him. It was he now who carried the Jinniyah; Richer had a lantern, unlit, and an empty bag. Gerbert only wanted to see what was there. Richer's ambitions were slightly more solid. Maybe there would be books; or a relic; or something magical.

The statue loomed much larger from below than from above. Its pedestal was carved with a word: either the Greek for *Strike here,* as the Jinniyah said and the book agreed, or—she allowed and Gerbert believed more likely—the name of some forgotten emperor or nobleman. Richer could not tell, blurred as it was, and hacked apparently with axes. The upraised hand pointed pointlessly wallward.

Not so pointless if the Secret History told the truth. Richer followed Gerbert to the stake, which pierced a crack in the paving. The wards blurred and frayed with the master's coming, and melted away. The moon was suddenly very bright; the image's shadow stretched, groping toward the interlopers. Gerbert bent as if in homage, laying his palms flat on the stone. Just as the shadow-finger seemed to touch him, he spoke a single word.

After the word was silence absolute. Even the wind had stilled.

Under his hands the stone shifted and sank. The world moved again; the wind resumed its restless wandering. Monk and archbishop regarded the mouth that had opened in the earth. Richer's hands were astonishingly steady as he lit the lantern and directed its thin beam downward. The shaft seemed as deep as a well, but behind his fear, where power was, he sensed that it was not so formidable. He set the lantern on the rim, and before Gerbert could stop him, slid over and down.

For an appalling instant he knew that he would fall without end or hope. Then he struck bottom. His hands, stretched to their fullest, could almost have touched the rim. "It's not far," he called up, his voice echoing in the shaft. "Here, master. Lower yourself down; I'll catch you."

It was done almost before he finished speaking. Gerbert was more solid than he looked, and stronger. He hardly needed Richer's hands, dropping down almost with a young man's lightness, one arm about his middle to protect the Jinniyah. When he was firm on his feet, he freed her from her wrappings and held her facing forward. "Come," she said with barely suppressed impatience. "What are we waiting for?"

The shaft opened on a passage just high enough for Gerbert, uncomfortably low for Richer. An overpowering odor of damp wafted out of it.

"Well?" the Jinniyah demanded. Well enough for her: bronze and not fastidious flesh, and protected in the fold of her master's cloak.

Richer could not even sigh: he would have gagged. He raised his lantern, bent his back, and braved the damp and the stink. It was revenge of a sort. Whatever there was to see, he would see it first. Even if it were nothing. He had already lost his hope of books. They would have rotted away long ago.

Before he had gone a furlong, he knew that he should never have begun. But Gerbert was close behind him, uncomplaining; and he had his own store of stubbornness. He set his jaw and went on. Step and step and aching, crouching step. Dark beyond the lantern's beam, foul-sheened walls, air which he breathed as shallowly as his body could bear. He began to think of going on all fours, though the floor was no more savory than the walls.

It began to slope downward; or perhaps he had merely noticed what had been so from the first. As soon as he noticed it, as if to mock him, it leveled. Richer nearly collided with a wall, swayed, stumbled, all but fell down a flight of steps into sudden, dizzying space.

The lantern had fallen from his hand and rolled clanking away. He neither needed nor heeded it. Light flared blindingly bright, so sudden that he tripped and fell, and lay on his face, trying to breathe.

First he was startled that he could. Then he was startled that he lay on dry stone. No damp here. No stink, perhaps, beyond his much-befuddled nose. His skin prickled with what he recognized as magic, though nothing like it had ever touched him.

Gerbert helped him up. The light was the color of blood; it gave the master's face a demonic cast. He had no eyes for Richer; they were all for this that must be the Treasure of Justinian.

"Not his Christian and orthodox majesty, I don't think," mused Gerbert. He was still holding Richer's arm, his Jinniyah set on the floor to stare her fill.

It was not so large a space except in the wake of the passage. As large perhaps as a side chapel in a great cathedral, round, with a domed roof. It was empty, its floor plain, paved with smooth pale stone. The walls were its treasure.

At first Richer took them for paintings. Then he decided that they were mosaics of wondrous subtlety. But no; were they carved in relief, painted and gilded, or—?

It was another chamber all about them, a dozen chambers, a hundred, a palace all of gold. Walls of gold, ceilings paneled with gold, everything all gold; golden guardsmen dicing with golden dice; a king of gold at table with his queen, food set beside them, servants standing about, all gold; and in the heart, in the center of them all, a great blood-red carbuncle that put the dark to flight. Across from it, facing it, stood a youth of gold, an archer with strung bow, arrow nocked, poised to loose. His eyes glittered in the stonelight.

"Illusion." Richer's voice was appallingly loud.

"Magic," Gerbert agreed, calm, but under it a swelling delight. "He was a great mage who did this, simply for the sake of doing it."

"Or she," said the Jinniyah. The ruddy light worked strangely on her, so that she seemed made not of bronze or gold but of living flesh. "You see the truth, master. This is no Christian thing. Justinian, says our historian? Not even Octavian, say I. This is older by far."

Truly, thought Richer, insofar as he could think at all. The guards wore strange armor; the courtiers and the servants observed no fashion that he had ever heard of. It was, now that he looked at it, shockingly immodest, men and women both wasp-waisted, kilted or skirted below, brazenly bare above.

There were beasts. Dogs; slender, haughty cats; serpents wound like ornaments about wrists, arms, necks; a great looming bull with which a company of youths and maidens seemed to dance, leaping over its horns.

"This is *old*," said the Jinniyah, and in her voice was awe and even, perhaps, a flicker of fear. "Can you feel it? Pride; joy. *See*, it sings. *See what my magic can do.* And yet . . . sadness, too. *Gone*, it laments. *All gone. All lost. All dead, forgotten, forsaken, sunk beneath the sea. Only I remember. Only I.*"

"And we, now," said Gerbert softly.

The light was changing. Not dimming, not brightening, but paling to earthly gold. Unearthly gold altered with it. Colors flickered into clarity. Metal warmed to flesh, cloth, wood painted and unpainted, food such as mortal man might think of tasting. Only the plates and bowls remained gold, and the ornaments of the king and his white-breasted queen. They smiled at one another, she fondling a jeweled serpent at her throat, he reaching for a cup.

Terror reared over Richer and fell, drowning him.

Alive—they were alive. And if they moved, if they spoke, if they turned their great kohl-darkened eyes on him, oh, surely, he would go mad.

He turned about, stumbling. Gerbert was rapt in wonder. Beyond him was a garden, a green hill, a sea so blue it hurt the eyes. No stair, no reeking, blessed, mortal passage. No escape. They were trapped. The magic had taken them. The air was warmer than March in Ravenna could ever have been. He scented grass, thyme, the sea.

"Mary, Mother of God!" he wailed, and bolted.

He hardly cared where he went. Out, only. *Out*. The table, the king, the lovely, wanton queen, loomed before him. His hands flailed. Cold stone. Warm air. Painted wall. Real and solid table, plates that scattered, a knife in his hand, cool hilt, white flame of magic.

The earth rumbled. The air shrieked like a woman. The archer bared white teeth in his sun-bronzed face, and loosed. The arrow flew as swift as sight; pierced the carbuncle; shattered it.

Darkness fell, abrupt and absolute. The world was a drum, and God's hand beating on it. Hands seized Richer, dragging him. His body yielded. His mind gibbered. Someone was shouting. It might have been himself. It might have been Gerbert, or the Jinniyah, or the outraged, violated magic.

He had no memory of the passage. Only of scrambling into blessed, mortal moonlight, and falling, and rising again, and being dragged anew. Behind him, in the rocking of the earth, the statue fell and shattered. Richer, who had quite lost his wits, laughed and clapped his hands like a child. Iron, oh, yes, indeed, but within it, pallid under the moon, the gleam of lovely, deadly, pagan gold.

Richer would gladly have slunk into the marshes and become a hermit for his shame, but Gerbert was having none of it. In the clear light of morning he was exactly as he always was, even in the midst of the most outlandish sorcery. He had taken a bruise or two in his flight, to which he was paying no attention. He had an archbishopric to look after, and a prodigy to be told of: how a forgotten square near the walls had been riven in the night by a demon's passing, and the ancient image had fallen, uncovering its golden treasure. Of shaft and passage there was no sign. The pavement had buckled over them. The magic that had endured so long was gone, shattered by one fool's helpless panic.

"Enough of that," said Gerbert with utter lack of sympathy. People were taking the statue's fall for an omen, though whether of good or ill they could not agree. Gerbert forbore to listen to them. The gold, he had decreed, would go to feed the poor of Ravenna. His chancellor thought him mad. His more pious servants were blessing his sainted generosity.

Richer was put to work overseeing the weighing and the stowing of the fragments, once Gerbert himself had sanctified them with his blessing and gone away to be archbishop. The archbishop's guard kept the people at bay, watching narrowly for thieves. But none was so bold as to lay impious hands on a miracle. They merely watched and whispered, and backed away when the wagon came through with Richer perched atop the wrapped and labeled shards.

When it was done, though Richer still burned inwardly with the shame of it, he had begun to think that he might not want to forsake the world after all. Not, at least, for a hut in the marshes of Ravenna. He washed his face and put on a clean habit. His stomach was entertaining thoughts of dinner: a prodigy in itself. He had been certain that he would never want to eat again, if it meant swallowing shame with every bite.

Men had suffered worse, he supposed, and lived to tell of it. He took a deep breath and went to face the world.

The archbishop's palace was always alive with people and voices, comings and goings. Richer was not surprised to see new faces—monks, priests, men-at-arms wearing badges which he did not recognize. Another embassy, no doubt, to the second most powerful prelate in Christendom. He could be proud of that, even after that prelate had seen him revealed as the rankest of cowards.

Gerbert was holding audience, as Richer had expected. He saw a pair of bishops, mitered and haughty, and a flock of babbling courtiers. He was in no mood to linger; the night's exploits had burned curiosity out of him. He merely sighed, for dinner would not begin until the archbishop was ready for it; and Richer was not ready to coax the archbishop's irascible cook to feed him out of turn. He took refuge in the library, which had the virtue of quiet, solitude, and a hypocaust which kept it blissfully warm.

Augustine was strong medicine for anything that ailed a man. Richer swam out of the *Confessions* to stare, blinking, at Gerbert. The archbishop was dressed still for high audience. His face was as white as the silk that lined his cope.

Richer forgot shame, guilt, even Augustine. He leaped up, catching Gerbert as he swayed.

Gerbert shook him off, steadying with an effort that wrenched at Richer's own body. "I'm not sick," he said sharply. But his eyes were dark, staring at something far beyond Richer. "I'm—" He swallowed. This time he let

Richer lay hands on him, though he would not sit. "Pope Gregory is dead."

Richer gaped. He could not say that he grieved. Surprised, yes—he was that. "Dead? So soon? But he was young. He wasn't even as old as I." And, belatedly: "God rest his soul."

Gerbert seemed not to have heard him. "Pope Gregory is dead. I," he said, "am summoned by my emperor. To Rome. To accept—" He was breathing like a runner in a race; like a man smitten in the vitals. "To accept election as his successor."

20

"I can't," said Gerbert. "My lord, I can't."

Otto would not hear him. He was all emperor to-night, even in the solitude which Gerbert had begged for and, more or less, received. There was an attendant or three. And Richer, who had not left Gerbert's side since they left Ravenna.

Richer looked at the Emperor of the Romans and tried to like what he saw. A youth whom an empire had brought early to manhood; a mingling of Greek and Saxon in the shape of his face, the set of his eyes, the reddish fairness of his beard. He pulled at it now and then: for tension, Richer suspected, though his expression was as calm as an icon's. His hands and his face were thin and pale. Too thin and too pale. Richer's eyes, trained to see such things, narrowed and sharpened.

"You must," Otto was saying. "No one else is so perfectly fit for it."

Gerbert threw up his hands. "*Anyone* is better fit than I! My lord, can't you, won't you see? An archbishopric is one thing. Ravenna can bear it, even knowing what I am: peasant's brat, Moor's pupil, master of more arts than any decent Christian should lay claim to. But to take the Chair of Peter . . ."

"That is exactly why you must take it. Because of what you are. All of it. And because—" Otto lowered his eyes. It was not humility. "Because I need you."

There, thought Richer. That would snare him.

He did not go down easily. "You need a young man who can rule your empire with you."

"I had one," Otto said. "He died. God took him; God showed me who must take his place. Do you question God's will?"

Strong medicine, that. Otto had a gift: he managed not to sound mad, or obsessed, or blasphemous. He said it as a simple truth.

He held out his hands to Gerbert, and softened his voice. "*Magister.* I knew what you would say. I tried to think of someone else. I prayed; I fasted. And all it came to was this. You are the one who must be Bishop of Rome. There is no better man for it. There will be none. Only you." He caught Gerbert's hands in his own, his face alive now, eager. "Can't you feel it? Can't you see what I see? All your life you've been preparing for this. Aurillac, Spain, Rheims—Rheims above all. God took it from you to bring you to me; to free you, to set you in the place He made for you."

Gerbert's head shook, but he did not try to pull away. "My lord—"

"Surely you knew. Surely you expected it, when I made you highest but one, of all the bishops in the world."

"But—to expect—to know that one is old, and one's pope is young—and then to know—to be— My lord, I can't!"

"*Magister.* Believe me. You can."

Gerbert sank down. He was crying like a child. Richer, appalled, lurched forward. Otto turned on him with cold words and colder magic. "Out. All of you, out."

He was strong. Richer could not even begin to muster resistance, though he burned and seethed. He was commanded. He obeyed.

When with a mighty effort he looked back, Otto was holding Gerbert, tender as a mother. But his eyes were steady, fixed on the dark beyond the lamplight, set on this course which his royal will had chosen.

Gerbert's storm passed quickly enough, once he had let it have its way. When it was gone he felt light and empty, hollow, almost serene.

He raised his head, drew a breath. Otto watched him in silence. He straightened; what little dignity he had left, he put on. "My lord," he said. "I'm not afraid that I'm not fit. I'm afraid I am. I want it with all that is in me; I know that I can hold it as well as any man living. And that is why I am afraid."

He met Otto's stare. It was dark, still, waiting. "I've always been prey to two great sins. The sin of pride, and the sin of despair. This is too high. It's too far to fall."

"That," said Otto, "is why I chose you. You know the price as well as the power. You won't fall prey to either."

"No?" Gerbert asked.

"No." Otto did not move, and yet he took it all in: the palace in which they sat, which he was building still, raw yet with newness, glittering with eastern splendor; the courtiers endowed with titles out of Byzantium; the rituals as intricate as the pope's high mass, through which they all moved from waking to sleeping, and he most of all, its center and its focus. He took it all in, and he made it as nothing. They were man and man here, master and pupil, friend and friend.

And, if Gerbert accepted this that was gift and burden and terror all at once, equal and equal, high priest and high king.

"I told you the truth," Otto said. "I need you. Ever since I sent you to Ravenna—" He rubbed his face. He looked tired to desperation, thinner and whiter than Gerbert had ever seen him, worn with endless labor. "I missed you, *magister*. I missed you with all my heart. It was like losing half of myself. And the things I did . . ."

He was going to break, as Gerbert had, helplessly. Gerbert reached for him.

But he had been a prince since he was born, an emperor since earliest childhood. He welcomed the steadying hands, but he did not weaken into tears. "Necessity is cruel, *magister*. The anger of a king—that is crueler yet. I was angry. I had had enough of war, rebellion, endless, poisonous, rankling sedition. Rome turned against me. It turned to Byzantium; it drove out the pope who was my cousin, calling him outlander and interloper and false priest, and set up a pope of its own who truly was all of those things, and defied me.

"I conquered that defiance," said Otto. "I cast out the antipope; I gave him into the hands of the Church. It proclaimed him anathema. It reft him of his eyes; it took his nose, his lips, his tongue; it bore him through the streets of this whore of cities, that horrible face turned to the tail of his donkey, and on his head the head of an ass. Then he stood trial, and I sat before them all, and I watched them strip him of all that had made him pope and priest and even human man, and shut him up in prison. He lives there yet, they tell me. He refuses to die.

"And I was glad, *magister*. Glad to see what my servants had made of him, because he turned against me. I fed—I fed on his torment."

His grip on Gerbert's hands was tight to pain, but the pain that was in him was infinitely greater. "And when I had fed, I was not satisfied. I laid siege to the lord of Rome in his stronghold of Sant'Angelo. I haled him out; I had him killed; I hung him where all his city could see what price he paid for his transgressions."

"That was justice," Gerbert said.

Otto shook his head wildly. "It was not! It was gluttony. It was power freed to raven where it would. It was the devil's claws sunk in me, tempting me to sin and sin and sin again. Even now, it wants—it hungers—"

Gerbert shook him until he fell silent. "Stop it! You're driving yourself mad. I know, my lord. I *know*."

Anger sparked, that anyone should dare speak so to the emperor. Then shame, and reluctant acceptance; though there was a little resistance left. "The power—"

"The greater the power, the greater the price. You failed, yes. But you repent. This is not canonical confession, and yet I grant you absolution."

"And penance?"

"You've walked barefoot to Saint Michael's shrine, and done penance there: the whole world knows it. Isn't that enough?"

"That was for the earthly sin: the torture of a priest of God. I never confessed the sin of power."

"Then let your empire be your penance. Rule it well, in mercy and in justice. Use your power for good as you used it for harm."

Otto bowed his head. Gerbert signed him with the cross. What sang between them was more than sanctity, more even than magic.

Gerbert laid his hand on his emperor's head. The amethyst of his ring, catching the light, flared suddenly, eerily red.

Otto leaped up, laughing for pure gladness, and kissed Gerbert on both cheeks. "Oh, *magister*! Now I have all I ever wanted. Between the two of us, we'll make a whole new world. You from Peter's throne, I from the throne of Charlemagne—no, greater: from the throne of Constantine, who laid the world under God's law, and ruled it hand in hand with Sylvester who was his pope; you in the spirit, I in the flesh—what can we not do?"

Make an old man young again, Gerbert wanted to answer. Mend a vessel broken under the heel of time and war and the world's waning.

And yet, as their eyes met, Gerbert tasted that joy and that hope. Maybe it could be. If they were strong; if they wielded their conjoined power.

"Without you I could never do it," Otto said. "With you I can move the world."

Gerbert's heart was cold. In the moment of his blessing, he had seen what no upwelling of joy or hope or sheer white power could deny. The spirit which he had summoned, to his long grief, was gone; but it had left its token. It was in Otto, a fleck of shadow like the mark of a claw, consuming him slowly from within.

There was death in him, and Gerbert's doing had set it there.

No, he swore to himself. Not while he lived; not while he had power. If he must take Peter's throne to defend the one who sat on Constantine's, then so be it.

He almost laughed. Even when he tried most to be humble, he could not help but be proud. "Your will be done," he said. No matter to whom he said it.

This was the summit of the world.

To be chosen in law and by the emperor's will. To rise from prayer in his majesty's chapel, to face the bishops who had led him from Ravenna, to hear them name him elect of God and of holy Church. "*Non sum dignus!*" he cried, thrice, with all his heart: "I am not worthy!" But that was ritual, for all the truth of it, and they would not hear him. They bore him into the palace of the Lateran where popes had ruled since the Church was new; they set him on the throne of Sylvester, of Gregory, of Leo who had crowned Charlemagne. They bowed down before him; they laid the world at his feet.

They gave him seven days to learn the taste of it, the sweet and the bitter both, locked like a prisoner in walls as splendid as they were holy. Even in sleep they did not leave him. He was his own no longer. He belonged now, wholly, to Mother Church: her master and her slave, servant of the servants of God.

Then they opened the gates and led him out to face the city of which he was bishop. He had fought one battle against this tide which overwhelmed him, and because they had looked for more resistance, or for none at all, he won it. He was not borne rocking and greensick in a litter. The white mule was old now and going blind, her eyes as moon-pale as her coat, but she could not have borne to pass this honor to another. Richer was at her head, his face as solemn as ever a monk's should be who led the lord pope to his crowning, but his eyes as they met Gerbert's were dancing. Even in the armor of his numbness, Gerbert mustered a small, tight smile.

It was an endless way from the palace of the Lateran to the basilica of Saint Peter, across the breadth of Rome, its ruins and its empty places, its spaces inhabited and uninhabited, its churches, its fora, its hills and its marshy hollows. A mighty press of people followed in his wake, swirled about him, lined the road as he passed. Their acclamations swelled and faded, swelled and faded. But behind him, tirelessly, chanted his priests and his novices. *"Tu es Petrus,"* they sang in the voices of angels. " 'Thou art Peter, and upon this rock I will build my church.' "

Tu es Petrus.

He sat on his throne in shimmering space, robed and vested, anointed, sanctified with prayer. The numbness that had brought him so far, in such unwonted docility, had gone away. And yet the fear had not risen to unman him. It was there, trembling deep within, chilling his hands in the jeweled gloves, but his mind was calm. The beauty of the ancient rite washed over him, clear as water. The world's eyes fixed on him, and he felt the weight and the heat of them, and yet his heart was light, glad; free. He had risen as high as living man could rise, and from that eminence, if he fell, he fell to death and worse than death; and he was not afraid. He had gone too far, flown too high. The lark had spread its wings and seen that, indeed, it was an eagle.

Brother Raymond who was Father Raymond now, lord abbot of Aurillac, would profess no surprise. Bishop Hatto, dead on the road from Rome to Spain, would perhaps have smiled. Master Ibrahim . . . if he lived still, would he be glad, or not displeased at least, to see his foretelling all fulfilled? *See*, Gerbert would say to him if he could. *I have done my penance. I have wavered in my oath, but I have never forgotten it, nor broken it beyond mending. I remember our dark rose who died for my magic's sake. I honor her memory. If you cannot forgive, will you grant me your goodwill, you who were and are my master and my teacher?*

The world's awe beat upon him. The choir's voices rose, piercingly sweet. " 'Feed My lambs; feed My sheep. . . . ' "

His body, well instructed, rose even as his deacons came to assist it. One was solemn to grimness. One reminded him of Richer who had vanished among the crowd, but whose awareness was there when Gerbert looked for it, like a spark in the night: decorous face, glinting eyes.

Yes, that was as it should be. Too much solemnity was a poison. Even a pope remained a man, try though his servants would to transform him into an icon.

The magic, numbed and quenched as Gerbert's will and wits had been, had roused with them. In the music and the holiness, the awe, the hunger for magnificence which fed it all, it swelled and bloomed. What had been mere exaltation, transmuted into glory. Walls of stone revealed themselves for walls of light. Light blazed within them, human souls laid bare, a field of flames as varied as stars, and more wonderful. There was Richer, a ruddy fire, mage and monk, loyal friend and loyal servant; and a great soaring brilliance that was Otto, mage and emperor, friend and pupil and—yes, in his way, son; and all about them the manifold marvels that were the priests and the bishops, the monks, the nuns, the clerks of all the orders, princes, lords of the city and of the empire, the senate and the people of Rome, all gathered to pay homage to the successor of Peter. And on them, about them, in them, the incalculable splendor that was the mind of God.

Thou art Peter, and upon this rock I will build my church; and the gates of hell shall not prevail against it.

Mortal light met the light of power, merged with it, became it: the air of Rome in spring, the portal of Saint Peter's, and the throngs of Rome before it, shouting his praises. Here beyond the dazzle of magic was pure and perfect clarity. He saw their awe of his office, of his vestments, of his face that shone with the light of his power. And he saw what would come after: cold sobriety, memory of rebellion, hatred of the foreigner set over them by a foreign emperor. They were his, and yet they were not. He would have to win them as every great prince must win his people; if he succeeded, they would barely thank him, but if he failed, they would destroy him.

He had fought that fight before. There was no one

now to contest his right to fight it. He would enter it; he would win it, or die in the trying.

The deacon with the mischievous eyes—more somber now, in honor of his office—knelt before him. In the man's hands lay the tiara of the Holy See. Neither crown nor miter, not quite a helmet, all white, high and rounded, circled with a coronet of gold. The deacon chanted in a clear strong voice, meeting Gerbert's eyes, making truth of time-smoothed ritual: "Receive this tiara; know that thou art father of princes and kings, ruler of the world, vicar of our savior Jesus Christ."

Gerbert took the tiara from his hands, held it up. It was not heavy, and yet the weight of the world was in it. Fear swelled anew, mounting into terror. *Drop it. Drop it now, flee, be free!*

He drew a breath, which caught, stumbled, steadied. Slowly he set the tiara upon his head. He bowed beneath it; and straightened, stiffening his back, raising his head. It was not pride. It was, when it came to the crux, plain peasant stubbornness. He would not shame his emperor who had laid this on him, nor his Church which had assented to it, nor his God Who had willed it.

The deacon bowed low before him, turned, faced the people of Rome and of the world. "Behold the lord pope, Sylvester, whom Saint Peter has chosen to sit upon his Throne. Long life; long life to the Holy Father!"

"Long life!" they roared back. "Long life! Long life! Long life!"

21

Night and winter and grey cold rain laid on Rome as near a semblance of peace as it was likely to know. Even its thieves had gone to haven. Its army of priests slept what sleep they might between compline and matins. In the palace of the Lateran, even the kitchens were quiet, the fires banked, the scullions snoring in their corners.

Richer had come from the school before the early dusk, as he often did; for though he had been made its master, he never forgot who was truly his master. Gerbert had been occupied with an embassy from the Rus. Richer, as often, had found his way to the library and settled there. Tonight, between the warmth of the brazier and the aftereffects of an ambitious working with a handful of his older students, he had fallen asleep over his book, and waked with a start to find the night well advanced. The brazier had died to a few dim coals. His body ached with cold and with lying sprawled over a table.

He groaned as he rose, flexing his aching shoulders. The whole palace slept: he could feel it in his bones. Neither rain nor cold had lightened since he braved them for the warmth of Gerbert's presence. His holiness would be asleep, if he knew what was good for him. Richer did not intend to trouble him. The guards knew the pope's friend, the gangling clown from the school near the great crumbling Colosseum of the pagans. What he taught there was no secret; nor was the Holy Father's part in it. They had a charter from his hand, the seal of holy Church; and never a thing the Curia could do, though its greater fools cited every text and transgression from Exodus to Simon Magus. Sylvester Magus had spoken, and he was the Heir of Peter.

They were calling him *Pontifex Magicus*. A fine title, and fitting, if somewhat sacrilegious.

Richer found his way by magelight, treading softly through the passages. In three years' time, even broken by long stretches when Gerbert was gone, on progress among his people or driven out by rebellious Romans, Richer had grown familiar with this most holy of palaces. The awe had abated a little; he had stopped creeping about in constant dread of breaking something.

He paused. At the end of the corridor, a door was ajar. Light glimmered through it.

His curiosity had restored itself since the treasure of Justinian burned it out of him. Surely there would be no such horror here, in the pope's own palace, lurking in the hall of his throne.

It was, if one insisted on precision, a *triclinium*, a dining chamber; and in fact the Holy Father presided over feasts there. Yet there also stood the lesser of his thrones, the chair of white marble that had come out of old Rome, on which he was set when he had accepted his election, and from which he received his audiences and took tribute. In that hall of three great bays, adorned with the porphyry of emperors, on which the map of the world lay spread in gold and jewel-colors, the throne was both center and focus. Behind it glowed a wonder of mosaic: Christ sending forth his twelve Apostles, and Peter above them all, seated upon a throne. At the Apostle's feet knelt

Charles the Great, receiving from his hand the banner of empire. But before and above the Frankish king knelt the man who had made him emperor, Leo the pope of Rome, and in his hands the Apostle had set the pallium with its blazon of crosses, the mandate of no earthly power but of Christ himself.

Under Leo's feet, wrapped in a scarlet mantle, the pope sat on his throne. Magelight glimmered about him. His chin was in his hand; he seemed deep in thought. He did not acknowledge Richer's coming down the length of the hall; but when the monk had nodded startled greeting to the glint of bronze half-hidden in the mantle and dropped down on the dais, he said, "You're late tonight."

Richer could not keep from blushing. "I was in your library. I fell asleep."

"To good purpose, I hope," said Gerbert.

"Hardly," Richer muttered. "I must be getting old. I ache in every bone."

"You? You're the merest pup."

Richer eyed him a little wildly. "You weren't waiting up for me, were you?"

Gerbert shrugged. "You know how little I sleep. I was comtemplating my sins."

"Sleep would do you more good."

"Would it?" Gerbert's hand encompassed that whole shadowed hall. "Look at this. It's hubris embodied in metal and stone. And all in honor of a faith that bids us forsake the flesh for the rewards of the spirit."

"Someone has to rule over that faith. He suffers enough for its sake. Why shouldn't he enjoy a reward or two of the flesh?"

Gerbert smiled wryly. "You should hear the Abbot of Cluny on the subject. If I listened to him, I'd be living in a cave under the Palatine, and subsisting on locusts and wild honey."

"Do we need another hermit, my lord? I'd rather have you here. It's warmer."

"And the food is better, besides." Gerbert sighed and straightened, uncovering the Jinniyah in his lap. She seemed all lifeless tonight, all mute, as if the chair of Peter had robbed her of her power to speak. Gerbert traced a molded ringlet with a finger, and sighed again; but then he smiled. "How fares the Art in Rome, *magister*?"

Richer always twitched when Gerbert called him by that title. But he was inured enough to it by now to answer sensibly. "It fares well, *magister*. We advanced a group of novices to initiates, and an initiate to master. Rabbi Ephraim says that that one will go far. Her magic is merely adequate, but she could teach a stone to sing."

"Would that happen to be his daughter?" Gerbert asked.

"Well," said Richer, "no. She has magic enough for three, but she couldn't teach a duck to swim. It's Hathumoda I'm speaking of—the nun from Gandersheim. She wants to go back there. Her abbess is tolerant, she says, and won't forbid her to practice her Art. Or, and that matters more, to teach it."

"No; that lady would not. She's the emperor's sister, you know. I hear she has a little of the family gift herself."

"So she does," said Richer. "But no discipline to go with it. Sister Hathumoda has hopes of altering that."

"God favor her cause," Gerbert said with a touch of irony. "They're strong-willed, those royal Saxons. Mulish, for a fact."

There was no delicate way to ask; therefore Richer was blunt. "Has his majesty done something, my lord?"

"No," said Gerbert. "No. Though he *will* drive his armies all over Italy when he's barely well enough to sit a horse. Romuald—do you remember him? The holy hermit from Ravenna. He tried to keep my lord there, where he could rest a little, but he wouldn't stay. He's marching on Rome. This time, he says, he'll quash their insurrections for once and for all." Gerbert's fists clenched and unclenched. "He knows how badly he fares in this climate. He *knows* what it did to his father, and to his cousin who sat here before me."

"But not to you."

"I." Gerbert shrugged. "I'm peasant stock. As long as no one's trying to rob me of my magic or my office, I'm as tough as old leather. But my lord . . ."

"You can knock sense into him when you see him. He always listens to you."

Gerbert's head sank onto his hand. "God grant he does." He sounded suddenly very tired. But, strangely, not sad; and not ever defeated. "Romuald, the old fox, inveigled a promise out of him. A few years more of empire, and then he takes the habit. But he's as clever in his own way. He'll enter orders, he says, when his empire is firm on its foundations. And when he has begotten an heir to take the crown."

"He may keep that promise yet. He's sent the Bishop of Milan to find him a bride in Byzantium."

"So he has, and so he may. And then we'll take pilgrims' vows and set out for Jerusalem."

"There's a dream worth dreaming," said Richer.

"Isn't it?" Gerbert's mood had shifted. He was light, almost joyous, as if the very name had given him peace. "Tell me, Jinniyah. Shall I die before I sing mass in Jerusalem?"

For a long moment Richer did not think that she would answer. Then, like a bell tolling, it came: the single word. "No."

She had startled Gerbert. He almost dropped her; Richer snatched, steadying them both. They stared at her. She had gone back to her immobility; her eyes seemed to see no more than bronze should ever see. Almost Richer might have thought that she was angry; but why should she be?

She was female, and Jinniyah. There was no accounting for her moods.

Gerbert patted her cheek. "Ah, old friend. I should take the binding off you."

"No need." She sounded faintly sullen. "Let be. It serves its purpose."

"Still—" Gerbert began.

He never said the rest of it. He had gone very still. Richer heard it then: swift feet, voices raised in expostulation. The door opened abruptly, letting in a knot of men. Gerbert's chamberlain in great disarray, remonstrating. One or two of the papal guards, hovering and not quite daring to interfere. And at the brunt of them, a man in sodden riding gear, slimed with mud, ignoring his escort to drop to his knees before the pope. "Holy Father," he said, breathing hard; but his voice was strong, rough with urgency. "My lord emperor begs you, if you will—he would not ask it, but his fever—"

Gerbert was on his feet. His face was stark white. His voice was frightening, soft as it was, and steady, and emptied of emotion. "Take me to him."

"But," said the chamberlain.

"But, my lord," said Richer.

Gerbert was not there to hear them.

The emperor's advance had halted at Paterno under Mount Soracte, a good day's march from Rome. His army had settled itself about the town; he had taken the most imposing of its houses, a moldering villa that gazed over winter-deadened gardens to the loom of the mountain. The rain that had turned Rome to mire had fallen here as snow; slopes and summit shone dazzling in the sunrise.

Otto had commanded that his bed be set in a chamber that faced the mountain, and its shutters opened, though the wind was cold. His physicians' expostulations moved him not at all. He lay propped up in the great bed, wrapped in furs; and for a moment as Gerbert crossed the threshold, he knew that he had ridden so hard and so far for nothing more than foolishness.

But the high color in the emperor's cheeks was fever; the light in his eyes was too bright, his voice too lively as he called out, "What, *magister*! So soon? What did your white mule say to such haste?"

"Alba takes her ease in my stable," said Gerbert. "I imposed myself upon a horse; and an iron-jawed son of Iblis he was, too."

Otto laughed and beckoned. "Will you forgive me if I don't get up to greet you properly? My knees are my Rome today. They keep turning rebel."

Gerbert sat on the side of the bed and cursed his brimming eyes. Otto was barely more substantial than a shadow; for all the liveliness of voice and glance, the rest of him barely moved. Beneath the fever-glitter was naught but dark; beneath the semblance of life and strength, sickness that had consumed him.

Gerbert's fault. Gerbert's grievous fault.

Otto could curl his fingers round Gerbert's hand, but he could not lift it. Gerbert raised it himself, so that Otto might kiss his ring. The emperor murmured thanks. When Gerbert tried to withdraw, his fingers tightened. "Stay with me," he said. "Don't leave me."

Gerbert swallowed hard and let his hand be held. He was aware, dimly, of people hovering, priests muttering prayers, a woman or a boy trying to sob quietly. They had recognized what power ruled here, as courtiers always did, by unfailing instinct.

As Otto had. For an instant, as he begged Gerbert to stay, the darkness filled his eyes; the old fear, the dread of death. Then he cast it down again and set his foot on it, and clutched at what life was left to him.

It almost broke Gerbert. That Otto did not blame him, not even as a saint might, with grief that all his dreams had come to nothing.

Not quite all of them. Pride, that might be, and Gerbert would pay its price. But he had grown past despair.

Richer had attached himself to Gerbert's riding, asking no leave and needing none. Now Gerbert felt his presence as a banked fire, his magic that was healing magic, his deft hands examining the emperor as much within as without. Otto allowed it with all apparent patience.

Richer drew back and lowered his hands. His eyes met Gerbert's. They were as somber as Gerbert had ever known they could be. "This is beyond my power," he said.

No. Gerbert did not know if he said it aloud. It was his whole being, that denial. He had held back this death before, or turned it aside. It could not conquer. It must not.

The monk offered a cupful of something bittersweet. "For the pain," he said.

Otto did not deny that there was pain: for that, Gerbert almost broke. He drank the dose with hardly a grimace, and smiled at Gerbert. "Look," he said, turning his face toward the mountain. "Doesn't it put you in mind of your lessons? Pagan Horace saw it just so—maybe from this very place. 'You see how Soracte stands all white with deep snow, the forests bow beneath their burden, the rivers stand still in the piercing cold.' Isn't it so? And now that you are here, we can live out the rest of it: put the cold to flight with wine and fire, and leave the rest to the

gods. 'Ask not what the morrow shall bring; take what the
day's chance shall give. . . .' "

"And shall we take the rest of his advice, too? 'Spurn
not sweet amours, my boy, nor dancing, until sullen age
takes away your youth.' "

Otto flushed even through the fever, but he smiled.
"Ah, well; he was a pagan. But maybe I can heed him
without seeming entirely depraved. I'm betrothed, did
you know it? The Bishop of Milan has found me a bride.
She's handsome, he tells me, and clever: a very proper
princess of Byzantium. They'll be landing at Bari in a day
or two. Imagine it, *magister*. An empress for my new
Rome. Sons; daughters. A dynasty." He drew a breath
that rattled, still smiling. "You'll marry us, of course.
Maybe she'll be like us. Or our children will. More pupils
for your school."

"God willing," said Gerbert. His magic would not
come to his hand. It was coy; it eluded him, sparking
where he did not need it, cold and lifeless where he would
have spent it all to keep his emperor alive. He was old; he
had lived as fully as any man could; he had risen higher
than a peasant's child might ever dream of. Why should
he not die in Otto's place?

Otto's own magic burned the hotter for his body's
failing. It sensed Gerbert's passionate outcry, all silent
though it was. "*Magister.*" Otto said it tenderly. His voice
was fainter now. "Whether I live or die, God has willed it. I
try to look ahead and see the simple light of day, but what
I see, what my bones tell me . . . Romuald knew. He told
me when I left him, 'Go, then. March to Rome. But if you
do it, you'll not see Ravenna again.' He's one of us, you
know; though he'd tear out my throat if I told him so. He
says it's all God in him. And so it is, if not exactly as he
sees it." Otto shifted. Gerbert helped him to settle more
comfortably, feeling the fire that burned him. His shirt

and his furs were sodden with sweat, and yet he shivered, huddling in them.

The magic, capricious creature that it was, offered a tiny mockery of comfort: it cooled the fire a little, soothing it to gentle warmth. Otto's gratitude washed over Gerbert. Their powers were coming together, slowly but inescapably.

One of the servants ventured to close the shutters upon the mountain and the cold. The darkness was abrupt and, for a moment, absolute. Otto's eyes had closed before the shutters; he did not start up, nor reprimand the servant.

Slowly the darkness lightened to dimness. Someone lit a lamp. Freed from the weight of the outer air, the hypocaust began to warm the room.

Otto had neither fainted nor fallen asleep. After a while he said, "My cousin Henry will be happy. His father fought a long and bitter battle for me and then for my throne; now the son will have all that his father fought for, except my person. He'll be a good enough emperor. But not . . . He's Saxon. He doesn't understand Rome."

Otto did not mean the city which Gerbert had ridden out of, which barely understood itself.

A hand touched Gerbert's shoulder, diffident yet persistent. He glanced at Otto's chaplain, whose hands were full: book, stole, candle, the oils of the Last Rites. Anger flared in him, turned his voice to a lash. "Not yet!"

The chaplain retreated, cowed. Gerbert forgot him.

Otto had fallen into a drowse. Sometimes he woke. He talked a little; less as the day waned. Clouds had come back with the sun's sinking. Rain began to fall as it had fallen on Rome, grey and cheerless. It veiled Soracte in fog; it hissed on the tiles of the villa.

"Now," said Gerbert to the chaplain, roughly, when grey had long since turned to black beyond the shutters. Otto barely stirred, though when Gerbert tried again to withdraw the captive hand, his protest was as sharp as a knife-cut. The chaplain performed the office with fitting reverence: the old, old words, and the anointing of the gates of the senses, and the entrusting of the soul to God. Gerbert murmured the words of the rite, softly, through the pulsing of magic. Otto's power bled out of him, slow yet inexorable.

Gerbert could not stop it. His scarred hand burned; he heard a shadow's laughter. *I give to you as you gave to me.* Blasphemous, those words; mocking; evil. *Mortal faith!*

"No," Gerbert said aloud. The chaplain's voice faltered. "Don't stop!" Gerbert snapped. The man stumbled, stammered, recovered.

There was nothing to grasp. No power. Only darkness and the broken temple of a body. What Gerbert's oath-breaking had loosed, had long since wrought its ill and gone. What remained was only memory. It could not even touch Otto's soul. It had no need. His life was enough; his dream ended before it was begun; all that he could have been and done and wrought. The light would be a little dimmer now, the night a little darker, for that he was not there to know them.

Otto was awake. For a moment in the lamplight he looked almost hale, blinking drowsily, peering at the people who bent over him. But Gerbert was closest, and it was to Gerbert that he spoke. "I'm sorry, *magister*. It was too much for me after all: too much dream, too much empire. God didn't will that I should win it. Someday, maybe . . ." He trailed off. The trickle of power was mounting to a stream. He drew a great, shaking breath. "Did I do well, *magister*? Did I not fail too badly? Did I, maybe, bring a little light into the world?"

The tears brimmed in Gerbert's eyes and overflowed. "A whole great galaxy of it," he said.

Otto smiled. The flood of magic crested. With one last, desperate leap of power, Gerbert grasped it, clutched it. It twisted in his grip; and suddenly, with a flicker of laughter, poured itself into him.

In vain he reared up his walls. In vain he strove to cast it back. It was as supple as water, as inexorable in its torrent. Just so had he done with his Jinniyah. Just so; but he had been hale and whole. And she was enchanted bronze, but he was flesh; he was not made to bear this weight of magic.

"You are," said Otto. "Take it, *magister*. It's all wasted, else."

As was he. A husk with open eyes, and a smile of—God help him—victory. "Now you have it all," he said. "Now you can dream the dream for both of us. Dream well, my friend, my teacher. Light the light I would have lit, that would have been Rome anew. Remember me; but don't grieve for me. I'm with you always. Always. . . ."

His voice was gone, his breath ebbing, sinking into memory. *I feel so . . . light . . .*

Gerbert was heavy, gravid, grieving. All power, and no joy. All the joy was Otto's. *Free,* he sang, down into the long dark. *Glad. Peace . . . oh,* magister! *I've found Jerusalem.*

But it was beyond Gerbert's knowing; and Otto was gone.

Gerbert looked down at the still body. The power had burned away his tears. It surged in him, sighing like the sea, vaster than he had ever known it. And he was master of it. He had paid for it in the purest coin it knew: the life of one he loved.

The throng about the bed was like a gathering of ravens. Gerbert did not try to hold his place there. The emperor was dead. The emperor waited in Saxony to take his new crown. Rome now more than ever would need a strong hand to settle it. The world could not wait upon grief or loss or a murderer's remorse. But Gerbert had killed his emperor as surely as if he had wrought it with poison.

Don't, he almost heard Otto say, impatient as he always was with Gerbert's foolishness. *Rome killed me, and my own stubbornness. The power is my gift and my inheritance. Use it well. Remember me.*

"How could I ever forget you?"

Otto's smile was warm in Gerbert's center. *We were the two halves of God, you and I. We were too much for this poor benighted world. Someday . . .*

"Not in our day," said Gerbert.

He looked up into Richer's face. His sadness had lost itself somewhere, though his grief was deep, and would never leave him. "They die," he said, "and I go on. That is the price I pay for what I am."

Richer said nothing, but he laid a hand on Gerbert's shoulder. Gerbert let it stay, though he straightened under it, setting his jaw and his will. "Someday, my friend, I'm going to have a word with the heavenly chancery."

"You're well placed to do it," said Richer.

Gerbert laughed, a sharp bark, edged with pain. "Yes, after all: I am. And while I'm waiting, I'd best see to my own chancery. Come, sir. We've work to do."

Even Richer could be taken aback at that. "Now?"

Gerbert glanced back at the bed, and to the press about it. His throat spasmed; his eyes flooded. He mastered them both. He was master of all the arts, maker of kings, prince of the princes of the Church. And he had a world to look after.

"Now," he said.

EPILOGUE

Rome, A.D. 1003

Gerbert's mind was made up. Nothing that Richer could say even began to shake him. "You need her," said Gerbert. "She wants to serve you."

"But she's *yours!*" cried Richer.

The bone of their contention gleamed bronze-golden on the table, conspicuously taking no part in the debate. She had spoken already. "I choose you. I belong to you."

Richer would not hear it. Now he tried sweet reason, somewhat frayed about the edges. "I can't do that to you, *magister*. I can't take your magic away from you."

"You won't," said Gerbert as serenely as Richer had ever heard him. "When my lord died"—Even after a year and more, he could not say it without a thickening of his voice—"when Otto died, he gave me all he had. I'm full to bursting with magic."

Even after a year and more, Richer could know the stab of jealousy. Grimly he quelled it. "But, *magister*. She—you—"

"It's time," said Gerbert. "I have all the power I need, and all the prophecies. She needs to be among young things again. To carry on what we two began. To bring the light into new places."

"Then why don't you just set her free?" Richer demanded.

"I don't want to," she said on her own account. Her voice sharpened. "I want what I have chosen. If you do not take me, I shall find a way to take myself."

No doubt she would. Richer looked about for reinforcements, but there were none. Only the pope's servants come to prepare him for the morning's procession, and the pope in his white robe managing to look both sturdy and translucent, like a clay lamp filled with light. His body had grown frail since Otto died, but his magic was stronger than it had ever been. His spirit shone out of him, clear and light and joyful. He might have been going to a festival and not to one of his endless pontifical masses.

Indomitable, that was Master Gerbert. Richer loved him to the point of pain; and would happily have throttled him.

Richer threw up his hands in disgust. "What choice do you leave me? I'll take her. And on your head be it."

They had the same smile, bronze and man. Damn it, he loved them both. He embraced Gerbert suddenly, to the servants' horror. Gerbert grinned up at him, wicked as a boy. "Come, lad, don't fret. You know I won't die till I've sung mass in Jerusalem."

"And a good long while from now may that be," said Richer, letting him go.

He did not linger over farewells. He laid his palm against the Jinniyah's cheek, briefly; that was all. She did not speak. Her face had gone still.

The servants bore him away to be pope. *Pontifex Maximus; Pontifex Magicus.*

Richer stood forsaken, trembling a little. He could not bring himself, yet, to touch the Jinniyah. His, now, insofar as she ever belonged to anyone. He felt as shy as a new bridegroom.

Slowly he stretched out a hand. She was cool, smooth,

lifeless; yet his fingers tingled. She was full to bursting with magic, and filling higher as he tarried.

"Take me," she said.

His hands moved for him. Wrapped her in the cloth which waited beside her, and lifted her, cradling her against his chest. His body thrummed with the power of her. She was too strong. He could not—he dared not—

"Take me," she said again, relentless. "Take me home."

The pope's procession had wound chanting through the gate. A tang of incense lingered still, an echo of the hymn, a servant or two idling in the master's absence. As Richer paused, dizzy with the power in his arms, beginning very dimly to understand what Gerbert and the Jinniyah had done to him, he heard the servants' voices, faint but bitterly clear.

"Where is he singing mass today?"

"Santa Croce."

"Holy Cross? Where's that?"

"What, Roman born and you don't know it? But there—they call it something else round about. It's a famous sanctuary. *Visio Pacis*, that's the name of it. Vision of Peace."

"Ah," said the Roman with an air of great enlightenment. "I know it now. It has another name in our part of the city.

"We call it Jerusalem."

Author's Note

Gerbert of Aurillac (ca. 945-1003)

All events in the life of Gerbert of Aurillac, except those which relate to his use of magic, are portrayed essentially as they happened. I have taken authorial license in a number of instances, most notably in the location of Bishop Hatto's see. He was bishop not of Barcelona (of which Count Borel was in fact lord) but of Vich, somewhat north and inland of the count's city. Gerbert did indeed study the Quadrivium under his tutelage, although the majority of his three years in Spain were probably spent in the monastery of Santa Maria de Ripoll, the library of which was justly famous.

The struggle for Rheims is based closely on the account of Richer of St.-Rémi in the *Historia Francorum*, and on the letters of Gerbert himself (available in Harriet Pratt Lattin's English translation, New York, 1961). Richer was not in fact in Rheims at the time of its betrayal to Duke Charles, but was tracking down his copy of Hippocrates in Chartres. It was Arnulf and not Gerbert who was found and captured atop the tower, to which Arnulf had ascended not to make astronomical observations but to barricade himself against his uncle's soldiers. I have simplified

273

the quarrel over the archbishopric considerably, stream-lined the very confusing sequence of events, and omitted the part played by Hugh Capet's son and heir, Robert, who had in fact been crowned co-king with his father—and who had indeed been Gerbert's pupil in the cathedral school of Rheims. Arnulf's deposition at the beginning of chapter 14 is translated verbatim from Richer's history.

Gerbert's misfortunes in Rheims after Arnulf's deposition were, in turn, considerably more complicated than I have shown them to be. After his meeting with the Emperor Otto III in Pavia, he did in fact return to Rheims, to face the interdict and to be driven out by the ostracism which it entailed. He rejoined his emperor in Germany, was given an estate near Sasbach which brought him nothing but trouble, and stayed with Otto until the resolution of the conflict over Rheims by the naming of Gerbert to the archbishopric of Ravenna. His relationship with his emperor was much as I have portrayed it; likewise the dream which they shared. Lattin's volume includes a very touching pair of letters (pp. 294-97) in which Otto invites Gerbert to become his teacher and encloses a rather clumsy but quite appealing verse of his own composition, and Gerbert responds with Ciceronian eloquence. Otto is always addressed as Caesar, as Emperor of the Romans.

The details of Gerbert's election and coronation as Pope Sylvester II are as accurate as possible; I am indebted to Nikolaus Gussone, *Thron und Inthronization des Papstes von den Anfängen bis zum 12. Jahrhundert* (Bonn, 1978). Election of the pope by the College of Cardinals in secret conclave was first prescribed in the latter half of the eleventh century. At the time of Gerbert, election was officially by the clergy and the notables of Rome, actually by the will of the Holy Roman Emperor; or by whichever strongman was currently ruling Rome. The office itself was as much secular as spiritual, and

Gerbert's actions during his reign, in accepting from his emperor a number of fiefs in southern Italy, laid the foundation for the Papal States of the later Middle Ages and the Renaissance.

Gerbert was probably not present at Otto's deathbed in Paterno, thirty miles from Rome.

The custom of a pope's taking a new name on election was very recent in Gerbert's time—he was in fact the second pope to do so as a matter of course. He refers to himself in his letters and papal privileges as "Sylvester, who is also Gerbert, bishop."

The magical elements in this novel are, of course, invented—but not, in general, by myself. The legend of Sylvester Magus is almost as old as Sylvester himself. It seems that a certain schismatic cardinal, an enemy of the great Pope Saint Gregory VII (1073-85), attempted to prove in polemic that all the popes since Gregory V were unworthy of their position. The charge against Sylvester II was that of sorcery and of service to the devil, and of founding and supporting a school of the black arts in Rome. William of Malmesbury in the twelfth century, in a long digression in his *Gesta Regum Anglorum* ("Deeds of the English Kings"), brings the legend to its fullest flower. Here is the Saracen magician and his daughter, the head of bronze with its oracular gifts, the magical golden treasure—of Octavian, William attests, and discovered not in Ravenna but in Rome—and the death of the pope after singing mass in the Roman church called Jerusalem. I have translated almost verbatim William's wonderful description of the treasure as Gerbert found it, all gold and lit by the great carbuncle. The oracular head, it is said, was passed down through the Middle Ages to the Franciscan alchemist and experimental scientist, Roger Bacon.

The magic which Gerbert is alleged to have practiced would have been the high learned magic of the medieval scholars. The incantation with which he summons the spirit, in chapter 13, is taken (somewhat facetiously) from the Grimoire of Pope Honorius III, quoted in E. M. Butler, *Ritual Magic* (Cambridge, England, 1949, rpt. 1980).

The Year 1000

Contrary to popular belief, there was no exceptional outpouring of millennarian fervor at the end of the tenth century. Gerbert, who was pope in the year 1000, seems to have regarded it as simply another year; likewise the secretaries of the imperial chancery. There was no apparent expectation of the end of the world. Gerbert at least was much too preoccupied with establishing his papacy, reforming a Church which stood in sore need of it, and playing Sylvester to Otto's Constantine. If they dreamed of any Second Coming, it was that not of Christ but of the Roman Empire.

Special preview of **ALAMUT**,
Judith Tarr's spectacular, new historical fantasy,
set in the world of the acclaimed
The Hound and the Falcon

Immortals of great magic in a world of very few,
Morgiana and Prince Aidan would seem destined
for each other. Yet each is strong in will as well
as magic, and neither bends easily to the other.
In the following pages, Morgiana renews her
battle to win over Prince Aidan.

When Morgiana came back from wherever she had been, she found a scene of striking domesticity. Sayyida sat on a cushion, plying her inevitable needle. Aidan was on the floor with Hasan. The baby wanted to walk, but he could not quite find his balance. And there were greater fascinations in his companion, whose hair, long uncut, hung down enticingly, and whose beard begged fingers to tangle in it. His mother rebuked him, but she was trying not to laugh. Aidan did not even try. He unraveled the impudent fingers and pretended to gnaw on them. Hasan whooped with mirth.

Sayyida saw her first. Morgiana set a finger to her lips. Aidan was engrossed in the game. It was Hasan who betrayed them with a cry of gladness. " 'Giana!"

Very slowly Aidan lowered Hasan's hands from his cheeks, and drew himself up. No more than he had on the clifftop, would he turn to face Morgiana.

Aidan's back was rigid. The lamp caught blue lights in

his hair. She wanted to stroke it, to smooth the tangles out of it, to slip her hand beneath and ease the tautness from his shoulders.

I would rather die, he said within, low and bitter cold.

She was, when it came to it, a coward. Or why had she left it to Sayyida for so long, to begin his taming? She flickered from the cavern, otherwhere.

And flickered back. This was her place. Let him see that she did not intend to leave it, or him, until she had won him.

"Then we will be here until the stars fall," he said, tightly, through clenched teeth.

"Not so long, I think." She came round to face him. He refused to play the child: he held still. His eyes were burning pale. Yet for all of that, he did not have the look of one who gnaws himself in captivity. While she had him to toy with, his kin were safe from her.

She nodded, unsmiling. "Your eye is clear enough. What would it take to convince you that I never willingly worked harm to you or yours?"

"Don't lie to me. You were glad to murder Gereint. Joanna—Joanna you would happily have rent limb from limb."

Her breath caught in her throat. "That great cow. What in Allah's name do you see in her?"

He uncoiled. It was splendid, how tall he was, how panther-supple; how oblivious he was to it. His anger rocked her. "What do I see in her? What can you know, you demon, you murderer of children? What do you see in me but what any bitch sees when she is in heat?"

It was brutal, that directness, and so he meant it to be. She said, "Very well. So it is jealousy, and the fire of the body. That was hardly a monk's cell in which I found you, or a monk's abstinence."

His skin was whiter even than her own; a blush was all the brighter for it. "And you think that I can possibly want you, after that? Or forgive you?"

"I didn't kill her."

"Not for lack of trying."

"But for you, I would never have tried at all." That stopped his tongue. Sayyida came quietly, relieved her of Hasan, crept away. Neither paused to notice. Morgiana lifted her chin, glaring up at him. The blood drained from his face. "I was commanded on my sacred oath and bound with words of great power to take her life. I had determined to break that oath; to find her, only, to see her face, perhaps to wound her lightly for my master's sake, then to go away. And how did I find her? That she took pleasure where she could—I could hardly fault her for that. Until I saw with whom she did it."

He knew madness, and jealousy. "You regret that you did it; but not for her sake. Because by it you lost me."

"She is human," said Morgiana.

His body snapped erect; his eyes glittered. "Then you'll never grieve if I break yon cubling's neck."

"You would not dare."

"He is human," Aidan said. The exact tone; the exact, subtle air of contempt.

Her fists clenched. He had her there; too well he knew it. There were humans, and there were one's own humans.

"You think that you would stop at murdering infants," he said. "And yet that is what you nearly did. She carries my child." He advanced on her, striking again, deeper, twisting the blade in the wound. "She was afraid to tell me; she feared that I would cast her off. And when she knew that I would not, that after the shock of it I was glad, that I welcomed her, and the child, and anything that might come of it, she was so happy, the air itself seemed to sing.

"Then," he said. "Then you came. You saw, and you struck. You killed any hope of winning me."

She would not weep or rage or cry denial. She was too proud. "Mortal women grow old," she said. "They die."

His face twisted. "Oh, you are cruel, and you are cold. You are nothing that human warmth can touch."

"No more than you," she said.

That struck home. He flinched; his lips set tight.

"I cannot help what the years have made me," she said. "I was alone; I made myself a slave, to lend some purpose to the long days. My folly, and my grief. How could I know what had been written for me and for you?"

He had heard all that he could bear to hear. He turned away from her without a word, and strode out of the cave.

She let him go. He could not escape, he knew it as well as she. He did not know, perhaps, that he did not want to. Much of his resistance was rebellion against its opposite.

How well you lie to yourself. His voice in her mind, bitter with scorn. She sent it back to him without the scorn. His mind closed like a gate shutting.

The three of them had made a world for themselves, small but complete. This most unwelcome fourth had burst it asunder.

The girl and the child never minded. He was the interloper, after all, the grown male, the stranger. He had to see how Hasan delighted in Morgiana's simple presence, and how Sayyida opened to her, close and warm as kin. What he had not chosen to see, was now painfully obvious. He had been accepted not as himself, but as Morgiana's.

He took to going out and staying there until hunger drove him in; and sometimes not even then. There was a little hunting, if he was patient. He began to test the edges of the ban, as he had in moving on Masyaf; but this would not yield at all. Its maker was within it, to sustain it, and she knew him now. Better by far, he suspected, than he knew her.

She was always aware of him, as he was of her. Often she followed him. She never tried to catch him. He was being hunted, but the hunter was patient. She seemed content simply to watch him; to know that she had him in her power.

Her mind was open to him. It was trust, implicit and complete. It drove him wild. But not mad, not that. That refuge was lost to him. He had to know how she loved him and wanted him; how deep the wound was, that he would not return the love and the wanting.

Could not.

Would not. She was certain. Damn that certainty. Damn her years and her strength and her obstinacy.

Stubborn, she said to him. *Fool.*

Murderer, he thought at her.

She showed him the first man he had ever killed, when he was twelve years old. She showed him the second, the third, the fourth. She showed him years of errantry, battles fought, cities sacked, foemen cut down without mercy in the blood-red exultation of war. The city—the name he had forgotten, had willed to forget—the city hammered down in siege, the gaunt starved women with weapons cobbled out of anything that would strike and kill, the one who charged shrieking upon him, he in his armor, she in filthy rags, and the baby on her back, but he never saw it until he had cloven her, and it, in two. And for a moment he was appalled, but then he shrugged and wiped his blade and went back to what was, after all, war.

She showed him himself crouched over the gazelle which he had hunted and killed as the cheetah does, by running it down, breaking its neck. Great graceful beast of prey with the taste of blood in his mouth, pale cat-eyes narrowed against the light.

"So has God made us," she said, cross-legged on a jut of stone, gazing down at him. "You no less than I. If you will hate me, then you must hate yourself. We are of the same blood and kind."

Bile burned his throat. "Would to God that you had never been born!"

"Why? Because I teach you to see the truth?"

"Clever lies. Twisting of what is so, to what you would wish to be so. I'm not your dog, Assassin. Let me go!"

Her head shook. "I am no Assassin now. I have forsaken it. I have no faith left to kill for."

It sickened him, that one would kill at all, for such a cause.

Something fluttered out of the air. A bit of cloth with a cross sewn on it, scarlet on black.

The silence stretched. She seemed to have turned her mind from him. He left the cloth where the wind had dropped it, and though his gorge rose, set to gutting and cleaning his kill. Her presence was a fire on his skin, her inattention a rankling in his middle.

She had an answer for everything. She would not, could not see the difference between cold murder and clean war.

Clean?

He saw Thibaut's body, serene as if in sleep; and the aftermath of bloody battle.

Not hers, that. His mind was locked shut. She had twisted him within as without.

"I make no apology for what I am," she said. "I only

sk that you see it clear, and not as your whim would have
t."

"I see clear enough. I see that it is your time for
nating, and I am here, and male, and of the proper kind.
There is no more to it than that."

"In the beginning," she said, "it was so."

She was before him in cold and enveloping white,
ike the Angel of Death. No maiden saint could have been
ess alluring. There was no seduction in her. She had
never known what it was.

She reached. He shied, caught himself. He saw the
swift wince of pain, the swifter flicker of a smile. Her hand
was warm on his cheek. For defiance, for bitter mockery,
e matched the gesture. Smooth; wondrous soft. Flesh of
is own kind, subtly yet deeply different from the human.
With one breath-light finger he traced the shape of her
ace. Not cold, her beauty, behind the mask she wore.
Oh, no. Not cold at all.

He recoiled. She betrayed no hint of triumph. She
urned and went away. Walking, as any creature would.
ny female creature. No male had that grace, that
uggestion of a sway, even scrambling over stones.

His face burned where she had touched it. He bent
ack to his fresh-blooded kill, shouldered it. The best way
ack was the way she took. He was not, he told himself,
aking it because she had.

For all her boldness and her wild ways, Morgiana
nared Sayyida's prudery in the matter of sleeping places.
he women spread mats in the kitchen. More often than
ot, Aidan had Hasan for a companion. Even so young, he
eemed to recognize that they were males together; and
e loved all the cushions and coverlets. "He's turning into
 little prince," his mother said.

"Then he is in proper company," said Morgiana.

Aidan, picking without appetite at a bit of roast gazelle looked up in time to catch Sayyida's look of comic dismay "Ya Allah! I'd completely forgotten."

His smile was wry. "Don't bow. You'll fall in the pot."

"I had no intention of—I mean—I—" Sayyida stopped in confusion.

"It's not as if I were real royalty," he said. She opened her mouth, indignant. He laughed. "I know I'm not. I've been told it on excellent authority. How can I be insulted by the truth?"

"That's nonsense," said Sayyida. "Royal is royal. And I never even thought. Ishak told me once—he was full of it. I didn't trouble to remember. What was a prince to me? I'd never come any closer to one than I already had."

Ardan gave up the meat and settled for cheese. "Go on, eat. I'm finished."

They tried to argue with that, but he had no appetite and they did. While they ate, he withdrew to the bath. It was a wonder to him, to have it there, always, for the taking. And wide enough to swim in.

He dropped his clothes, but he did not go into the pool. Where the stone poured down in a curtain like ice blue and palest green, he settled on his stomach, chin on folded arms, watching the play of water in the light of the lamp. Idly he made a light that was his own, and shattered it into embers, setting them to dance atop the water.

He yawned, rubbed his cheek against his arm. He was forgetting how it felt to be clean-shaven. Maybe he would go back to it. It would shock the women; it would prove that he was a Frank and a barbarian. And, in body, monstrously young.

Time left no mark on him. Even scars faded and vanished. He had taken a blow to the mouth once, long after he was grown. The stumps of teeth had loosened and fallen; he learned to smile close-mouthed, and contemplate long ages of beauty marred. It was illuminating, and humbling, to know how much it mattered. But a day came when he ran his tongue along the broad ugly gap, and felt a strangeness. In a few months' time they had all grown back, all the shattered teeth, sharper and whiter than ever. Sometimes in his wilder moods he was tempted to sacrifice a finger, to see if it would grow again without a scar.

He would never do it. He was too tender of his vanity. He troubled little with mirrors, but he liked to know what he would see there. He liked the way people, meeting him, drew back a little and stared, and doubted their eyes. Even the way they judged him, mere empty beauty, with no need to be more. It was always amusing to prove them wrong.

He always knew, now, where Morgiana was, as he knew the whereabouts of his own hand. He said to the water, but in part to her, "I'm a very shallow creature, when it comes to the crux."

She dropped something over him: a robe of heavy silk, glowingly scarlet. "But very good to look at," she said, "and no more modest than an animal."

"Why not? I've nothing to hide."

"The Prophet, on his name be blessing and peace, was a modest man. We follow his example."

Aidan sat up, wrapping the robe about him. It was lined with lighter silk, pale gold; it was embroidered with dragons. It was perfectly suited to his taste. "Was he ugly, then?"

"Oh, no!" She seemed shocked at the thought. "He was very handsome. He looked a little like you: being noble, and Arab, and slow to show his age."

"You knew him."

"I was never so blessed." She was in green tonight. She looked much better in it than in white. Much warmer; much less inhuman.

She had not denied that she was old enough to have known Muhammad.

"I may be," she said. "I don't remember. I was little more than a wind in the desert, until my master found me and made me his own. I remember nothing of being a child. Who knows? Maybe I never was one."

"My mother was like that," said Aidan. "A wild thing, nearly empty of self, until a mortal man gave her a reason to live in mortal time."

"Did she die with him?"

"No. She . . . faded. She went back into the wood. Us—my brother and me—she left. We were half mortal, and raised mortal, though we knew early enough that we were not. As our sister is."

"You have a sister?"

It twisted in him, with pain. "Gwenllian. Yes. Ten years younger than I, and growing old. You killed her son."

"I was oathbound," she said. "Surely you know what that is."

He drew up his knees and laid his forehead on them. He was tired. Of fighting. Of hating. Of grieving for human dead.

"It is what humans are. They give us pain."

"And joy," he said. "That, too. Surely that is what it is to be alive?"

"I don't know. I don't think I've ever lived. Empty of self—yes, that is I. I was a dagger and a vow. Now I am less even than that."

His head flew up. His anger flared, sudden and searing. "You are not!"

He had astonished her. It soured quickly; her mouth twisted. "No. I am something, still. A thing to hate."

"I don't—" He broke off. He could not say it. It would be a lie.

Except . . .

He shook himself. "You *are* more than that! Look about you. Look at your friend; look at Hasan. Aren't they worth something?"

"One friend," she said, "in a hundred years."

"A hundred years of what? Being a dagger and a vow. Serving masters who never saw you as anything else. But you are more; your heart knows it. It found Sayyida, and she had the wits, and the quality, to know you for what you are."

"A murderer of children."

It hurt, to have those words cast back in his face. It was not supposed to hurt. It was supposed to be a triumph. "Yes, damn you. And more than that. None of us is simple, my lady."

"You can say that?"

"You wanted me to see you clearly."

She stood. She shook; it had the heat of rage. "I wanted you to love me."

He cut his beard short, but he did not get rid of it. It was not worth a battle; and his vow was not kept. Not yet.

He decided that he rather liked it, once it was short enough to show the shape of his face. It added years and dignity, both of which he could well use. Besides, as the women said, he was a man, and a man's beauty could not be perfect without it.

Sometimes Muslim customs made surprising sense.

Morgiana left them on occasion, walking her paths that no one else could follow, to fetch food, and drink other than water of the spring, and the odd treasure. Once she brought back a jar of wine, and a lute.

Aidan regarded the lute when she laid it in his lap, and gently, most gently, caressed the inlay of its sounding board. "Where did you get this?" he asked her.

Steal, he meant. She refused to be baited. "I went to a place where such things are known, and asked where I might find the best maker of lutes. I went where I was shown. I paid," she said, "in gold. My own. Fairly and honestly gained."

He looked down. He had the grace to be ashamed. Lightly, almost diffidently, he plucked a string. The lute was in tune.

"I can't accept this," he said.

"Did I say it was a gift?"

He flushed.

"Play for me," she commanded him.

He was angry enough to obey her, defiant enough to choose a tune from his own country. But she had traveled far; she had learned to find pleasure in modes which were alien to those of the east. This was properly harp-music, bard-music, but he fitted it well to the supple tones of the lute.

She watched him in silence. He was out of practice: he slipped more than once. But he played very well, with the concentration of the born musician, head bending farther as the music possessed him, mouth setting in a line, fingers growing supple, remembering the way of it.

When he began to sing, she was almost startled. She did not know why she had expected a clear tenor: his voice in speech was low enough, with the merest suggestion of a purr. In song the roughness vanished, but that new clarity resounded in a timbre just short of the bass. A man's voice beyond doubt, dark and sweet.

It took all her strength to keep from touching him. He resisted her abominably easily; he only had to remember his Frankish woman, and what she carried. He was not like a human man, to be led about by his privates.

But he watched her. She knew that. He found her good to look at. He was beginning, not at all willingly, to forget how to hate her, if never to love her. And he wanted the power she had, to walk in an eyeblink from the wastes of Persia to the markets of Damascus.

She was pleased to teach him lesser arts, to hone the power he had never thought of as more than a child's toy, but that single great art, she would not give him. She knew what he would do with it.

Just this morning, he had tried to trick her out of it. Then when she vanished, she felt the dart of his will, seeking her secret. It was not as easy to elude him as it had been. He was a clever youngling, and he was growing strong.

The lutestrings stilled. He raised his head. His eyes were dark, the color of his northern sea. "Why?" he asked her. "Why teach me at all?"

"Why not?"

"What if I grow stronger than you?"

She laughed, which pricked his pride terribly. "I don't think I need to fear that. But that we may be equals . . . that, I think very possible. I would welcome it."

"Even knowing what I would do then?"

"Ah, but would you do it?"

He was mute, furious.

"My sweet friend," she said, "if you were half as wise as you like to imagine, you would know what it means, that we move so easily in one another's thoughts."

"It means that you will it, and I have no skill to keep you out."

She shook her head and smiled. "You know better than I what it is. Remember your brother and his queen."

He surged to his feet. "We are not so mated!"

He took care to lay the lute where it would be safe, before he flung himself away from her. She saw that; she saw quite enough apart from it. She allowed herself a long, slow smile.

Alamut is Judith Tarr's sweeping, new historical fantasy, set in the same world as *The Hound and the Falcon* trilogy. Here is the tale of Morgiana and Prince Aidan, two powerful and immortal mages living in a time when alliances of kin and country bind as surely as spells. Destined to be enemies, Morgiana and Aidan discover another choice—as lovers.

(*Read* Alamut, *on sale in November 1989, in hardcover and trade paperback wherever Doubleday Foundation Books are sold.*)

ABOUT THE AUTHOR

JUDITH TARR is the author of a number of novels of high and historical fantasy, including *A Wind in Cairo* from Bantam Spectra, and the award-winning trilogy, *The Hound and the Falcon*. She holds a Ph.D. in Medieval Studies from Yale University, where she was introduced to the life and legend of Gerbert of Aurillac; she has done research there and in France, and certifies that, yes, indeed, the light in Rheims is exactly the color of champagne. She lives in New Haven, Connecticut, and is completing *Alamut,* a new novel for Bantam and Doubleday.